# HOME TO YOU

## A SUSPICIOUS HEARTS NOVEL

## TAYLOR SULLIVAN

GOOD HOUSE
PUBLISHING

*To my husband. You are my rock. Thank you for loving me exactly the way I am. I would be lost without you.*

# CHAPTER ONE

With shaking hands, I slammed the car door, and the sound echoed through the parking garage behind me—I cringed. It was almost midnight, and even though I was moving in the morning, I didn't want pissed off neighbors tonight. I didn't want them any night, but especially not now. Not when I already dreaded each step more than the scale after Christmas.

I took a deep breath, slung my messenger bag across my chest, and pushed myself forward. It was heavier than normal—heavy because of the burden it carried more so than its weight—but I couldn't help myself from adjusting the strap over my shoulder anyway.

Kevin's Dodge Charger sat in our shared spot at the front of the garage. Just like it was every other night that week, but this night was different—he was home, and all my sleepless torment, my lying awake to plan out each word would finally come to an end. But I hated not knowing what awaited me—hated it more than anything. I was the girl who loved spoilers and read the *end* of a novel before the *beginning*. Presented with the blue pill or the red pill—there was no question; I took the blue one every time. I

1

liked my safe, normal life. I liked predictable. I didn't want to know how far the rabbit hole went—yet here I was.

My flip-flops slapped against the hard pavement, and my fingers itched for a hand to hold—someone to tell me I could get through this night, someone to tell me I was strong. But I didn't have anyone like that right now—I wasn't even sure I'd believe them if I did.

When I finally reached the third floor, I hesitated at our apartment door. Kevin would be waiting for me, and that fact twisted my stomach in knots. But it was now or never, and on the count of three, I shoved the key in the lock and pushed.

The smell of his cologne hit me first. The expensive scent of citrus and musk now lingered with the unsettled dust of packed books. Darkness filled the room I'd left littered with boxes only hours before. The only light—a sliver cast through the open door; like a shining beacon to my late arrival.

"Were you just going to walk out on me like that? Without saying goodbye?" His voice cut through the darkness like cold steel, and I had to remind myself to breathe.

"If that was my plan, I'd be gone by now." My voice shook, but I hoped he hadn't noticed. I stepped over the threshold and flicked on the light.

He stood against a stack of boxes, his sandy blond hair a disheveled mess, but his clothes pristine and freshly pressed like they always were. He smiled at me—that charming smile that made everyone love him, but one I found terrifying in that moment.

His chin lifted as he took a swig of his beer. "Where have you been?"

"Nowhere." Which was the truth. I'd been everywhere, and nowhere, all at the same time.

"Where, Katie?" He pushed himself upright, stalked toward me with long strides, and stopped when his polished black shoes touched the edge of my simple brown flip-flops. He stood only two inches above my five-foot-ten-inch frame, but there was an anger in his stance that was terrifying.

"I should be the one asking you that question."

His eyes narrowed and he moved even closer. "What's that supposed to mean?

"It's over, Kevin. I know the truth." Disgust spewed out of me —for him, for myself, for believing his lies for so long.

He shook his head. "I don't know what you're talking about." But he retreated a step, and I grew a little stronger.

"Don't give me that. Don't stand there pretending to be innocent. *I'm done.*" I'd imagined myself screaming those words, but in that moment, they came out in a broken cry.

"Darling, what's this about? Talk to me." His eyes searched mine, his charming smile back in place.

I almost wished I could believe him. Things were easier when I didn't know, when I lived in blissful oblivion. But I was an idiot, and as much as it hurt now, I couldn't stand the thought of going back to that again.

Shoving my hand in my messenger bag, I pulled out a manila envelope that contained my proof and pushed it to his chest. It fell to the ground and dozens of photographs scattered across the hardwood floor. Recognition transformed his features as the faces of multiple women stared up at him. But not just women—he was there too. In fancy restaurants, hotels—in bed. "I can explain."

"Screw you!"

He grabbed my arm, his fingers tearing into my flesh. "Who knows about this?"

His eyes were wild, his jaw constricted, and my heart stopped beating. He'd never hit me before, but for the briefest second I thought he might. I could've destroyed him with those photos; not only had he cheated on me, but he was playing with fire. The boss's secretary, the copy editor who pretended to be my friend, and even the owner's wife.

"No one," I whispered. Because even though the thought had

crossed my mind, even though he'd lied to me and made me look like an fool, I still couldn't strip him of the career he loved more than life.

Relief washed his features, and his grip eased. "It didn't mean anything, they don't mean anything."

He smiled again, the one I knew held anger under its surface, and bitter acid crept up my throat. I looked to the floor, unable to meet his stare any longer, and yanked my arm out of his grasp. "Why, Kevin?"

He took a deep breath and shook his head. "Don't do this."

"I need to know." Because being in the dark was torture. A poison that saturated my mind, telling me all the reasons I'd failed. All the reasons I wasn't good enough. Maybe it was because I didn't have blond hair like the rest of them. That my boobs were too small, or because I sucked at laundry. The truth would hurt, but nothing could be as harsh as my own insecurities.

"Katie, being with those women was good for us. It all made me realize what I have at home with you." He dropped to one knee. "I love you, darling. Don't let one silly mistake ruin that."

His words hit like a punch to my stomach. *Silly mistake?* I closed my eyes and stepped back.

"I want to grow old with you. I want you to have my babies. They'll all have big blue eyes *just like you*. Marry me."

Tears blurred my vision as I looked down at the man who knelt in front of me. The man that up until five days ago I thought I could spend the rest of my life with.

"I'll give you everything you've ever wanted, we'll buy a house, get a dog—"

"Get up!" Sobs wracked my body and my voice shook. "It's over, Kevin. Over!"

He stood slowly, hands held up in a silent surrender. "How can you say that? Have the last two years meant nothing to you?"

"Don't you dare try and turn this around on me!" My hands clenched at my sides, my nails tearing into my palms.

"We're a team, Katie. We'll get through this. We look good together, honey—"

"Is that all I am to you? A pretty face?" My gut twisted; I couldn't breathe.

He shook his head. "You know that's not true." He ran a hand through his thick hair, scanning the boxes that cluttered the room. "Don't move out. I'll go. We'll work on things. I'll win you back, just give me a chance."

"I don't trust you anymore." My voice was raw, my hand settled on my throat. "I've already resigned. I have an interview in LA on Monday."

"LA?" His blue eyes narrowed. "Are you going to Jake?" His words boomed like thunder, and his gaze locked on the picture that lay in the center of the coffee table.

He yanked the frame off the table and threw it against the wall with a crash. "Are you fucking him?"

"The only one fucking other people is you!" I rushed toward the picture and dropped down on shaking legs to pick up the broken frame that held some of my most cherished memories. "You need to leave."

"You can't kick me out of my own apartment."

I stood, walked across the room, and opened the front door. "Get out."

He laughed, one that was haunted and held no humor.

"Get out or I'll call the police."

The corners of his eyes crinkled with amusement, but I knew he wouldn't risk it. His reputation meant more to him than anything.

He turned slowly around the room—taking in the empty walls and stacked boxes. "This is what you really want?"

I nodded, though it wasn't true. What I wanted was to go back to Monday morning, to *not* find that note in my inbox, to have none of this nightmare be true—but that wasn't an option.

He came closer, stopping only inches from my face—so close I could see the blond stubble on his usually smooth cheek. "You want to know why, Katie?" He whispered in my ear. "Why I went to other women?" He trailed a hand down my bare arm and a shiver of disgust ran up my spine. "Because you've never satisfied me. You just lay there like a dead fish—what'd you expect?"

I closed my eyes as bile burned the back of my throat.

"No man will ever be satisfied with you."

I swallowed, not allowing him to see how much his words tore me up inside. "The movers come in the morning. I'll be gone by noon."

"You'll regret this." He looked me up and down, and for a second I thought he may say more, but he remained silent as he walked out to the hall.

I didn't hesitate before bolting the lock behind him. The invisible barrier offering me the limited closure I craved so much. I pressed my back against the door, my body so weak I practically melted into the wooden floor.

*No man will ever be satisfied with you.*

The broken frame was gripped in my left hand and I brushed fragments of shattered glass to the ground. All the faces I'd loved so much but hadn't seen in years stared up at me.

*The Gang.*

The photo was taken twelve years earlier, the summer after Dad passed. My brother, Dave, and his friends Jake and Justin were all high school seniors, shirtless, and shamelessly flexed their biceps for the camera. I was there too—my friends Sarah and Megan by my side. We all stood in our practiced supermodel poses that were supposed to be slimming—and me...I still wore a training bra even at fourteen.

I'd only been five foot three then, soft around the middle, and a little girl in both body and soul. I was the shortest of the bunch and hated it, but now at five foot ten I wished I could knock off a couple of inches—or five.

It was a time of innocence, a time of discovery, and my whole world had been wrapped up in that handful of people. I thought we'd be together forever. But that was when I trusted people with my secrets—when I trusted them with my heart. When I was young, full of hopes and dreams, and so in love with the boy who lived next door.

Jake Johnson.

The first boy I ever loved—the man who still held a piece of my heart. I let out a breath and pressed my head back into the apartment wall as memories of a fourteen year old girl flooded me. My pink bedroom, the sweltering heat of summer, and the AC Mom would never run...

---

*TWELVE YEARS EARLIER*

I threw the covers from my sweaty legs and rolled in the direction of my closed door. Muffled voices seeped through powder pink walls and I wondered if that was what awoke me. I considered getting up to turn on the air conditioner, but Mom's stressed face filled my mind and I couldn't do it. No matter how uncomfortable I was, I didn't want to make her worry any more about money than she already did.

It was nearly two in the morning, and even in the dark I could see that Sarah was no longer in my room. She was supposed to be my best friend, but lately she'd been spending more time with the boys than me. I wasn't sure how I felt about that.

I turned to my side, trying to find a comfortable spot, but it was too late. That familiar sadness had already begun to creep over my skin like a thick blanket. If I lay there much longer, it would suffocate me like it had the first few months after Dad passed.

Stumbling out of bed, I walked down the hallway running my hand along the textured paper walls. I heard more laughter and followed the voices until I stopped at the living room. Their backs were to me, and my heart instantly sank.

Sarah was on the ottoman holding an old guitar, and Jake was so close she practically sat in his lap. "Like this?" she asked, her hands positioned at the neck of the old Fender.

I thought about clearing my throat to tell them I was there, but I was too shocked.

*He's only teaching her how to play. That's all this is.*

"No, no." He laughed. "Here, let me show you." He wrapped his arm around her, then helped position her fingers on the frets. He was shirtless and his dark hair damp. They must have gone swimming.

"Is this right?" she asked.

"Mmmhmm." He nuzzled her neck, humming his response against her skin.

My breath caught. A burning sensation tickled my nose. Sarah? Why Sarah?

She giggled, "Stop it, Katie likes you."

He moved closer. "No, she doesn't."

Sarah giggled again. "She'll be so mad if she finds out."

"Katie's like my sister. She won't care."

His words came on a whisper, but I heard them like they were meant just for me. All the air left my throat and my chest heaved. I always knew Jake felt that way about me, but I'd never heard him say the words before.

Sarah leaned back and placed a hand on his strong jaw. "I guess she never has to find out."

---

Twelve years later, and I could still feel the sting of finding them like that. Ironic, considering I was facing a whole new kind of betrayal, and the first person I turned to for comfort had been Jake.

I pressed my head against the door and rubbed slow circles at my temples with my thumbs. Sarah had snuck back into bed that night around three in the morning. She never did say anything to me about what happened, and I never asked.

The photo still rested in my lap—scratched and flawed from the broken glass, and I bushed broken pieces to the floor with my thumb. My muscles were so tense they felt bruised. Bruised and battered—what I imagined my heart to look like. I pushed myself from the ground, removed what remained of the broken frame, and deposited the picture to an open box.

Not bothering to change, I crawled into my unmade bed and pulled the covers up to my chin. I was broken and weak—shattered—just like the glass covering my living room floor.

*No man will ever be satisfied with you.*

Kevin's words played in my head again and again, and eventually I cried myself to sleep.

# CHAPTER TWO

The early afternoon sun streamed through the windshield of the moving truck, and I pulled down the visor hoping to block out some of its harsh rays. The movers had come right on time that morning. Eight a.m. Exactly eight hours after Kevin walked out of my life forever, only three after I relaxed enough to fall asleep.

It was surreal really. Knowing that every earthly possession, everything that mattered to me, was now contained within a twenty-four-foot moving truck and the car that trailed behind it. In hindsight I should have paid the money and had someone drive the thing. I'd never done anything like this before, and all that could go wrong kept running through my mind faster than a freight train. A flat tire, a pothole, a gust of wind that would blow me over, taking my Ford Focus with it. But my rapidly deflating bank account told a different story. I needed to do this. I only had a few thousand dollars left to my name, and I needed that for an apartment, to set my feet on the ground—to start over.

I took another sip of my caramel macchiato, and my eyes locked on the sign that read "Los Angeles: 126 miles." After all these years, I was finally going back. It was the place of my childhood, the place that held a thousand memories, and my heart picked up speed just thinking about it. But that seemed to be my normal these days. I walked through life with that tight ball of panic settled between my heart and throat waiting for the next thing to happen.

I couldn't quite figure out how I found myself in this position. My life, usually so predictable, had turned into a blur. A blur that was more like Lifetime television than of my own reality. It just wasn't like me to storm into the office and give my resignation without notice. I was the responsible type. The one who was never late, the one who didn't break promises and always paid her bills on time. I didn't cheat, always sent thank-you cards, and had never smoked a day in my life. I was the *good girl*, the one you'd bring home to your mother. The type who saved her virginity until the age of twenty-three—for the man who never wanted it in the first place.

It wasn't that I never had the opportunity. I had many boyfriends, and lord knows they all tried. I just always wanted something more. Something special. There was always that one man I held everyone else up against. Jake.

When Kevin came along, I thought things had finally changed, that I'd finally gotten over the boy I'd loved my whole life. It was six months after my move to San Diego; I'd been assigned to cover a local food drive, and Kevin was the brand-new reporter in the office. He was the type who could sweet talk his way into any situation, and it only took two weeks to talk his way into my pants. I didn't even tell him I was a virgin until months later... I'm not even sure why, maybe to save myself from having to explain the reason.

Three months after our first date, Kevin and I moved in together. I thought he was my forever, that he was the one. But now, two and a half years later, I realized I couldn't have been more wrong. I trusted the wrong person. Which unfortunately, seemed to be a pattern in my life. But as the miles ticked by, I was filled with both fear and longing for what awaited me. Jake. My Jake. The Jake I hadn't seen once in three years. What would it be to like to live with him again?

I moved in with them right before I turned twenty-three. I'd wanted to get my own apartment, but Dave asked me to move in with him and Jake instead. I think it was his brotherly way of keeping me under lock and key. But with the stress of tuition, classes, and work, I couldn't have afforded my own place anyway. Looking back, I'm sure Dave knew that too.

He and Jake were a year into the launch of JM construction, and we were all constantly broke. They'd been making plans about the business since they were ten, when they'd taken all Dad's lumber from the garage and built that tree house in the backyard. Dad had been annoyed at first; he'd purchased the wood to build Mom those garden boxes she'd been wanting. But when he saw what a good job they did, his expression quickly changed to one of pride.

Jake wasn't as lucky though. He'd been on the fast track to becoming a lawyer like his father. Actually made it all the way through school before he came to the realization he hated it. When he presented his plans to his parents, they were pissed. Said he was wasting his life and education. But building things was where Jake came alive, and even though it meant his parents cutting him off, he took all he had, and dumped it into the company

We lived in a junky old three-bedroom house in Northridge, California, and it was never a surprise to come home and find Jake working out in the garage, or even asleep shirtless on our couch. I loved it. Even with the lack of money, that house held some of the best memories of my whole life...

---

*THREE YEARS EARLIER*

With my feet tucked under me on my bed, I chewed on my pencil and read the same sentence for what felt like the hundredth time. *Finals week.* I'd been surviving on coffee for the past three days. But it was worth it. In a few weeks I'd finally graduate, and join my peers with the BA I was supposed to have two years ago.

A knock pulled my attention, and I glanced up to see Jake open the door. He wore his faded gray sweatpants with the hole in one knee and a white tank top that left his perfectly sculpted arms bare.

"Why are you always hiding in here, Kit Kat?" He walked into my room, lay on my bed, and took a bite of apple like he owned the place.

"Why do you think?" I waved my hand over the textbooks that littered the mattress and tried to ignore the butterflies beating away inside me. But he smelled so good, like soap, clean skin, and testosterone. Or what I imagined testosterone would smell like anyway. It was impossible.

He made a face, then turned to his side, and propped himself on one elbow. "What are your plans tonight?"

I cleared my throat. "I'm going out with Phillip."

He cringed. "You're still seeing that guy? He's such a douche." His teeth sunk into his apple and his lips curved in a smile.

I inwardly groaned. I loved his mouth. Those lips I was sure tasted like a Fuji apple right about now. I sat back on my heels and cursed my lustful thoughts. "He's sweet. And besides, you shouldn't talk."

He flipped to his stomach, his eyes twinkling. "What's that supposed to mean?"

I glanced up and had to stop myself from rolling my eyes. "Like Candace is such a prize." She was Jake's flavor of the month. I couldn't even say I was jealous. She would be gone soon, just like all the rest of them.

13

He grinned. "What's wrong with Candy?"

Now I did roll my eyes. "She laughs like a hyena." My tone daring him to deny it.

"Yeah, well… At least she doesn't cry as much as Phillip."

I wanted to laugh, but instead I threw a pillow at his head. "Shut up, he's sensitive."

"So feisty." He narrowed his eyes.

I bit my inner cheek, trying to hide my grin. "Why are you always barging in here bothering me, anyway?"

"I didn't barge, I knocked."

"That wasn't a knock, that was a tap—and besides, you're supposed to wait for an answer."

"Why does it bother you so much, Katie? Are you hiding someone in here?" A quick smile turned his lips, and he rolled over to check under the bed.

"Yeah, like I could sneak anyone past Tweedle*dee* and Tweedle*dumb*."

His smile grew wider, and he tossed the rest of his apple in the trash. "Which one am I?"

"Definitely Tweedle*dumb*." I matched his smile and raised my brows.

"Oh Kit Kat, that's the wrong answer." He rose to his knees, a mischievous look crossing his beautiful face.

My heartbeat quickened as I recognized the game we were about to play. Without hesitation, I bolted from the bed, ran to the living room, and leapt over the couch in two seconds flat.

He stalked into the room, his long legs and an easy grin turning my insides to butter.

"You think that couch will protect you?"

I began to giggle. "Fine, you can be Tweedledee!"

"Too late, Katie, you'll have to pay the fine."

And I knew what the fine was; he'd tickle me until I couldn't breathe.

"Jake." I used my sternest voice to warn him off, but he wasn't swayed.

He ran to one edge of the couch, and I ran to the other. I looked into his eyes, barely able to contain my laughter, and knew without a doubt I was trapped. In a pathetic effort to get away, I grabbed one of the pillows and threw it his chest. He caught it in mid-air and arched one brow. I narrowed my eyes, picked up another pillow, and soon we were whacking each other in the middle of the living room. I laughed so hard my eyes watered, and he didn't hesitate before taking advantage of my weakness. Grabbing the pillow from my hands he tackled me to the floor.

"No, Jake!" I screamed, falling back to the brown shag carpet.

He straddled my hips while his fingers ascended to my ribcage. "Oh Kit Kat, I just can't help myself."

"Please." I laughed. "Stop! I'll do anything."

His hands stilled, and my breath instantly caught. "Go to the game with me and Dave tonight."

He wasn't laughing, and the seriousness in his expression made me still. That familiar tingle was low in my belly, and I became hyper aware of his position on top of me. "I can't Jake, I already have plans."

"Tell him you have to study." His expression confused me. It was too serious. What happened to the playful Jake I felt safe with? And why was he looking at me like that? Like he wanted to devour me like that apple in my bedroom.

"Okay," I replied between breathless pants, but this time it was no longer from laughter.

"Good." He pushed himself off the ground and pulled me to stand.

"You're such a jerk." I looked to the floor, knowing my arousal was plastered all over my face.

"I know." He reached up to tuck a strand of wild hair behind my ear, and my heart beat so fast I was sure he could see it beating inside me. "We leave at five."

"Fine—but now I have to study." I brushed past him to my room, needing distance to catch my breath.

"Katie?"

"Yes, Jake?" I feigned annoyance.

"Let him down easy."

---

Phillip and I broke up a couple weeks later. I told everyone it was because we grew apart, but I knew the truth. I pushed him away hoping beyond hope that one day, something would happen between Jake and me.

Things were always like that with us. Playful, comfortable, but at the same time, there was that part of our relationship I had no control over. A part so deep inside me I couldn't quite reach the off switch. The part that wanted him to love me as much as I loved him.

It had only been an hour since leaving San Diego, but my bladder felt like it was a balloon ready to pop—the Venti caramel macchiato had been a *bad* idea. With two hours still ahead of me, I pulled the beast of a truck into a gas station, did my business, and bought a banana to appease my grumbling stomach. But I could only muster a bite or two; I was too nervous for more than that.

Back in the truck, the salty beach air rushed through the open window as I pulled onto the freeway. I was still too far from the water, but I'd know that scent anywhere. The beach. We'd spent every possible moment there back then. Actually, we spent every day together, period. Dave, Jake, and I—we were inseparable.

---

*THREE YEARS EARLIER*

16

"I'm starving," I called over my shoulder as I rummaged through the empty cupboard.

"Me too," Dave said, standing at the open fridge. "Do we have any of that potato salad left?"

I laughed. "That's over a week old."

"So?" Jake asked from the doorway. "Where's your sense of adventure?" He'd just gotten home from work, his arms were stretched up high up on the frame, and his sideways smile gleamed at me. I grinned. Things had been different between us for a couple of weeks. Little touches, flirtation I wasn't used to, and for the first time in years, we were both single. I bit my lip and turned back to the empty shelves.

"I seriously can't believe we're out of food again," I muttered, trying to hide how much he affected me. But the truth was, we'd been living together for three months, and I'd grown used to empty cupboards.

"It takes a lot of calories to maintain these muscles," Dave replied, flexing his chest and biceps to annoy me.

"You're such a dork." I laughed, pushing him aside to move my search to the fridge. I wasn't sure if Dave suspected anything between Jake and I. He didn't seem to notice, either that, or he didn't want to know. I was his baby sister, and Jake was his best friend. That would be a hard pill to swallow for just about any man... but especially Dave.

"What about this?" Jake asked, and I turned around to see him holding a bag of popcorn kernels.

My eyes narrowed. "Where'd you find those?"

He pointed to the very top of the pantry I wasn't tall enough to see. "Up there."

"Did we even buy those?" I directed my question to Dave, who shrugged in reply.

"I don't know..." I shook my head. "I really don't think it's a good idea."

But he ignored my warning and began tossing the bag from hand to hand. "How do we cook these babies?"

"Microwave?" Dave suggested, his expression along the lines of I-don't-know-what-the-hell-I'm-talking-about.

"Yes!" Jake shouted, then threw the bag in the microwave and shut the door.

"You can't do the whole bag." I moved across the kitchen and pulled them back out. "If we're going to do this thing," I cocked my shoulders like Fonzie, "we need to find a paper bag or something. You know, like microwave popcorn?"

"How about this?" Dave asked, holding out a large brown bag from the grocery store.

I shrugged, then grabbed the bag from his hand and opened it up to put a couple tablespoons of kernels inside.

"There's no way that's enough. I'm starving." Jake picked up the bag and added what must've been a half a cup more.

"How long should we put it in for?" He looked back at me over his shoulder.

I lifted my shoulders. "Five minutes maybe?"

"Works for me." He put the folded-up grocery bag in the microwave, entered the time, and pressed start. When he turned around, his eyebrows were raised with mischief, and his fists rested low on his hips.

"Why are you standing like that?" I questioned.

"Like what?" he asked, his smile producing that adorable dimple.

"Like Superman." I grinned.

His smile turned shy and he shook his head at me. "Whatever."

"You want to be him, don't you?" I couldn't help laughing a little.

"Umm... Of course I do. Who doesn't want to be Superman?"

"Do we have any butter?" Dave asked, ignoring our little conversation and opening the fridge.

"We *did*, but you guys probably ate that too." I jumped up to sit on the counter.

A couple minutes passed with no popping and I began to grow wary. "Why isn't it popping yet?"

"Patience, Kit Kat," Jake replied, and wagged his eyebrows at me.

As if on cue, the microwave started to make a few faint popping noises, and Jake looked at me with an *I told you so* smile.

"Do you smell that?" Dave asked.

"What?" I sniffed the air and my eyes instantly widened.

"Shit!" Jake said, opening the microwave door.

When he pulled out the bag it was smoking, and a small red hole revealed blackened kernels inside.

"Well, I guess that didn't work," Dave murmured.

Then the hole grew bigger, and before I knew what was happening, the bag ignited to flames in Jake's hands.

I panicked and began to wave my hands, and blow at the same time.

"Stop waving your arms and get the damned fire extinguisher!" Dave yelled.

"Where is it?" I screamed, frantically spinning in circles.

"Fuck this." Jake threw the burning mass into the sink. The smoke alarm screeching as the flames grew bigger and bigger.

Jake and I began opening every cupboard searching for the extinguisher when Dave stepped toward the sink, flicked on the faucet, and extinguished the growing flames. "Idiots!"

Jake and I turned to one another and burst into fits of laughter.

"It's not funny!" Dave yelled as he pulled the battery from the alarm. "We almost burned down the damned house!"

Jake and I sobered as we watched Dave storm out of the kitchen.

"He looks really mad," I said, trying to suppress the laughter that bubbled in the back of my throat.

"He just has a stick up his ass 'cause we burnt his dinner."

We both started laughing again, and I had to cross my legs because I was afraid I would pee my pants. "Oh I love you."

Jakes eyes twinkled and he looked at me sideways. "Well, that's a first."

I sobered. "What?" But I knew what he was talking about. I hadn't meant to say the words. They just slipped out.

"No one has ever said that to me before."

That wasn't the answer I was expecting. Sure, I'd never said the words before, but there was no way I was buying it. "Whatever." I rolled my eyes. "Everyone loves you."

He shrugged. "It's true." Not seeming to care if I believed him or not.

"Your parents?" I pointed out, as if to say *duh*.

"Nope. They're just not the type. I know they love me, they just don't say it."

*Wow.* Hearing that made me a little sad. I always knew his parents were a couple of jerks, but to never say *I love you* to their own child? I suddenly understood so much about him. Understood why he always swore he'd never have a family of his own. Why he spent everyday at our house growing up.

Even though I hadn't meant to say the words the first time, in that moment, I was compelled to say them again. "Well, it's true... I love you, Jake Johnson." I smiled a big cheesy grin, trying to lighten the words I'd held inside for nine years.

His eyes crinkled at the corners—but his stomach growled at the same time, breaking some of the seriousness that had settled over us. He patted it like it was its own life-form, then glanced at the burnt mass in the sink. "I'm gonna taste it."

"No, you're not. It's all burnt and disgusting." I looked down at the puddle of soggy, blackened popcorn in the sink.

He raised an eyebrow like I'd dared him, picked up a large chunk, and tossed it in his mouth.

My eyes widened with shock and disgust as I watched him chew and swallow.

"Not bad." He shrugged, then smiled his crooked smile again.

I shook my head at his willfulness but couldn't help feeling amused. "Come on, I think I have some money stashed in my room. Let's go see what we can get off the dollar menu."

"I knew you were holding out on us." He threw his arm over my shoulder, kissed my cheek, and we walked out of the kitchen.

My heart soared high that day. I was the first person to ever say I loved him. He never said the words back, but something else changed between us that afternoon. There was a closeness, an understanding that went so much deeper than it ever had before. It was after that day I began to think something might actually happen between us, and it was after that day everything fell apart.

# CHAPTER THREE

*THREE YEARS EARLIER*

**D**ressed in the boxers and a cami I'd worn to bed the night before, I searched the crowded emergency room for a familiar face. My heart was in my throat as I scanned from seat to seat, my legs like gelatin as I stepped over someone's outstretched legs looking for a glimpse of my mom.

When our eyes locked, it was as if I floated over to her. Not even remembering the movements it took to get there. She looked pale and gray, much like she had nine years earlier when we waited for news about my father. Though this time maybe even worse. Not because she was older, but because she waited to hear the news of her only son.

"We don't know anything yet." Her eyes filled with tears, and she squeezed my hand.

"What happened?" I sat down, not knowing if I wanted answers, only that I needed to say something to fill the void in my chest with noise so I wouldn't fall apart.

"He was talking with an inspector—someone lost control of

the crane—" Her voice cracked, unable to continue, but I'd heard enough. Whatever happened was bad enough that he was in surgery. So bad that we hadn't heard anything in an hour.

My eyes burned with unshed tears, and I felt like a ton of bricks landed on my chest. I didn't want to cry. Crying meant that something was wrong, and I wasn't ready to accept that. God wouldn't do that to me. He'd already taken my father. He couldn't have my brother too.

I glanced around the waiting area, spotting Jake in a far-off corner of the room. He was all alone, and blood covered the front of his shirt. His eyes were fixed and glassy, and I wanted to go to him. For him to hold me, for me to hold him, but my mom began to tremble next to me, reminding me of how she was after Dad died. I wrapped my arms around her and squeezed. Mom needed me. I needed to be strong. I was okay. Everything would be okay.

With senses on high alert, I heard the electric doors before the doctor pulled down his mask and entered the room.

He called my mom's name and we both stood, using each other for support. He came toward us, and before he uttered the words, I knew.

"I'm sorry, Mrs. McGregor, we did everything we could."

My mom sagged in my arms, and my mind filled with static. I watched the doctor's mouth move, unable to comprehend anything else he said. All I knew was that my brother was gone, and nothing else mattered.

Mom and I were invited back to say our goodbyes, and I looked over my shoulder, scanning the room for Jake. He wasn't in the corner where I'd last seen him. He needed to be there. Dave was his best friend; he needed to be able to say goodbye.

People were everywhere, nurses rushing back and forth, and there was a baby crying in her mother's arm—so many people. I spun around among the chaos, and the whole room began to echo. Then I saw him, way at the other side of the room. His back was turned, and he was walking down the hall on his way out of the hospital. I wanted to call out, to run to him and tell him not to leave, but I felt Mom shaking in my arms beside me and knew she needed me calm. I held her tightly, my heart ripping farther out of my chest with each breath, but I was in shock. I hadn't shed a single tear.

When I returned to the house hours later, Jake was sitting forward on the couch, his head in his hands, and I dropped my bag to the apartment floor.

He looked up, and the torment I saw in his eyes caused a ball of tears to thicken the back of my throat.

He needed me.

I needed him.

We needed each other.

Before I could say anything, he was on his feet, crossing the room in two powerful strides. "I'm so sorry." He crushed me hard against his chest, and my whole body sagged against him.

He gripped me to him, and I pressed my face to the smooth cotton of his shirt. I could feel his heartbeat, the warmth of his breath, the deep rumble of his voice. I needed all of it. Needed confirmation that the only other man I'd ever loved in my life was still alive.

"I was supposed to be there," he whispered.

His words came like a confession, laced with guilt and pain. Then his strong hands trailed down my back, and he sunk to his knees in front of me. "It was supposed to be me."

My hands fell to his hair, and he wrapped his arms around my waist. "I couldn't get to him, Katie."

My chest heaved. "No, Jake...don't." I was choking, every word painful. "No..."

"He told me, but I didn't listen." His voice was raw and hollow.

Hot tears began to fall for the first time. I had no idea what he was talking about, but I couldn't stand to hear him blame himself. "It's not your fault, Jake. It was nobody's fault." My voice was strange and broken. I tried to lift him to his feet, but he was too heavy, and his shoulders began to shake. I'd known him for seventeen years, since he was little boy, and never once had I seen him like this. It terrified me.

I sank to the floor next to him, pulling him to me with strength I didn't know I had. My fingers found his damp hair, and I smoothed it back from his face. "It'll be okay, Jake, it'll be okay." Even as I said the words, I wasn't sure I believed them. How could the world be okay without my brother?

He looked up, his eyes red-rimmed and wild with pain, and I trailed my hand down the side of his jaw. "I'm so sorry."

"Shh…" he whispered, and in an instant that part of him was locked away again.

He stood, lifted me in his arms, and carried me to the couch. I buried my face in his neck, and he sat with me in his lap. My body began to tremble with my grief, and the tears I'd been trying to hold back began to flow. He gripped me tighter, held me secure, and rocked me gently.

He told me everything would be okay. That he would always be there, that he would take care of me, and I felt my hair grow damp with the wetness of his tears. He held me well into the night, when exhaustion finally took me. I awoke early the next morning, tangled in Jake's embrace. But my heart was empty. My brother was still gone.

---

Three weeks after Dave's death, the escrow closed on our childhood home. The deal had already been in place, and Mom had already purchased another home in Colorado—but I pleaded for her to back out.

She was moving with her boyfriend, Paul, who was already there waiting for her. I knew she needed him, that she was grieving too, but I couldn't help feeling like she was choosing him over me. Over the memories of her own son—the memories of my father.

Jake became my rock. The only thing I had left in the world. We spent every night together, every weekend, and when the nightmares started, he began sleeping in my bed...

---

My heart slammed in my chest and I couldn't breathe. The room was thick and foggy, like walking through a funhouse filled with a cloud of dry ice. Off in the distance was a dark hall, but I couldn't see its end. I grew frightened and nervous. *Why was I here? Why was I alone?*

Then up ahead, surrounded by puffs of white smoke, was Jake. His back was to me as he walked down the hall.

*Come back,* I wanted to yell, but panic squeezed my throat, and I couldn't make a sound. I began to run, chase after him, and my heartbeat came faster and faster.

But it wasn't fast enough, wasn't good enough...I couldn't catch him.

*Jake! Don't leave me. Please don't leave me!*

"Shh." Jake's deep voice filled my ear, and he pulled me to his solid chest. "I'm here. Shh."

I opened my eyes, thankful it was only another nightmare, and pressed my hot cheek to his bare skin.

"It was just a dream." He ran a hand down my back. "Shh..."

His blue eyes locked with mine, and the backs of his fingers caressed the side of my face. "Don't cry," he pleaded, his calloused thumb brushing away a single tear.

His voice calmed me. The soft light of dawn allowing me to see how much he cared about me. My dreams affected him more than they did me.

"I'm so sorry," I whispered, knowing this wasn't the first time I'd woken him this way.

"Don't be sorry." His voice was deep and groggy and he began to smooth my hair away from my face.

I could smell the familiar scent of his skin and my heart began to pound again.

"I haven't had one in a while." I looked up at him. His eyes were closed, and I thought he might want to go back to sleep.

"Yeah."

My eyes shifted to the dimple of his chin, then slowly up to his full lips. He hadn't shaved since the morning before and already had a scruff of beard. I ached to be able to run my hand along his jaw. To touch him the way I'd always wanted to.

When I looked up again, his eyes were open, and he was watching me. My chest tightened with embarrassment, and I tried to pull away, but his hand caught me behind the neck, holding me firm.

My breath grew heavy under his gaze, and his hooded eyes moved to my lips. I was frozen, unsure of what was happening, and then his mouth came down to mine. Softly at first, like I could blow him away with an exhale, but then the kiss became firmer, sweeter, and he sucked softly on my bottom lip until I whimpered.

When his velvety tongue slipped into my mouth, he groaned, sending a pulse of need straight to the pit of my stomach. My hands trailed down his back, and his muscles flexed under my touch. I couldn't think. My whole body was alive from his kiss, and all I wanted was more.

He rolled me to my back, his body heavy on mine, and looked deep into my eyes. For a second I thought he was going to pull away, but then he placed a gentle kiss on my forehead, my nose, and found my mouth again.

A soft moan escaped me, a low, primal sound I'd never made before. I arched against him, my body more alive with each touch, his erection pressing into my hip.

My insides turned to liquid, and I wanted to touch him. I

wanted to give him an ounce of the pleasure his kiss gave me. With trembling fingers, I found the strings of his sweatpants, but the next thing I knew, he rolled away from me and sat on the far edge of the bed.

"Katie, I can't."

His words came on a breathy pant, but I felt them like a hard slap.

Embarrassment and pain surged through me, and I moved to the end of the mattress. "I'm sorry," I whispered, not knowing what else to say.

"No, damnit." He reached out to touch me, but I rolled my shoulder to shrug him off.

"Jake, it's okay." I took a deep breath, trying to force down the hurt, but bile crept up my throat. "I need to get ready. I have work this morning."

As if on cue, the alarm beeped to life on my nightstand, and I reached out to silence it. The tension was palpable, and I didn't waste a minute before pushing myself to stand and running to the bathroom.

"Katie!" He called out, but I didn't answer. I closed the door behind me and turned on the shower so he wouldn't hear me cry. When I returned twenty minutes later, my emotions locked away in the safe place I usually didn't hide from Jake—he was gone.

---

As I pulled off the freeway, I took a deep breath and tried to process all that had happened. Everything changed after our kiss. It was in that moment, alone in my bedroom, I accepted the fact that nothing would ever come of us. That no matter what I did, he'd always think of me as someone to take care of, like the little sister he had to protect. Every contact became painful, and nothing remained of the playful banter we'd always shared. He never came to my bed again. Didn't come into my room without knocking—didn't seek me out at all. I was depressed, alone, and knew it was finally time to move on.

After graduation, I got the first job I applied for. A position as a photojournalist at a small paper in San Diego. Within a week, I'd packed my bags and had my car loaded. I was ready for a new start. Finally ready to put that needed distance between us so I could get over him...

Jake placed the last of my boxes into the back of my car, then shoved his hands deep in the pockets of his jeans. "Are you sure this is what you want?"

The tension was so thick I almost couldn't breathe. "Yeah. It's a great opportunity."

His lips lifted in a smile, but his eyes were hard. Just like the wall that ran a thousand miles between us. He stepped forward and tucked a strand of hair behind my ear. The thing he'd done a million different times, but a touch I hadn't felt in weeks. "There are jobs here too, you know."

My throat burned, my heart clenched, and fear bubbled inside me. Could I really do this? Move away from the last person who really knew me? The man who owned my heart? "Yeah, well. There's nothing here for me anymore."

I wanted him to say it wasn't true, that *he* was still there. I wanted him to be angry, or hurt like I was. I wanted him to have any other response than what he did.

His jaw flexed, and he opened the door to my car. "I'm happy for you, Kit Kat. Call me if you need anything."

I promptly got inside without giving him a second glance. It was easier that way. Easier not knowing if he was sad to see me go. Easier not knowing if he watched me as I drove away.

I cried the whole drive to San Diego, and continued every night for the first month I was there. He finally called to check on me a few months later, but I knew he was only doing what he thought he should. His *brotherly duty*. Just like he'd been doing every day since.

As I turned the moving truck down Jake's street, my hands burned from my vise-like grip on the steering wheel. I pulled to a stop on the opposite side of the road and watched him. He was arranging boxes around in his garage, completely unaware of my presence.

*I won't fall for you this time, Jake Johnson. This time I'll know better.*

# CHAPTER FOUR

As soon as I cut the engine, the whole cab silenced, and some of the tension melted from my shoulders. Jake still hadn't noticed me, and for the first time in the twenty years, I was thankful for his oblivion. It was ironic really. I used to ache for him to notice me, and now I sat there needing more time before he did.

He'd called me out of the blue six months ago, telling me about his new house. Actually, he'd called a lot over the years. Every birthday, Christmas, and even the anniversary of Dave's accident. Though he never said it was the reason.

When he invited me for a visit, I'd been so nervous. I began pacing back and forth and rattling off all the reasons I couldn't go. That I was too busy, that I couldn't take the time off work, or even leave Kevin that long. But now as the butterflies swarmed an angry flurry inside me, I realized it was more than that. I'd stayed away on purpose. I stayed away too long.

He was still in the garage, and I could just make out the flex and shift of his muscles as he stacked one box on top of the other. He wore a pair of old jeans that were frayed at the cuffs, and a plain white T-shirt spread over his broad shoulders. I'd secretly hoped he'd changed a little bit. Maybe put on a few pounds, developed a bald spot, or even lost a few teeth. But even from ten yards away I could tell my wish hadn't come true. He was beautiful. Well, in that very masculine and rugged sort of way. His dark, wavy hair was longer now. Curled at his nape the way it always had been when we were kids. People thought we were related back then. Not only because we were always together, but I guess we had similar features. We were both tall, had dark hair and blue eyes. Other than that, I just didn't see it. He was gorgeous, and I was just me.

The sound of the Dodger game carried across the warm breeze, and I realized that was why he was so blind. The world could be ending, but if Jake was listening to a ball game, he wouldn't notice. Some things never changed I guessed. I could still get lost watching him, and his blood still ran Dodger blue.

After five minutes, and a few cleansing breaths, I decided it was time to stop procrastinating and pushed the door open. The strap of my tank top sagged to my shoulder, and I brushed it back up before hopping to the asphalt. I closed my eyes, cursed my racing heartbeat, then took a deep breath and crossed the street to Jake.

"Hey, stranger," I called out. My voice sounding strained and hoarse even to my own ears.

He looked up, seeming not to notice, and his handsome face transformed into a huge smile. He walked over, meeting me halfway, and lifted me off my feet in a firm hug. "Hey, beautiful."

I gripped him tighter. Not realizing how much I needed this. It had been so long since he'd lifted me like that. So long since I'd been held by a man who actually made me feel small. My heart leapt to my throat, and he lowered me to the ground.

He held me at arm's length and his smile faded. His rough fingers brushed across my left cheek causing a stir low in my belly. "You look like shit, Katie."

"Thanks." I laughed then swallowed. "What happened to beautiful?"

He let out a breath. "What did he do to you?" His voice was soft, but I heard the protection under its surface. The protection I both loved and hated at the same time.

My throat thickened, and I turned out of his arms toward the house. "Aren't you going to show me around?" I needed time. How could I tell him about another man who didn't think I was enough?

"Same old Katie, always avoiding the question."

My stomach clenched, but when I turned to face him, he was smiling again.

He pulled on one of my braids—the way he always did when we were kids—and started walking toward the house. "I'll let you off the hook this time. Follow me."

His driveway was void of cars, and I did a quick scan down the street looking for his old Mustang. All I came up with was a black truck with a JM construction logo on it. Johnson McGregor—the company he'd started with my brother, our names forever linked even after we grew apart.

"What happened to Bessie?" I asked, wondering about the old car.

He only shook his head and kept walking. I was concerned by this reaction and about to ask more about it, but then he unlatched the gate off the driveway, and we both stepped into the backyard. It was so beautiful I lost my train of thought.

A mixture of pine and birch trees lined the redwood fence, and lush fern and hydrangea mingled among their trunks. It looked like something you'd find in a Better Homes and Gardens Magazine, and I didn't want to leave—but Jake quickly climbed the front steps and beckoned me to follow.

"Five-four-eight, five-two-eight. The code to the house." He had me recite the numbers a few times so I wouldn't forget, then opened the door, and gestured for me to go inside.

The living room was large and very masculine, with brown leather furniture and a big-screen television. A rustic-looking rug sat in front of the couch, and I ached to slip my sandals off and feel the tall pile between my toes.

"Wow, you're a big kid now." I looked up at him and smiled. "A big step up from that old house in Northridge."

The corner of his mouth lifted, but his forehead wrinkled in a way that made me instantly regretted my words. Why did I have to go bringing up the past? The house that held too many painful memories for the both of us.

We continued through a doorway to the left which led us to the kitchen. It wasn't large, or fancy, but the natural light streaming through the open windows gave me chills. It was a good size with simple design. Crisp white cabinets, butcher block counters, and all stainless, top-of-the-line appliances. Exactly what I would have I picked out myself. I raised my eyebrows. "All this for a guy who doesn't cook?"

"It's all about the resale value, Katie." He grinned.

I breathed a sigh of relief. That was the Jake I needed right now. The smiling one. Though I couldn't quite push all the memories from my mind. I trailed a hand over the smooth surface of the counter and his words hit me all at once. I turned around. "You're planning to sell the place? But it's perfect." In the few minutes I'd been there, I was already attached. After six months, how could he even think of leaving?

He moved to lean against the counter and his bicep flexed as he braced himself there. "It's *only* a house."

The way he said it made a knot form in the pit of my stomach. His inflection making me wonder if he was hinting about me— but then I remembered. Jake didn't get attached. He didn't commit to anything; why would that change for a house?

I cleared my throat and gestured toward a small dining area just beyond the kitchen. It was surrounded by a large bay window that flooded the room with warm light.

"This is beautiful."

A broad smile covered his face as he pushed himself from the counter. "Come on, let me show you the best part."

We stepped out of the back door to a huge stone patio that could easily fit a hundred people. There was a built-in barbecue off to the left and a large table and chairs to the right. A rustic wood awning covered the deck closest to the house, and the thick beams let in the perfect amount of light. Past the patio was a sizable pool, and all the landscaping made it feel just as raw and organic as the front.

"There's a hot tub up there." He gestured to another stone patio secluded by plants. "And way over there will be a garden one of these days. I just haven't had time to set it up yet."

I didn't know why, but seeing all he'd achieved in my absence caused my throat to thicken with emotion. "It's absolutely perfect, Jake."

"Come on, I'll show the rest of the house."

Leading me to the other side of the patio, he took me through a set of double doors to the master bedroom. Aside from the large sleigh bed and nightstands, the room lacked other furniture. The same wood flooring had been carried throughout the house, and a few random pieces of clothing were scattered across it.

"Sorry," he muttered as he began picking the pieces off the floor.

"You do remember we used to be roommates, right? This is nothing," I teased.

He looked up, a gleam of recognition and humor in his eye. "You're right." Then promptly dropped the clothes where he stood. "Come on, Kit Kat." He threw an arm over my shoulder. "I'll show you to your room."

My stomach fluttered from his closeness, but I laughed as he ushered me down the hall. The first room we came to was filled with a bunch of boxes. A couple surfboards stood on end in the corner, and a desk was stacked high with papers and random junk. His arm slipped from my shoulder and he pulled the door closed.

"Storage," he muttered, but I caught a glimpse of embarrassment I didn't like. Why would he care about that? Especially with me—the girl who couldn't keep up with laundry to save her life.

The second door was a guest bath, but I only caught a glimpse before we moved to the end of the hall. I peered into the living room off to the left and realized we'd come full circle.

"And this one's yours." He opened the last door on the right, and I followed him inside. My immediate impression was that it was too girly to be a part of Jake's house. A four-poster bed stood in the center of the pale blue room, and a white down comforter was spread on top. The room was cast in a soft glow from the large window, and it looked so relaxing I realized for the first time how tired I was.

"You have your own bathroom," he said, pushing past me to open another door on the right. "I've put some things in there for you. I wasn't sure how long it would take you to unpack."

"Thank you," I said softly. I was taken aback. He'd always been there for me, but there was something so domestic and personal about picking out someone's toiletries that I would've never expected from Jake. I'd lived with Kevin for over two years, and he'd never once done anything like that for me.

A woman's voice called from the living room, and I turned just in time to see a petite blond enter the room. "There you guys are."

She threaded her arm around Jake's waist and peered at him adoringly. "Hey," she whispered. But it wasn't a normal whisper. It was a comfortable one—one that told me they were more than friends.

"Katie, this is Grace." He smiled down at her, but when he looked back to me, his brows furrowed, and I knew my shocked reaction must have been plastered all over my face.

I cleared my throat and shook my head a little. "Nice to meet you."

"Nice to meet you, too," she replied, but her eyes were fixed on Jake. "He's told me so much about you."

"Good things, I hope?"

"Of course." She glanced at me a second before turning back to Jake. "I just saw John pull up outside."

He clasped his hands together and smiled at me. "Perfect timing. Katie, where are the keys to the truck?" He flashed his white teeth and held his hand out expectantly.

"Why?" I asked, my eyebrows knit together as I tried to recover from the fact he had a girlfriend. It shouldn't have bothered me. I'd seen him with dozens of women over the years. Maybe hundreds.

"So we can unload."

I shook my head. "I only need a few boxes. The rest can go to storage until I find a place."

"That's ridiculous, where are your keys?" His tone more serious now.

"Jake…" I pinched the bridge of my nose, feeling very uncomfortable. He was already giving me a room. How could I take over his garage too?

"Either you give them to me, or I'll have to get them myself. You're not going to win."

I smiled at the familiar banter, and he grinned back.

"Fine." I pulled the keys from my pocket and slapped them to his outstretched palm.

He flashed his sideways smile like he'd just won a pillow fight, then looked to Grace. "You guys get acquainted, I'll be right back."

I watched as he bent to softly kiss her forehead before leaving the room. My jealous gut twisted. She was adorable. At least eight inches shorter than me, short and sassy blond hair, big blue eyes, and killer curves. The kind of girl you could toss in the air and give a piggyback ride to without breaking a sweat. Just like the girls Kevin cheated on me with.

"How long do you think you'll be staying?" She smiled with

her question, but her eyes told me she wasn't happy about my visit.

"Umm... Not too long, just a couple weeks. *I hope.* I have an interview on Monday." I shook my head. "I see Jake is as stubborn as ever."

"Yes, he is." She looked to the bedroom window just as Jake walked through the front gate. "He's been so nervous about having everything ready for you."

She said it like a statement, but I heard the fleck of apprehension lingering under the surface. I tried to think of something to ease her mind, but what could I tell her? There was a history between Jake and me even I didn't understand. A history that three years separation couldn't heal.

"I hear you're a photojournalist?"

I cleared my throat, thankful for the change in subject. "Yes. Though actually I'm trying to switch fields. That's why I'm here. I'm trying to break into the wedding market."

"How wonderful." Her face lit up. "Maybe Jake and I will end up needing you one of these days."

A knot twisted in my stomach. "Are you guys engaged? I hadn't heard—"

"Oh, no." She cut me off. "But a girl can always hope, right?"

"Of course," I whispered.

The whole room fell to an uncomfortable silence, and I turned to the window again.

"Well, I better go see if they need any help." My tone was awkward, but she didn't seem to notice.

"Alright." She gestured over her shoulder in the direction of Jake's room. "I just have some calls to make..."

I nodded, thankful she wouldn't be joining me, and we both left in different directions. I should've been grateful he had a girl-friend. I didn't need the complication of knowing he was available when my life was already falling apart. But I couldn't help the bubble of jealousy that grew inside me like a lovesick teenager. Just like it always had.

I entered the garage through the door off the living room to see the truck already backing up into the driveway. I rushed to the middle of the garage, waving him back with one hand as I kept an eye on each side to make sure nothing was hit. When he'd backed up far enough, I gestured for him to stop. The door opened, but the man who jumped from the cab wasn't Jake.

"Hey, thanks," he said, wiping his hands on his jeans as he walked toward me. He was younger than Jake, but not by much. His shoulders were broad, body fit, and his smile infectious.

"No problem." I smiled back. The way he was looking at me made me a little nervous, and I bit my inner cheek to keep my smile from spreading to a full grin.

"You must be the little sister." He held out a hand to shake. "I'm John. Jake and I work together." His hand was still extended, and I quickly recovered enough from the sister reference to not be rude. Of course Jake would introduce me as his sister. I shouldn't have been surprised...but I was.

"Katie," I said, finally finding my voice and giving him my hand.

"It's nice to meet you, Katie."

The way he said my name made me blush. Like he was talking about chocolate, or ice cream, or something else equally as delicious. I looked to the ground to hide my embarrassment. "Thanks for the help."

"No problem," he replied softly.

The door to the house opened, and we both turned to see Jake step into the garage. "Hey. You didn't tell me your sister was such a fox," John said.

Jake raised one brow, then walked toward me and draped an arm over my shoulder. "I see you've met John."

I cleared my throat. "Yes, and you didn't have to rope him into helping me, I'm pretty strong, you know." I glared up at him, but his attention was focused on the truck.

"How many of these boxes do you need inside?" he asked, pulling away to grab one of the dollies from the back of the garage.

"Umm, just a few. I marked the ones I need with red tape."

He looked down at me, his eyes creased with amusement and surprise. "Wow Katie, I'm impressed."

I gave him a playful punch in the ribs. I guess I wasn't always the most organized in the past.

"See what I put up with?" he asked John.

"It's okay, Katie, Jake's just a wimp. You stick with me, I like my women rough." John winked, and I couldn't help but laugh. *What was going on?*

Jake cleared his throat, and I could tell he wasn't happy about John's flirtation. He never liked it when guys flirted with me though. Neither had Dave.

When Jake lowered the ramp of the truck, he peered into the back and looked over his shoulder with an arched brow. "Dirty?" he asked, referring to the box in the very front. "I don't even want to know."

"Shut up." I shook my head. "I didn't have time to do laundry."

"Yeah, okay," he teased.

John grabbed the other dolly and smiled at me as he climbed the ramp. "Dirty and rough. My kind of girl."


It didn't take me long to realize I wasn't needed, plus John kept making comments that made my cheeks flame red. When Jake came out of the house for the third load, I dismissed myself and headed to my room for a shower.

As I waited for the water to warm, I caught a glimpse of myself in the mirror. There were bags under my eyes from little sleep; my hair, which started in long braids, now looked like something a bird had tried to nest in; and there was a coffee stain on the front of my light blue shirt. *Great.* I closed my eyes and began to work the tangles from my hair until loose waves fell to my shoulders.

When I stepped under the hot stream, I let some of the past week wash down the drain and tried to force myself to relax. It had been one of the worst of my life, but at least it was over. I needed to move on and focus on the next chapter. I grabbed the shampoo and conditioner Jake left for me and couldn't stop myself from inhaling the clean herbal scent. It smelled like him. There was something intimate and comforting about that.

Five minutes later, I wrapped one of the white towels tightly around my body and stood in front of the mirror again to brush my teeth.

*Jake has a girlfriend.* For some reason my mind couldn't let that go. He hadn't said anything about her when I called last week, and you'd think that would've been an important detail not to forget. Well, to me anyway.

But to be fair, I guess I didn't give him the chance. He'd been the first person I thought of when I got the confirmation of Kevin's infidelity, and when I talked to him, I might have been slightly hysterical. I probably scared the shit out of him. Actually, I know I did. He wouldn't let me hang up the phone until I promised that Kevin hadn't hurt me. To be honest, I think I called him because I wanted that kind of reaction. I knew he'd want to break Kevin's arms, and there was something strangely comforting about that.

When I finished combing through my hair, I peeked out to the bedroom to see a stack of boxes already inside. The door to the hallway was closed, so I opened the first box hoping to find something clean to wear.

The door to the bedroom flew open, and I let out a little scream.

"Oh shit," Jake muttered, shifting his eyes to the floor. "This is the last of it, I'll just come back later." He turned to leave, but I shook my head determined not to make things awkward between us.

"Jake, it's okay." My voice was tight, and I held the edge of my towel firmly at my chest, but we'd lived together almost a year, for Christ's sake. He'd seen me like this a thousand times. "You can just put it on the bed."

He nodded, then placed the box on the bed before he turned around. "Eaton and I are going to return the truck, is there any paperwork we need?"

"Who's Eaton?"

He scratched the back of his neck and looked into my eyes. I almost laughed at how obvious he was about not looking down. "Sorry, I mean John. There are a few of them at work, so I call him by his last name there."

"Oh." I chewed on my nail when he continued to stare at me.

"So...?"

"What?" I felt the blood rush to my face.

"Do we need paperwork for the truck return?"

Oh, God! Idiot!

"Oh—no—I don't think so. Do you need me to go with you? I just need to get dressed. It'll only take a minute." I pulled open the box and began shifting through my less than stellar pack job.

Jake laughed. "No, we're good. I don't think there's room in the cab anyway. Stay here and get settled."

I covered my face, feeling like a jerk. "Okay."

He bit his lower lip and smiled at me. "Are you up for company tonight? We thought we'd pick up a few pizzas."

"Sure, that sounds great."

"It's good to have you back, Kit Kat." He looked at me sideways as he walked out of the room, and I was left grinning, breathless, and completely in over my head.

# CHAPTER FIVE

J ake unnerved me. He turned me into a quivering mess
simply by his presence in a room. No other man had ever
done that—not even Kevin.

When I was in San Diego, it was easy to convince myself it was
all just something my body had become accustomed to. Like
Pavlov, and his theory of classical conditioning. Jake was the
ticking metronome, and I was the salivating dog.

I thought with three years of separation I'd be able to control
myself, but the minute I felt the backs of his callused fingers run
across my cheek, it was over.

What was it about him? How could he make my toes curl and
all the air leave the room with one of his smiles? Standing there
with only a towel shielding my naked body, my only thought had
been of running a finger along the cleft of his chin. To reach out
and touch the scruff of his face and the masculine edge of his jaw.
I didn't dare venture any farther south.

Digging through my boxes, I searched for the rest of my
running gear. Jake would be back from the truck return soon, and
I needed to get rid of some of this tension coursing through my
veins. I threw my still-damp hair in a ponytail, dressed in my

shorts and tank top, and slipped on my running shoes before heading out the door.

When my feet hit the pavement, I felt the familiar burn of my thighs and knew it would only be a few minutes before my mind went blank and peace washed over me. I'd started running in San Diego, when I hadn't known a single person and needed a way to escape from the grief of losing Dave. But if I was being completely honest, it was the loss of Jake, too. Yes, moving had been my choice, leaving my doing, but it still felt like abandoning another piece of my already shattered heart.

As I settled into my familiar stride, the sound of rustling leaves filled my ears. The streets were lined with enormous mulberry trees that must have been forty years old, and American flags flew in just about every yard. It reminded me of the neighborhood we grew up in, and I wondered if Jake made that same connection.

The sweet scent of star jasmine drifted in the breeze, and even though I didn't see any around, I would know that smell anywhere. It made me think of childhood, of home, of that hot August morning when I was six. Dad had brought the plants home, and I begged him to let me help dig the holes. Though thinking back on it, I'm pretty sure I did a lot more twirling than digging. My dad never seemed to mind, though. I don't think he was bothered by anything I ever did. The morning he passed, I sat out on the front steps in tears, the jasmine vining up the side of the house in bloom. I felt as though he were still there. Wrapped around me with memories of days playing in the front yard, spinning around in circles—but I was lost.

It was Jake who found me again. Late one night, a few days after Dad's passing, he walked into my room, pulled me into his arms, and hugged me so hard I felt whole again for the first time in days. In the silence of my pink bedroom he gripped me, his touch almost painful, but felt so good. It was that real human contact that told me life still had to be lived. That I could go on because even though I lost my dad, I still had people who loved me.

We didn't talk that night. No words could've been as meaningful as his touch. He held me for hours, and I let all the tears I kept bottled up fall to his shoulders. I couldn't let my mom and brother see them. They had their own grief, and I didn't want to worry them with mine. But Jake was strong; he could take my hurt, and I let it all pour out of me like a roaring river in spring. I didn't have to tell him how much I missed my dad, or about feeling consumed by guilt for being thankful it was over. I didn't tell him seeing my dad so sick at the end of his life had been too much for me to take, and I was almost happy when he finally found his peace. I didn't have to, because he already knew. It was in that moment, held in his capable arms, that I began to breathe again. That I began to feel like myself. And it was that night I decided I wanted to spend the rest of my life held in his capable arms.

Rounding the next corner, I saw a large field of grass with a play area on the other side. The park was filled with families enjoying what was left of the summer sun, and I recalled what Grace said about her and Jake getting married. Were things really that serious? Would Jake marry her? Have children? Surely not. Jake had always been so vocal about never wanting kids. Never wanting the family life he'd hated so much.

I pushed the thought of Grace from my mind and began running laps around the park. As I picking up the pace, my mind began to calm. Perspiration covered my skin like dew, and the summer breeze cooled me. The sun had begun to set on the horizon, and I relished in the soft rays as they kissed my face. A blue jay fluttered across my path, and for the first time all week, my fingers itched for my camera.

My love for photography started when I was ten years old, when I picked up my dad's camera for the first time. I had no idea what I was doing, but I felt important with it in my hands and loved to watch life happen through glass. Somehow limiting my view to that tiny window helped me see things a little differently, a little better. I often found hidden details that everyone else missed. To this day, I still heard my dad's voice every time I pushed the shutter.

*Slow down... Don't rush... See the shot... Breathe.*

When my legs began to tire, I turned back down the street to Jake's house. Each pound of my feet on the pavement rejuvenated me, and I felt lighter than I had in days. When I was only a few feet from the house, Jake walked out of the gate and waved. My foot caught on something on the sidewalk, and all of a sudden I flew through the air landing on hands and knees.

"Holy shit, Katie! Are you okay?"

In a second, Jake was at my side, pulling me into his arms and carrying me into the house through the entrance from the garage. "What happened?" His voice was rough with concern, but all I could think about was the feel of his warm breath on my neck.

"I tripped." I rolled my eyes, as heat sweep up my cheeks. He was making a fuss over nothing, and all I wanted was for him to put me down so I didn't embarrass myself further.

But he didn't. He continued into the kitchen and sat me on the counter.

My heart skipped a beat when he began to run his hands over my legs, inspecting them for damage. His touch was gentle, and I was suddenly very grateful I'd remembered to shave.

"Well, it doesn't look like anything's broken." He flicked on the faucet as he began rummaging through a cabinet.

"You don't have to do this, Jake," I said, wishing there was a drawer big enough so I could climb inside and never come out.

A smile lurked at the corner of his mouth as he pulled the first aid kit from the top shelf. "You always were accident prone."

*Only with you around.*

He moistened a paper towel under the cool water, rested one hand on my bare thigh, then ran the damp cloth over my skinned knees. Goosebumps covered everywhere he touched, and my breath hitched in my throat.

"Does that hurt?" He looked up at me through thick lashes, and I shook my head.

"Just a little," I lied. But I knew my reaction had nothing to do with pain.

"Do you remember that time Dave and I tied the skateboard to the back of my bike?" A lazy smile tugged at his mouth, and he brushed his thumb over my knee to remove some lingering debris.

I inhaled sharply as my nerves began to protest. "How could I possibly forget?"

"Sorry," he said with a wince, and I began to recall holding on for dear life as Dave pulled me at rapid speed down the middle of the street. No helmet, no protection. *Kids.*

"We were so lucky you didn't get seriously hurt." His eyes flashed to mine, and I swallowed.

He stood right in front of me, and my bare leg brushed against his jeans. He grabbed a tube of ointment out of the kit, applied a dab to his finger, then smoothed it over my roughened flesh.

I closed my eyes, overwhelmed by his closeness.

"I'm almost done," he said softly, but all I could think about was how clueless he was. How could he not see how much he affected me? Everyone else could. Why couldn't he?

I opened my eyes again when I felt the first bandage hit my knee. "Do you really expect me to walk around like this?" I asked, inspecting the large brown swatch with my fingers.

"You can take it off later." His blue eyes sparkled, and I couldn't help but smile. That was the Jake I knew. The Jake I'd missed every day for the past three years.

Just as he placed the last bandage, Grace appeared in the doorway.

"What's going on?" Her voice was calm, but she shifted her eyes from me to Jake, and I couldn't help feeling as guilty as the time Mom caught me in the closet playing doctor with little Billy Pratt.

"Just a couple of skinned-up knees," Jake replied. But the way she looked at us made me think she didn't buy it.

Just then the back door opened, and I gingerly climbed down from the counter to see John.

"I'm going to run to the store to get more beer, you guys need anything?" He was looking at us oddly, and I knew he could feel it too. The tension in the room was as thick as my grandma's split pea soup.

"Can I come with you?" I asked, needing to remove myself from this simmering pot.

"Of course," he replied, and I didn't hesitate before grabbing my purse and walking out the front door.

---

"What happened?" John asked as I climbed into the cab beside him.

"I just tripped." It was crappy answer. I knew he wasn't talking about my fall, but I really didn't want to think about what happened back there. I wasn't sure myself.

"I mean in the kitchen." He raised his eyebrows, and I knew he wasn't going to give up.

"I don't know." I turned toward the window and busied myself looking for the seatbelt. I still felt embarrassingly aroused from the whole ordeal and didn't feel like talking.

"Grace looked pretty pissed." He backed out of the driveway, shifted into gear, and pulled out to the open road.

"I hadn't noticed," I lied. It wasn't like she had anything to worry about. No matter how lustful my thoughts, Jake would never think of me as more than his sister.

"It's not like you can blame her."

"Blame her for what?" I couldn't read his expression.

"For being jealous."

*What?* "Why do you think she's jealous?"

"Oh come on, Katie. A beautiful woman just moved into her boyfriend's house. I think it's only natural." He turned the corner, and my chest tightened.

"Jake doesn't think of me that way." I shook my head and turned back to the window.

"Oh." His brow lifted. "So he's not your brother?" I could hear the amusement in his tone and cringed.

"Jake's a man, sweetheart. There's no way he doesn't notice you."

He pulled into the parking lot of the grocery store, and I practically jumped out of the truck as soon as it stopped moving.

He must have noticed the effect he had on me, because when he closed his door behind him, he was laughing. "Come on, Katie, let's go get some beer. Looks like you could use a few."

The next few minutes were spent with John throwing various microbrews and alcohol in the bed of the shopping cart.

"How many people are coming over anyway?" I asked, counting ten six-packs and all the fixings for margaritas.

"Just a few, but it would be a crime if we ran out." He flashed his easy grin, and I felt my mood lighten.

"So how long have you worked with Jake?"

"A few years," he responded, then pushed the cart to another aisle.

"Is he a good boss?" I caught myself smiling as I followed behind him, not able to ignore the way his ass looked in those jeans. He was very attractive, and I wasn't blind.

"He's grumpy as hell"—there was laughter in his voice—"but he's a good guy." He threw some plastic cups and plates into the cart before moving on. "Jake doesn't take any shit, but there's no one who works harder than he does. I mean...I don't know anyone who's built what he has in such a short amount of time."

49

I had to agree; Jake was a hard worker. Maybe his drive for success replaced the spot others reserved for family.

"So what's your story? I mean, now that I know you're not really his sister." He turned to look at me, and I noticed the scar between his lip and chin. It sort of reminded me of a dimple, but not... no, it was definitely a scar of some sort.

I cleared my throat, grabbed the cart from his hands, and started pushing it myself. "We grew up together."

"I'm sorry," he teased, then pulled the front of the cart, so we turned into the produce section.

John went off to grab a bag of lemons, while I busied myself knocking on watermelons.

"What the hell are you doing?" he asked, coming to stand beside me.

"I'm picking out a watermelon." I tried to keep my face serious, but I'd always felt silly when I knocked.

"Do you expect it to answer you?" He bumped me with his shoulder like old friends.

"Yeah, you go ahead and laugh now, but when this is the best watermelon you've ever had, I expect you to bow at my feet."

He raised his eyebrows, and I turned away before he could see me blush. *What the hell was I doing?*

He grabbed a watermelon of his own, held it to his ear, and began tapping. "What am I listening for?"

"Okay, you've had your fun. We can go now." I placed my watermelon in the cart and began to push.

"No, I'm serious." He reached out to grab my arm. "Tell me all your secrets, Katie." I looked up at him, and something in his expression told me he wanted to know more than about watermelon.

I laughed a little, grabbed the melon out of his hands, and started examining it. "Okay, the first thing you do is check to see if it feels heavy for its size."

He picked up another and did as I instructed, his face calm and serious.

I shook my head, feeling completely silly, but forced myself to continue. "It's also good to check for brown spots and pieces of sap."

"Does that mean it's bad?" he asked, his deep brown eyes both serious and reminding me of a puppy at the same time.

"No"—I laughed—"that actually means it's sweet."

"Like you." He smiled again, and I had to resist the urge to chew my lip.

He examined the dark green skin a while, and I couldn't help but be amused by how seriously he was taking the job. "When do we get to the knocking?" He looked up, and I laughed.

"Go ahead."

After a round of knocking from the both of us, he held his selected melon to my ear and tapped. "Is that right?"

I nodded. "Sounds good to me."

His arm brushed mine as he placed his melon in the cart, and I wondered if he'd touched me on purpose. I grabbed the melon I'd chosen, and put it back on the shelf.

"What are you doing?" he asked, seeming almost insulted as he took the melon off the shelf and returned it to the cart. "We'll need this for the competition."

My brows furrowed with suspicion. "What are you talking about?"

"One of us will be bowing tonight, remember?" A devilish smile spread across his face. "From the look of those brown spots, I think I have a good chance."

My jaw dropped. "But that's not fair." I followed behind him in complete shock. "I just showed you all my tricks."

"I never said I played fair, Katie." He looked back at me over his shoulder, his eyes alive with mischief, and pushed the cart into a checkout line.

*What the hell had I gotten myself into?*

# CHAPTER SIX

A half hour later, I stood in front of Jake's refrigerator and let the cool air rush over me. The feeling reminded me of the days when Dave and I used the fridge as a makeshift air conditioner. When everything was so simple.

The beer had begun to sweat at my feet, and I hurried to stack the bottles on empty shelves. Jake had spent nearly every day at our house back then. We ate boxed mac and cheese and hot dogs, while his parents prepared gourmet meals next door. I never questioned why. He grew up in a house that was more like a museum than a home. So much to see, so little to touch. I placed the last beer in the spot in the door, picked up one of the watermelons, and laughed. *Shit.*

"There's another fridge out in the garage."

Jake's voice startled me and I turned around. He smiled in that easy way of his and snaked an arm around my waist to grab a couple beers from the bottom shelf.

"Where's John?" he asked.

I closed the door and hoisted the melon a little higher. "Out back." I cleared my throat.

"Oh." He raised one brow, then glanced between the watermelon I held in my arms and the one still on the floor. "That's a lot of watermelon." He popped the caps off the beer and handed me one.

"So?" I carried the melon and beer to the center island and pulled a knife from the block. I'd spent the whole drive home trying to figure a way out of the whole situation. I didn't think John was serious, but I wasn't planning to find out either. "Do you have a bowl?"

He set his beer on the counter, then dropped to his haunches. "Will this one work?" he asked, pulling out a large silver bowl from the cupboard. He looked up, a glint of light hit his eye, and that same smile that always made my pulse race flashed at me.

I cleared my throat again. "Yes."

"How's work?" I asked, turning back to the cutting board and placing the bowl on the counter. The watermelon was large, and I had to use all my weight to get the knife all the way through.

"Busy. Which is good I guess." He was amused for some reason, and I shifted my weight to the other foot.

"Yeah, it looks like it's a good thing." I pulled out the knife and waved it around to indicate all he'd built, but his eyes went wide, and he stepped toward me.

"Careful." He removed it from my hand and placed it back on the counter. "Don't hurt yourself."

I wrinkled my nose, remembering the time I nicked Dave while slicing apples. It had been an accident of course, but there were some things you never lived down.

I laughed under my breath. "Sometimes it sucks knowing people so long. They know every mistake you've ever made."

His eyes crinkled with understanding. "Why are you so nervous anyway?"

I glanced down at the cutting board, hating the fact he knew me so well.

"I—" he began, but the back of his jeans started to buzz, and he muttered an apology as he shoved a hand in his pocket to fish it out his phone. He glanced at the screen, turned it off, then shook his head. "Sorry. Work."

I picked up the knife and began slicing again, hoping he'd forgotten about his last question. "You could have answered it."

He tucked the phone back in his pocket and shook his head. "It's the weekend, whatever it is can wait."

I nodded. "What are you working on these days?"

He raised his brows, my change of subject not going unnoticed, but he humored me anyway. "Right now? A shopping complex. The inspector's been riding my ass—I'm sure that was him... He doesn't like me too much."

"Do you think it has anything to do with you not taking his phone calls?"

He chuckled. "Maybe."

He continued to tell me more about work and all the jobs he'd completed while I was gone. I listened eagerly for every word. Not only because we weren't talking about me and my nerves anymore, but because I loved hearing about the company. The part of my brother that lived on through the hard work of his best friend. John was right. Jake had built a lot in a very short amount of time. Last I'd seen him, it was only he and Dave. Now there was a whole crew working under him.

When the bowl was piled high with fruit, I covered the mound with plastic wrap, and Jake grabbed the trash and threw it over his shoulder. "Come on, Kit Kat, I'll show you the other fridge."

We walked down the two steps to the garage, and he flicked on the light. It cast a faint glow over the empty space, and I began to feel uneasy about being alone with him for so long after the Band-Aids incident earlier. "Where's Grace?" I asked, my voice pitched a little higher than usual.

"She's out back." There was an irritation in his tone, and I wondered what happened while I was gone. Was John right? Was Grace upset I was here?

"I'll look for a place on Monday," I said softly, placing the bowl on the top shelf.

"What?" He threw the bag of rinds in the trash, and when he turned around, his eyes darkened.

"I don't want to cause any problems for you guys."

He came closer, and I noticed a lock of hair curled up by his ear. I wanted to touch it, to play with it between my fingers, but I resisted the urge and tried to brush past him before I did something stupid.

He grabbed my arm, placed one finger on my chin, and lifted my face to meet his. "Did Grace say something to you?" His voice was soft, and my heart began to race.

I exhaled a shaky sigh, exhaustion finally taking its toll on my emotions. "She's been nothing but nice to me."

"Katie, she's been upset with me all week. That had nothing to do with you."

I searched his face. *So they had been fighting.*

"Besides…" He dropped his hands, setting me free. "I just got you back. You can't leave me yet." His lips cocked in a lopsided grin, and I nodded, not knowing what else to say.

"Come on, there's someone here I want you to meet."

When we passed the kitchen, I took a long pull of my beer and followed him to the backyard. The sun had already set, and the patio was illuminated by small lights that ran over the slatted wood awning. I heard John's laughter, then saw him over by the table talking to a brunette seated on his lap. He was shirtless, and my eyes ran over his broad chest, which was partially shielded by the soft curve of a woman's back. Who was that?

There was a stack of pizzas on the table beside them, and when the smell reached my nose, I realized I hadn't eaten all day. Jake closed the door to the house and they both turned toward us. The woman hopped from John's lap, laughing at something he'd said as they walked over. The woman was very attractive, her hair short and sleek, her body soft and feminine. She wore a black bikini and a sarong tied at her hips that matched her blue eyes perfectly.

"Em Garland." She introduced herself. "You must be Katie."

I shook her hand. "Katie McGregor. Nice to meet you."

Her face lit up, and she threw her chin to the backyard. "We were just about to jump in the hot tub, want to join us?"

"My suit's still packed." I gestured a thumb to the house, but inside I was grateful for the easy out.

"I have one you can borrow." I turned to see Grace coming from Jake's room, and inwardly cringed. Not only had she ruined my easy out, but she also looked better in a bikini than she did in her clothes.

John walked over, draped an arm around her shoulders, and grinned. "I knew you were good for something." He kissed her forehead, then raised one brow at me.

She ducked out of his embrace, seemingly annoyed by his touch, and beckoned for me to follow her before disappearing through the double doors leading to Jake's bedroom. *Great.*

I awkwardly followed after her, stepping from the stone patio to the hardwood floor. "I'm not sure your suit will fit me."

"Oh, don't be silly." Her voice was soft and just a little too sweet. She pulled a suitcase from the corner of the closet, and her towel dropped to the floor. I tried not to notice, but it was impossible. Her body was perfect. Her breasts spilled from her aqua bikini like something you'd see on the cover of the swimsuit edition of *Sports Illustrated*. Even if the rest of me fit, there was no way I'd fill her top. I imagined it would look like a little girl trying on her mother's high-heeled shoes.

"Here it is." She tossed a clump of purple fabric at me, and I caught it at my chest.

"Thanks," I responded, then turned toward the hall that led to my room. "I'll just go put this on."

"You can use Jake's bathroom, I know he won't mind."

I cringed, feeling uncomfortable, but nodded anyway. When I

entered the bathroom, I locked the door behind me and noticed a lacy black bra hanging from the towel rack. I laughed a little—even though the situation really wasn't funny at all.

I placed my beer on the counter and threaded the fabric from finger to finger. I was wrong. The top would fit—barely. It was made up of two purple triangles and some string. How the hell she fit herself into it was beyond me. Though maybe she didn't care. Or maybe she only wore it for Jake. I shuddered at the thought; I really didn't want to think about that part of their relationship, or any part of their relationship actually.

I removed my clothes, folded them neatly on the counter, then jumped when I heard Grace's muffled voice calling through the door.

"What was that?" I asked. And why the hell was she talking to me anywhere? She was like one of those strangers who took up conversation in public restrooms. *Creepy.*

"I was wondering if it's working for you?" Her voice came louder this time, and I knew she moved closer to the door. *Great.*

"Umm...I think so?" I should have told her the truth, that I wouldn't even wear it to a gynecological exam, but I didn't want to cause problems for Jake.

"Great!"

I pulled on the bottoms, immediately blushing at how tiny they were. They fit because they were tie-on, but for the second time that day I was thankful I remembered to use my razor. As I struggled into the "cups," or whatever you would call something so small, I caught a glance of myself in the mirror, and froze. *Holy fuck!*

I wasn't ashamed of my body, but the top was miniscule. I pulled my ponytail out and shifted my hair forward to cover some of the exposed flesh. "Umm... What towel do I use?" I called through the door, both hoping and dreading that Grace was still on the other side.

"There should be some in the cabinet to the right of the shower."

*Yep. Still there.*

I opened the cupboard, grabbed one of the gray towels, and wrapped it around me before pounding the rest of my beer. When I opened the door a minute later, she stood in the center of the room. Her towel was still by the closet, and I couldn't help notice her suit was much less revealing than mine.

"Do you like it?" She looked amused as her eyes scanned over me from head to toe.

Anger flushed my cheeks, and my chest puffed up. She'd done this on purpose!

"Perfect," I answered sweetly, but inside I was livid. I wanted to yank her aqua bikini from her body and see how she liked it. She'd intentionally given me this suit to make me uncomfortable. What kind of person did that? I clenched my jaw, pulled the towel from my body, and walked out to the yard. *Screw her.*

I'd always been rebellious. If you told me to do one thing, I was likely to do the other. And it had seemed like a good idea in the moment, but that was only until I stepped out on the patio.

John noticed me first. He grinned appreciatively, raised his eyebrows, then took a swig of beer.

Jake and Em turned in unison, and I watched in slow motion as his gaze swept over me. His eyes smoldering blue as he took in every bit of my exposed skin. When he finally met my face, I was blushing. He cleared his throat, and I wrapped the towel around my body again.

"Do you know how to make a margarita, Katie?" Em asked, averting my attention.

"Sorta," I responded, forcing my eyes from Jake's heated stare.

"Well, that's a hell of a lot better than me." She grabbed my arm and pulled me behind her to the kitchen.

She placed a couple of shot glasses on the counter and immediately filled them with tequila. "I've had a shitty week," she explained, "how about you?"

I nodded. "You have no idea."

"Do you want to talk about it?" Her eyes searched mine as she handed me one of the glasses.

"Not really." I crinkled my nose, hoping she didn't take offense.

"Yeah, me either." She held up her shot and waited for me to do the same. "To new beginnings."

I laughed, thinking about how appropriate that was. We both threw back our drinks, and I coughed as the caustic fluid burned my throat. She gave me a couple pounds to my back, and I laughed again. "Sorry, it's just been a long time since I've done a shot."

"Well, we'll just have to remedy that," she replied, filling my glass for the second time.

"So are you and John—"

"God, no!"

"I'm sorry, I just saw you together and assumed."

She laughed. "John's great, but he's not my type." She threw back her second shot and gestured for me to do the same.

We spent a few minutes gathering all the necessities for margaritas. She hopped up to sit on the counter, and I began filling the blender with ice.

"What do you think of Grace?" she asked, looking at me in a way that said she was still trying to figure me out.

I cleared my throat, not sure how to answer. "She seems nice."

She nodded, but there was a glint in her eye that made me a little nervous.

I opened the bottle of sour mix, examined the back pretending to read the directions as an excuse not to speak.

"She's new," she said after a pause.

I cleared my throat again, realizing we were still talking about Grace, but remained silent. I was always so transparent about my feelings for Jake, if I said a word, she'd know.

She jumped off the counter and began measuring out the tequila. "I don't know what he sees in her, but she won't last. They never do."

We spent the next few minutes pouring ingredients into the blender, while I agonized about Grace. Em was right. Jake's relationships never did last. Maybe because he had horrible taste in women.

When we joined the others out back, my eyes immediately found Jake over by the fire pit. Grace sat on the seat beside him, and her hand rested on his thigh. A pang of jealousy grew in the pit of my stomach, and I took a cleansing breath. Why was I acting like this? It wasn't as if I had any claim on him. I never did.

Disgusted with myself, I placed the blender on the bar and poured myself a full cup of margarita.

John stood on the other side of the counter and smiled when I caught him watching me. He came closer, grabbed the drink from my hand, and took a sip. "Not bad."

"Thank you." I took it back, not sure what to do with him. The attention was flattering, but it was the last thing I needed right now. I turned around, needing a second to clear my thoughts, and noticed Jake walking toward us. His chest was bare, his swim shorts low on his hips, and I couldn't help my eyes from wandering over his hard chest and sculpted abs.

"You should eat," he suggested.

I cleared my throat and forced my eyes up. He was staring at the drink in my hand, and I was instantly annoyed. I knew he was right; I was known to be a lightweight, but that was none of his concern. I was sick of him being the big brother I never wanted him to be, and the temptation to go without dinner almost won out. But my head was beginning to feel a little foggy from the shots, and I decided now wasn't the time to be stubborn. I filled my plate with a couple slices of pizza, then noticed the bowl of watermelon sitting on the counter.

My eyes flicked to John, who raised a brow at me and laughed.

I couldn't help but giggle a little. The whole thing *was* kind of funny. Either that, or I was already more drunk than I thought I was.

"What's so funny?" Jake asked, obviously witnessing the exchange.

"Katie's a cheater," John responded, and I choked on a mouthful of margarita.

In spite of trying to avoid it, we eventually made it over to the hot tub. The alcohol was beginning to loosen my nerves, but nothing could make me forget I was practically naked in Grace's pathetic excuse for a bathing suit. I sunk deep under the water, did a quick check of my girly parts to make sure they were still covered, then glanced up to see John watching me.

He grinned. "Tell me about yourself, Katie?"

In spite of myself, I found him amusing and couldn't help but smile back. "I hate that question. It feels like an interview."

"Well, maybe it is." He winked.

His chest was bare, and I couldn't help my drunken eyes from wandering over his body. He had a cherry blossom tattoo over his left shoulder. I never thought a branch of flowers could look so... manly—but they did. I giggled into my cup, then forced my eyes in another direction. Which turned out to be a mistake. Jake sat directly across from me, the tips of his hair damp and sexy, but Grace was nestled between his parted thighs and ruined the whole thing.

I turned back to John.

He leaned forward and gave me all his attention. "What do you do for a living?"

I eyed him over my cup, noticing Jake shift in my peripheral vision. "Photography."

"Really?" Em asked, and she climbed in and sat to John's left. "Do you do head shots?"

I nodded, noticing again how striking her features were. "Are you an actress?"

She laughed and shook her head. "Not even close. I'm a web designer. *But* I do need some head shots."

"Oh. Well, I'd be happy to trade for tech help. I need a website... I mean, if you have time."

"I would *love* that!" she answered.

"Do you do parties, Katie?" Grace cut in, and I reluctantly turned to face her.

"Yes," I replied, though the thought of working for her made my stomach turn.

"She's *not* shooting the party," Jake interjected.

I frowned. "What party?"

"I'm throwing a party for Jake's thirtieth—"

"And Katie will be there as a guest," he stated. "I don't want you to worry about taking pictures," he said to me.

"I really don't mind—"

"No." He cut me off. Then his voice softened. "It's not a big deal."

"Not a big deal?" Grace scoffed. "It's your birthday. Everyone will be there." She turned to face him, and her voice lowered to a muffled whisper.

I averted my attention back to John and Em, trying to ignore the conversation between Jake and Grace. But my heart was heavy. I'd almost forgotten Jake's birthday.

As the night grew to an end, we made our way over the seating area. I curled up at the end of one of the loungers, my towel tight around my chest, as the fire burned low and steady between us. Jake pulled out his old guitar and began strumming the chords to "Ain't No Sunshine" by Bill Withers.

This used to be the norm for us. Nights much like this around the fire, and days filled with little sleep and pots of coffee because we stayed up to watch the sun rise.

John came over and lifted my feet. He sat down beside me, then returned them to his lap. "You look tired."

I laughed under my breath. "I am."

His strong hands took my feet and gently began to knead. "Relax."

I thought to protest, but my eyes grew heavy, and I felt my body sink deeper into the cotton seat of the lounger. "Okay…"

The next thing I knew, Jake stood over me and pulled the covers up to my chin. I took in a sharp breath and looked around my bedroom. He must have carried me to bed.

"How long have I been asleep?" I asked.

"A couple hours," he whispered.

I cleared the sleep from my throat as I remembered all the times he or Dave had put me to bed when we lived together. "Sorry." I sat up a little. "Is everyone gone?"

"Yeah." His voice was low and relaxed.

"They must think I'm so rude."

He shook his head. "Don't worry about it. They understand. Now go back to sleep, Kit Kat." He flicked off the light. "I'll see you in the morning."

I nodded, flipped to my side, and for the first time that night, did what he asked without arguing.

# CHAPTER SEVEN

The next morning, the alarm woke me at my normal time. Eight a.m. The same time I took that little green pill for the past two and a half years. The pill that allowed me to walk away from Kevin without the complication of a child, but couldn't protect me from the questionable practices of his infidelity.

I rolled to my side, reached from the seclusion of the sheets, and tapped the alarm. The room fell into blissful silence.

It had been over a week since I found out about Kevin, but the fear of the unknown kept me from seeing a doctor. I'd trusted him with my life, and thinking about all the women he'd cheated with over the years made my stomach turn. Had he used protection with any of them?

Soft light filtered through the bedroom window as I examined the small pill in the palm of my hand. In some ways I wanted to kiss the thing for preventing me from getting pregnant; in others, I wanted to throw it across the room because of the reminder I was alone.

*Today I would make an appointment. I'd procrastinated long enough.*

The covers were twisted around my body from sleep, and I threw them to the foot of the bed. Grace's bikini loomed under their surface, and I muttered a curse as I shifted the fabric back over my exposed breast. I bit my lip. *Had it been like that when Jake brought me to bed last night?* Surely not. He would have said something. Wouldn't he?

Dismissing the thought, I dragged my aching body to the restroom, discarded Grace's bathing suit to a pile of laundry, and quickly dressed in a pair of cutoffs and Dave's old Dodger hoodie. It was practically threadbare in spots and way too large, but it was one of the only things I had left that reminded me of my brother.

The wood floor was cool beneath my feet as I padded down to the kitchen. The counters were cluttered with bottles and discarded plates, and the sight of the empty tequila bottle made my stomach turn. Alcohol had seemed like a good idea last night, but as I tried to calm my aching head, I cursed the man who invented tequila, vowing never to drink it again.

Jake's kitchen was stocked in a way you'd expect of a bachelor. Lots of beer, very little food. But I was somehow able to rummage together a box of Bisquick and the rest of the ingredients for pancakes.

After doing the dishes, I set a pot of coffee to brew, and a calmness I hadn't felt in days washed over me. The house was so quiet I could hear the sound of the hot water percolating through the rich grounds as I began mixing up the batter.

When I had it all ready, I went in search of a skillet, and spotted one in a low cupboard. I dropped down to retrieve it from the bottom shelf, but Jake's voice startled me, and I bolted to my feet like I'd just been caught searching his underwear drawer.

"You scared me," I said, my hand on my breast as I tried to calm my rapid heart.

"Sorry," he chuckled. "I thought I smelled coffee."

He wore a pair of pajama pants tied at his hips, and his bare chest reminded me of the fact he'd carried me to my room last night. I swallowed, then I glanced up to see a smile tug at the corner of his mouth and realized I'd been staring.

"I was just making pancakes," I explained, placing the skillet on the burner. I sliced a pad of butter from the brick, added it to the pan, then struggled with the knob of the range.

"Here, let me help you." He came to stand behind me, a hint of amusement in his voice, and brushed my side as he turned the knob to ignite the flame. "You have to push it in first."

I inhaled the rich, earthy scent of his skin and closed my eyes, trying to force down the growing feelings inside me. "Thank you," I whispered. Both relieved and disappointed when he moved away.

"When did you learn to cook?" he asked, resting a hip against the counter, watching me.

"It's just Bisquick, Jake. I'm not sure if that qualifies as cooking."

"I don't know... I still remember that frozen lasagna."

I shook my head at the memory. "It wasn't that bad." The butter now sizzled in the pan, and I ladled a spoonful of batter on top.

"It still gives me nightmares." He grinned.

I narrowed my eyes. "You better watch it, Jake. Your food could easily become compromised."

"I think I'll take my chances."

Right then, with his hair wild from sleep and his eyes twinkling with mischief, he looked so young, like the Jake I had pillow fights with. The Jake who teased me about my nerdy boyfriends. I hadn't realized until that moment, but he'd seemed different since I'd come back. Harder, tired, closed.

"A lot can change in three years." I turned back to the pan and flipped the first pancake to a waiting plate.

He shifted a little. "It's been too long, Katie." His tone causing a knot to form in the pit of my stomach.

I'd lost count of how many times he'd invited me to come back. But I always knew seeing him again would be painful—I was right. He looked at me expectantly, but what could I even say?

*Because just the sound of your voice makes me quiver.*

*Because I was afraid you'd see the longing in my eyes.*

*Because I was terrified of falling in love with you again...*

But I said nothing, and ladled more batter into the pan. The coffee maker beeped, breaking the silence between us, and Jake retrieved a couple of mugs out of the cupboard. "Will milk be okay? I don't have any half-and-half."

I shouldn't have been surprised by the fact he remembered how I took my coffee, but my heart still squeezed a little. "Yes, thanks."

Flustered, and not knowing what else to say, I answered his earlier question. "I took a class," I said, trying to ignore how easily he affected me.

He shook his head, and I realized it had been a while since he asked it.

"To learn how to cook."

"Oh yeah?" He took a sip of his coffee, but the corner of his mouth lifted from behind his mug.

"Are you laughing at me?" I narrowed my eyes, though inside I was smiling too.

"I'm just happy you're here, that's all." His dimple flashed, and I had to clear my throat before continuing.

"It was when I moved to San Diego. The flyer said it was a great way to meet people." I flipped another pancake, thinking of how I was the only person in class under the age of sixty-five.

"Is that where you met Kevin?" His voice was tight.

"No," I said softly, then wanting to chance the subject asked, "Where's Grace?"

He raised a brow and took another sip of his coffee. "She went home last night."

"Oh, yeah..." I vaguely recalled him saying so last night. "How long have you guys been together?"

"A few months. She sold me this house."

"Real estate agent?"

"Yep."

"So she sells you this house and you fall madly in love?" I laughed, trying to hide the fact that seeing him with another woman still made my blood flow green.

He topped off his mug with more coffee and smiled. "She works for the agency that sends us most of our clients."

*Oh.* My brows furrowed. "Doesn't that make things complicated? Mixing business with pleasure?"

He shrugged, then completely ignored my question and nodded toward my hoodie. "I remember that shirt."

I cleared my throat and poked a finger through a hole on the sleeve. "Yeah, it's seen better days." But inside a bubble of fear grew in my stomach. *Did Jake love her?* Getting into a relationship with someone so close to his business didn't seem like the Jake I knew.

"I think this was from when Dave and I painted the old house together." He ran a hand down a streak of brown on my arm, and my worries about Grace were replaced by memories of my brother. My chest tightened.

"Yeah, I think you're right." It had been so long since anyone mentioned Dave that the sound of his name caught me off guard.

"It looks better on you." He smiled his crooked smile, then excused himself to get the paper.

When he turned the corner, I leaned against the counter and tried to collect my thoughts. Being around Jake brought back so many feelings I hadn't been prepared for. Feelings I thought had dulled but in reality were as sharp as a razor. I blew out a breath, told myself to calm down and got back to work flipping pancakes.

With the table set, I looked out of the bay window, taking in the view of the backyard. It was beautiful, and after I finished my chores, I thought I might treat myself to a dip in the pool. When I turned around, Jake was right behind me, and I slammed into the wall of his chest.

"Ooof!" He laughed. "Are you okay?"

"Yes." I squeezed my eyes shut, trying to ignore his warm skin that was so close to my lips I could taste it.

"Did you need something?" His voice was deep and smooth, and I looked up to see him smiling.

*You.*

"Butter." The familiar tug twisted in my abdomen, and I let out a shuttered breath.

He smoothed a lock of hair away from my face before turning toward the fridge. "Syrup?"

"Yes, please," I muttered, then grabbed my coffee and took a long sip. Only a week ago I planned to spend the rest of my life with another man. But sitting there in that kitchen, a plate full of Bisquick pancakes in front of me, I realized the last three years had been a total lie. My heart had never been Kevin's. It couldn't have been. It lived over a hundred miles away—here with Jake.

When he returned to the table a minute later, he wore a pair of black-rimmed glasses that made him look like Clark Kent. A very sexy, half naked Clark Kent.

"Nice glasses," I said, unable to contain my grin as I sliced a pat of butter and spread it over my pancakes.

"Thanks." His brows furrowed, but a smile lingered at the corner of his lips. "They're for reading."

"You need glasses for reading now?" I raised my brows in that teasing way that told him he was getting old. The one thing I held over him and used whenever possible as payback for all the times he and Dave called me a baby.

"I know." He scratched his head. "I'm almost thirty, how'd that happen?"

I smiled, then stood and grabbed the coffee pot to refill my mug. "So what's this party thing Grace was talking about last night?"

"I don't know. Something she's been planning for a while." He shrugged.

"Here? At the house?"

"Yeah..."

"Oh." I frowned. It wasn't like him to have big parties. In fact, he hated them... Sorrow gathered in my chest, and I poured syrup on top of my pancakes. So much had changed since I'd been gone.

---

By twelve o'clock I had most of my clothes unpacked, my laundry sorted, and a doctor appointment scheduled for Monday afternoon. Jake was in the living room watching a Dodger game, and I could periodically hear him yelling at the screen. Just like the old days. Before one perfect kiss tore us apart.

I gathered a load of laundry from the floor, stopped to add the purple bikini to the load, then headed out to the garage. As I passed him on the couch, the sound of Kevin's unmistakable voice filled my ears. Adrenaline pumped through my veins, and I whipped around, scanning the room for his face. My body stiffened, and my eyes locked on the television.

A wildfire blazed on the screen, and Kevin's smooth voice reported the devastation. My hands dropped, and the laundry slid from my arms to a pile on the floor. There he was, that gorgeous face that used to make me swoon, now projected on the sixty-inch television screen.

"Katie?"

I barely heard Jake's voice as I wrapped my arms around my stomach. This wasn't the first time Kevin had been on TV, but it was scarce enough that I wasn't expecting it.

"I found condoms in his pocket once—I'd already been on the pill for over a year." I laughed a little, a hollow laugh with no humor. "I actually believed him when he said he'd forgotten to take them out."

I felt Jake move behind me but didn't turn around. "Then someone left a note in my inbox, warning me that he hadn't been faithful—that's when I knew." I turned to face him. "There were three of them that I know of, but probably more." I closed my eyes, not sure why I was telling him all this, but in that moment, it was important to me.

He tried to speak, but I shook my head, needing to finish. "People in the office actually covered for him. One of the women was even supposed to be my friend." My throat constricted, and I had to swallow before I spoke again. "I hired a private investigator. A fucking PI—like one of those cheater shows we used to watch as kids." I looked into his eyes. "I didn't know what else to do."

My body began to shake, and he pulled me into his arms. His grip so tight it almost crushed me.

"That fucking asshole." His voice was low, mixed with a protection for me, and a hatred for Kevin.

"He said he loved me." My voice cracked on the words, and I closed my eyes. "What kind of love is that?" It felt good to share my burdens, to know that others knew my secrets, but at the same time—I was ashamed. I pulled away and wiped at my face with the back of my hand. "Yeah, so…" I looked down to the laundry on the ground, desperate to lift the cloud that filled the room. "Maybe if I wasn't so bad at laundry," I joked.

He caught my hand and stilled me. "You did *nothing* wrong."

His voice was soft but held an edge. I closed my eyes, swallowed the bitter tears that threatened the back of my throat—but it was too late. I was fighting a losing battle.

My chin began to quiver, and he crushed me to his chest again. "Shit… Don't cry. That asshole doesn't deserve your tears."

I nodded into his chest and accepted the comfort I'd been needing all week. The comfort I knew would be here when I came back. A knock sounded at the door, and I immediately pushed away.

John peered through the screen door, his brows furrowed, and he shook his head a little. "Should I come back later?"

Jake turned to answer, and I picked up my pile of clothes, ran to the garage, and threw the laundry to the top of the machine. I heard Jake enter a couple minutes later, but I couldn't face him. I'd made a fool out of myself, made things look so much worse than they really were. "Sorry." I cleared my throat. "That looked really bad."

He ignored my words and came closer. "Are you okay?"

I nodded, using every bit of my self-control not to lose it again.

"I can tell him to go away. He's just here to watch the game."

I shook my head, turned to face him, and forced myself to take a breath. "Don't do that. I'm fine. Really. Go enjoy your game."

"Katie..." His eyes were filled with sympathy, and I looked down at my hands. That was the last thing I wanted from him.

"Please?"

He nodded. "Okay. But I'm here if you want to talk."

"I know."

I thought he might say more, but he didn't. He dropped his hands to his sides and walked back into the house.

When I heard the click of the door, my body sagged, and I dropped to the garage floor. *Jake knew.* There was something so final about that. Something that made the whole thing so much more real. My lips began to quiver again, and I finally allowed myself to grieve. To mourn the loss of a life I'd started to believe in.

# CHAPTER EIGHT

The next morning, standing in a terry cloth robe, I looked down at Kevin's name glowing neon green across my phone. I had to leave for the interview in an hour. My hair was still damp, my face naked, and I had no clue what I was going to wear—I didn't have time for more excuses, not that I wanted to talk to him even if I did. I swiped the screen, sending Kevin to voicemail, and pulled another top from my closet.

I should've decided on an outfit last night, but Jake and I ended up eating cold pizza and watching movies until midnight. I'd been worried things would've changed after I told him about Kevin's infidelity. That he'd look at me in that same sympathetic way he'd done in the garage. But when I came inside, we both went on like I hadn't just crumbled to pieces in his arms.

My phone buzzed with a new text, and I closed my eyes, knowing it was Kevin again. I looked down to the screen on the dresser and froze.

KEVIN: Pick up the fucking phone!

What the hell? Who did he think he was?

ME: I'm sorry, you must have mistaken me for one of your WHORES. I'm busy.

KEVIN: Cute. Where the fuck are they, Katie?

My chest tightened, and I looked around my room wondering if I'd packed something of his by mistake.

ME: I don't know what you're talking about.

And I didn't. I had no clue.

KEVIN: Don't play games with me. You don't know who you're dealing with.

"Having problems?" Jake's amused voice startled me, and I spun around to see him standing at my bedroom door.

My heart was running crazy, but I shook my head and turned off my phone. Whatever was bothering Kevin wasn't my problem, and I certainly wasn't going to bring it up to Mr. Fix-It. "I can see you still haven't learned to knock."

Jake's adorable smile gleamed at me, and he held up two mugs. "My hands were full."

I pressed my lips together to hold back a grin and walked toward him. "Let me get this straight, you couldn't knock, but you were able to open the *door* just fine?"

He shrugged, and I took a mug from his hand.

"Thank you."

He nodded, then gestured a chin to the mess all over my bed. "What are you doing in here anyway?"

"I have an interview, remember?"

"So you decided to throw your clothes all over the room?" He raised one eyebrow, clearly amused.

I looked around, taking in the scene through different eyes. My clothes were on every surface, my blow dryer and makeup on the floor by the mirror, and my shoes in a large pile in front of the closet. "Oh, be quiet." I yanked another shirt from the closet and held it under my chin. "This is important. I have to look perfect."

He glanced from my bare feet to my wet hair, then took a sip of his coffee. "You already do."

The seriousness of his tone made my breath catch. "Thanks."

He'd always said stuff like that, and a part of me wished he wouldn't. That's what made him so easy to love.

I hung the top back in the closet, determined to stay on task. "What are you doing home anyway? It's already nine thirty. Shouldn't you be at work?"

"Paperwork," he said, running a hand through his hair. "I decided to stay home so the guys wouldn't bug me every two seconds."

"You mean the way you're bugging me?" I raised my eyebrows, then grabbed another top.

"Very funny." He shoved a hand in his pocket and grinned. "You know you can't get enough of me."

He was kidding, but his words couldn't have been more true. After all these years I still craved his company more than chocolate—even the peanut butter filled kind.

He turned toward the door. "I'm going to make some eggs, you want some?"

I shook my head. "No thanks, I'm too nervous."

His forehead creased. "You can't survive on coffee, Katie."

*Katie.* I was always Katie when he disapproved of something I did.

"Would you stop. I'm a big girl. I can take care of myself."

He shook his head, as if he was laughing at himself. "You're right." Then his eyes met mine and he smiled. "Knock him dead."

I smiled back. "I'll try."

---

Two hours later, I stood in front of the upscale café downtown and shifted my gear bag to my other shoulder. I hadn't been sure what to bring this morning, so I decided on everything. Now with my camera bag on one arm and portfolio in the other, I was worried it might be too much.

I set my portfolio to the ground, balancing it against my leg as I simultaneously tried to open the heavy door. The hostess must have taken pity on my struggle, and she rushed to the entrance, holding the door wide so I could fit through with all my stuff.

My cheeks bloomed with embarrassment as I nodded my thanks, stepped inside, and glanced around the café looking for Rick Henderson—the brilliant photographer I hoped to assist for.

The restaurant was unlike anything I'd never seen. Soft light streamed through a wall of windows and made the indoor space feel like I was still outside. The gray textured walls were covered with boughs of ivy, and small tables with mismatched chairs sat on the polished cement floor. The whole scene looked like something from the streets of Europe, instead of a small shopping center in downtown Los Angeles. Not that I would've known. I'd never been anywhere outside of the US.

The smell of freshly ground coffee and sweet pastries hit my nose at the same moment I saw him. He sat at one of the far tables in the corner, leaning back in his chair, and looked exactly like his profile picture online. Handsome, probably mid-forties, and even though I was still over ten yards away, I felt the confidence radiating off of him.

A waitress approached his table, and something he said caused her to blush and drop the menu. He picked it up, seeming amused, then handed it to her as she rushed away.

His brown hair was on the long side, but very fashionable. And the long legs stretched in front of him were covered by faded designer jeans. I had to admit, he was sexy. But he knew it. His button-down white shirt was left casually open at his throat, and he looked every bit the artist I knew him to be—it was intimidating.

"Mr. Henderson?" I asked as I approached the table, even though I knew exactly who he was.

He glanced my way, pulled himself to stand, and eyed me up and down.

I had decided on black slacks and white bohemian top, but as I took in his brown flip-flops, I wondered if I'd overdressed.

"You must be Ms. McGregor." Amusement turned his lips as he took in all my stuff. He slipped my gear bag from my shoulder and gestured toward one of the chairs. "Please, sit down."

I awkwardly placed my portfolio under the table and smiled. "Thank you, Mr. Henderson."

"Call me Rick."

I nodded. "Rick." Then sat.

He set my bag on the table and took his place across from me. "I looked over your resume." He leaned back in his seat again. "But I have to ask—why are you applying for this position?"

I blinked, feeling like a kid who just jumped in the deep end without floaties.

"Why the change of direction?" he clarified.

Crap. I was drowning. I pulled myself a little straighter while I tried to think of my reason. I had one—I'd gone over a million different questions on the drive over, but now sitting across from this confident man, my mind went blank.

*Don't screw this up, Katie. You need this job.*

After what seemed like an eternity, but in reality was only about thirty seconds, I spoke. "I like to tell stories." My tone rushed and tight.

He seemed to enjoy watching me squirm, and smiled as he leaned back in his chair. "I gathered as much. Considering you were a *photojournalist.*"

*Oh God, I'm going to die.* Would he notice if I just crawled under the table and hid?

"You have a lot of talent, there's no denying that fact." He considered me from across the table. "Why weddings?"

I took a deep breath, then moistened my dry lips. "Because it's the happiest time of a person's life."

He seemed to be intrigued by my answer, which gave me confidence to continue.

"There are so many emotions wrapped up in that single day. Hundreds of hours have gone into meticulously planning each detail. Months—sometimes years—yet when it comes down to it, there are no guarantees. Life doesn't always turn out the way you plan, and that's where *we* step in."

I made eye contact, looking for signs of boredom, but he seemed interested, so I continued. "It's our job to tell their story. The hopes, the dreams—the good and bad—to deal with the stuff that goes wrong, and to be there for the things that go *right*. To capture the emotions, the fears, and the love…"

"Ahhh. So you're a romantic." He leaned forward again, his arms braced on his knees, and pressed his fingertips to his lips. "I like that. I like *you*, Ms. McGregor."

His tone made me uneasy, and I sat back in my chair. "Thank you."

"Are you willing to travel?"

"Of course."

"Out of the country?"

I considered this for a moment. "Yes."

"Are you sure?" he asked, obviously detecting my apprehension.

"Yes," I replied with a little more confidence.

"What do you shoot with?"

I'd sent a list of my equipment with my resume, but I wasn't about to point that out. I reached for my gear bag, but he stopped me with a wave of his hand. "Just tell me, Katie."

My heart picked up speed, and I rattled off my less-than-stellar list. So much of what I was accustomed to had been on loan from the paper—all returned when I quit.

He listened, his fingers once again pressed to his mouth.

"You'll need to add a 70-200mm 2.8. Can you handle that?"

I swallowed. That was a twenty-five-hundred-dollar lens, but I had the money. I nodded.

He smiled, seeming pleased. "I'll be needing an assistant next weekend. Will you be ready by then?"

"Yes, of course."

"Good." He leaned back in his chair once more. "I'll have you know, I don't give second chances. One mistake and you're out."

"Yes, I understand. Thank you for the opportunity, I've been a fan of your work for years."

He nodded, like he'd heard the words a thousand times.

"Okay, that's enough business for today." He smiled across the table and signaled for the waitress. "What would you like to drink?"

"Just coffee please."

When the waitress approached the table, Rick ordered for both of us, then turned his attention back to me. "Tell me about yourself, Ms. McGregor." His tone softened, and he once again leaned back and got comfortable.

I straightened. "What do you want to know?"

The rest of the meeting carried on more like an awkward blind date than an interview. A date I would have walked out of. The way he watched me sent a creepy feeling up my spine, and I reminded myself this was only temporary. I was using this job to learn the business and pay the bills. That was all. As soon as I got settled, I never had to see Rick Henderson again.

An hour later, seated in the waiting room of the obstetrician's office, I dialed Shelly's extension. She had been my partner at the paper and the only reason I held any regret for my less-than-optimal exit. I needed to explain what happened, or at the very least, say goodbye.

"Shelly Hanson," she answered in a rushed tone.

I cringed—she was obviously stressed. Stressed because *I* had left her alone with double the work.

"Hey Shell, it's me." I pinched the bridge of my nose and waited for her response.

The phone muffled, like she was cupping it with her hand. "Katie? Where are you?"

I took a deep breath. "LA, I—"

"Oh my God. You don't know!"

Bile crept up my throat, and I pushed back against the textured upholstery of my seat. "Know what?"

"Shit, Katie... Hold on a sec."

More rustling noises came through the receiver, and my stomach twisted with anxiety. I heard the sound of a door closing, then Shelly picked up the phone again. "Katie, I hate to be the one to tell you this, but Kevin's been cheating on you, honey."

I adjusted in my seat and let out a sigh of relief. "Oh, Shelly, I already know. We broke up. That's why I'm in LA."

"Shit. I'm so sorry."

My brows furrowed. "How did you find out?"

There was a pause, followed by more rustling. "When I came into work this morning, there were photos of Kevin *in bed* with Mr. Olson's wife plastered as everyone's interface," she whispered.

My eyes bulged and the texts from Kevin that morning ran through my mind. "How?"

I barely got the word out before she continued. "I think Olson's wife did it. She came in about an hour ago with her lawyer. She said something about making a fool of him the way he made a fool of her."

"Holy shit," I muttered, then immediately regretted my foul mouth when I locked eyes with a toddler jumping up and down on his mother's lap. They were seated across from me, her stomach hard and round with pregnancy, her eyes drooping with exhaustion. But she still smiled and sang into the ear of the boy who reminded me of a cherub, both seemingly unaware of my inappropriate language.

I lowered my voice. "What about Kevin?"

"He was fired and gone before most people got in this morning."

*Wow!* He must have thought it was *me.*

"Katie," her voice softened, "are you okay?"

I nodded, then realized she couldn't see me through the phone and swallowed the lump that always formed when people asked that question. "Yes."

"He got what he deserved. Don't you dare feel bad about this." She knew me too well. She knew I'd internalize everything and blame myself.

I let out the breathy laugh, knowing she was right. "Thanks, Shell. I'm gonna miss you."

A commotion of voices sounded from the other side of the receiver, and Shelly cupped the phone again. "Hey babe, I hate to do this, but I really gotta go. The shit has hit the fan around here. You keep in touch, okay?"

I smiled. "Okay, I will."

"Bye, babe."

I clicked off the phone and picked up a magazine from the coffee table. Mr. Olson's wife did what I was too chicken to do. Made Kevin look like the fool he was—yet I was being blamed for it. *Figures.*

My phone began to vibrate beside me and I jumped. But it wasn't Kevin like I'd expected; it was Mom. *Great.* I hadn't told her about Kevin, and I knew she'd have questions. Questions I didn't really feel like answering in that moment. But I took a deep breath, swiped open the screen, and let out a sigh.

"Hi, Mom."

Her clipped voice came immediately. "I called your house, but it was disconnected. Is everything okay?"

I shook my head, wondering why Kevin had disconnected the phone. Probably to avoid reporters—which was both ironic and hilarious. "Everything's fine, Mom. Kevin and I broke up." I crunched up my face, waiting for her reply. She wouldn't like this. She was always fond of Kevin.

"*What?*" she screeched.

"It's okay." I paused. "It's for the best."

"But weren't you guys going to get married?"

"No," I shook my head, "we were never getting married." I just hoped we would. Big difference.

"Where are you now, honey? Do you need to come stay with me and Paul? You know things are crazy here, and he's in a lot of pain from his back, but there's always the couch..."

She continued on about doctor's appointments, work, and her busy life—all reasons I hadn't called her in the first place. But how could she think I could possibly move in with her and Paul? She knew how I felt about him. Sleazy, gold-digging Paul.

Okay—so he wasn't *that* bad, but he hadn't worked a day of the five years they'd been together, and Mom still did *everything* around the house. But if I was being honest, and as childish as it might seem, the reason I didn't like Paul was because he took my mom away when I needed her most.

I stared into the center of the room, remembering the worst days of my life, while Mom went on about Mary Lu, and how she was jealous because Mom was promoted before her.

"...so I guess we could clear out a space in the front room. Get a blow-up mattress. What do you think?"

"Mom, it's okay. Really, I'm fine."

"Oh, okay..." Her voice lowered, but I could tell she was still worried.

I closed my eyes and let it out. "I'm staying with Jake, Mom."

She was quiet a minute. "Our Jake? Jake Johnson?"

I rolled my eyes, and the little boy bouncing in his mother's arms giggled. "Yes, that's the one." I twirled my finger at my ear and mouthed the words "crazy" to the little cherub. He snorted a laugh, then covered his face with the chubbiest little hands I'd ever seen.

"Oh honey, I'm so happy to hear that."

She knew—just like everyone else—how much I loved Jake. She also knew this was my first time seeing him since Dave passed.

"How is he? Is he still handsome?"

"Mom..."

"Okay, okay. I'm just happy you two are talking again."

The nurse walked into the waiting room, and I sat up at attention. She glanced at her clipboard, then out to the waiting room.

"Katie McGregor?"

I stood and picked up my bag. "Mom," I said, already feeling breathless with fear. "I gotta go."

# CHAPTER NINE

It was late afternoon by the time I made it back to the house, and my blood still boiled from the judgmental comments the doctor made about protection. I didn't know why I let it bother me so much; it wasn't like she knew me, *or* knew my reason for being tested. But for the briefest of seconds I considered telling her about Kevin. Though what would've been the point? I needed to stop worrying about what other people thought of me.

I popped the trunk, got out of my car, and began filling my arms with gear and the groceries I'd picked up on the way home. I felt guilty for needing a place to stay and wanted to make dinner for Jake to say thanks. It was small comparatively, but it would make me feel better knowing I was contributing in some way.

When my arms were completely full, I looked down at the carton of milk still sitting in the corner. I knew I should make two trips, but the stubborn side of me wouldn't let that happen. I set a couple bags to the top of the car, grabbed the milk, closed the back, then somehow collected everything between my shoulders, arms, and fingers.

I made it to the walkway before my phone began to buzz in my pocket. I bit my lip, trying to figure out how to get the phone to my ear without having to start completely over. But my arms began to tremble under the weight of the groceries, and I decided to ignore it—I'd already made it halfway and was determined to make it to the finish line. I entered the code to unlock the door, pushed down the handle with my fingertips, then forced the door open with my foot. It thudded against the wall, and I shimmied inside, trying to balance the bag that had ripped on the walk over as I dropped everything to the floor.

Jake was lying on the couch, and even with my less-than-graceful entrance, he was still fast asleep. Which wasn't surprising. I'd once done both his hair and makeup on a slumber party dare without so much as a flinch.

A black binder was settled on his bare chest, and he was wearing those damned sexy glasses again. My stomach fluttered. This whole living with him thing would go a lot smoother if he didn't insist on lying around looking so delicious all the time. Okay, so this was the first time I'd seen him lying around, but it was enough! Hopefully it would be the last.

My phone buzzed with a new message, and I pulled it out of my pocket. *Kevin again.* I closed my eyes, contemplating whether I wanted to hear what he had to say or not. He'd lost his job today, and judging by the texts I'd received that morning, he blamed me for it. Well screw him. If he hadn't gone and slept with half the office, he wouldn't have been in this position. It wasn't my fault. I quickly erased the messages before a weak moment could force me to listen, then went into my settings and blocked his number from ever contacting me again. *Out of sight, out of mind.*

Leaving my gear by the front door, I began putting the groceries away, taking a couple trips to appease my protesting arms. But when I was done, Jake still hadn't moved.

In spite of my better judgment, my unauthorized feet stepped closer. Like a magnet to a pile of nails, I couldn't stay away. When I was a girl I used to study him when I thought no one was watching. I had him memorized—like a road map to my aching heart—the deep cleft of his chin, the dimple on his right cheek. His straight nose, and those eyelashes so thick I imagined he grew tired just holding them up. He'd been my idea of perfect then, and if I was willing to admit it, I guessed he still was.

My heart clenched, and I brushed his hair back from his forehead to reveal the small birthmark along his hairline. So often I wondered if anyone outside of me and his own mother knew it was there. My heart picked up speed at the idea of being caught, but my fingers didn't listen and traveled to the crease above his brow—probably formed from long hours of studying, or maybe too much stress—but they were deeper now, and a sadness welled in my belly. I'd missed so much while I was away. Memories I could never recreate, and time I could never get back. There were parts of him I didn't know anymore. That saddened me more than I cared to admit.

I took a deep breath and ran my hand through his glossy hair once more. His face moved toward my hand like a kitten. So trusting, so sweet, and dead to the world. I slowly removed the glasses from his face, folded them up, and settled them on the coffee table.

*Damn him and his sexy face.*

I picked up the pens that had fallen to the floor, placed them on the table, then turned to the front door to put my gear away.

"How was your interview?"

My eyes widened, and I picked my bag off the floor. *Had he been awake?*

"It was good," I said, cautiously turning around to face him.

He sat up, scrubbed the sleep from his face, and looked at me expectantly. "Oh yeah?"

I shifted to my other foot. "I got the job."

"I knew you would." He smiled sleepily and sat forward. He didn't look like he knew I'd just lusted over him like a psycho while he slept. My shoulders relaxed.

"The only thing is," I bit my lip apprehensively, "he wants me to buy a new lens."

His brows furrowed, and he placed the binder on the coffee table. "Do you need money?"

"Oh no, that's not it at all. I have the money, but I'd planned to use it for an apartment after landing the job."

"You know you can stay here as long as you need."

"I know." I shifted my eyes to the floor, somehow feeling sad when I knew I should be happy. I found a job in this messed up economy. Even if my plans had changed, I should have felt lucky when so many people were unemployed.

"Are you still worried about Grace?" His voice held an edge that made me glance up.

I shook my head. "No."

"Then what's wrong?" He came toward me and rested a hand along my neck.

"I don't know. It's just that nothing in my life ever goes as planned. I've given up everything, and it's never enough." I was feeling sorry for myself, and I knew it didn't make any sense, but deep down I think I wanted him to know all that had happened since we were apart—just like I wanted to know everything that happened to him.

His mouth set in a firm line, but his eyes were kind. "What's not enough, sweetheart?"

I blinked back tears. "I sold Dave's baseball cards, Jake." The words poured out like a confession. "I didn't have a choice." I shook my head. "I had no savings, I used all my credit hiring the PI, and it was the only thing I had that would sell quickly enough." I searched his face, waiting for the disappointment I was sure to come. They'd built that collection together since they were boys. Spent endless hours mowing lawns to afford them, but all I saw reflected in his blue eyes was sadness.

"You should've called me. I could have helped you."

My throat burned, and I continued on as though he hadn't

spoken. "Once I have the money I'll get them all back. Every last one of them. I promise."

He searched my face. "Why didn't you come to me, Katie?"

I looked down at the floor, willing the tears not to spill over. "What? So you could rush to my aid and fix everything for me?" My tone was harsher than I intended. I wasn't being fair, but I was tired of being the girl people took care of. I'd never wanted that, and I certainly didn't want it from him. "I'm a grown woman. It's time I start figuring things out for myself."

He removed his hand and let it drop to his side. "Asking for help doesn't make you a failure."

"When's the last time you let someone help you?" I challenged.

His eyes shifted to the window, and something in his expression made my heart constrict. "Friends have helped me a lot over the years."

Friends. But not me. My stomach twisted. I wasn't there. "I'm sorry, Jake."

"For what?" He looked back at me.

"Acting like this."

His eyes crinkled at the corners, and he reached up to touch my face again.

"It's just hard for me. Taking from people."

"I know."

"I'm going to pay you back for everything."

"I know."

"And I'm going to start by making dinner tonight."

He arched one brow, and I ducked under his arm to grab my bag by the front door.

"Trust me. You'll love it." I bit my lip and began to walk backward. "Unless you have plans— but you can invite Grace if you want."

He grinned. "I'm looking forward to it." He picked his glasses and binder from the table before turning to face me again. "Grace is out of town for a couple days."

*Oh.*

I continued backing toward my room, my bag hanging from my shoulder, when it suddenly hit me that we'd be alone. I swallowed. "I'm just gonna go change into something more comfortable." My eyes bulged as the words left my mouth. "No, I mean, I'm just *hot.*"

*Damnit!*

"I'm going to change." I rushed into my bedroom and closed the door, but not before I saw that adorable grin spread wide across Jake's face.

———

An hour later, freshly showered and dressed in a pair of shorts and a tank top, I stood in the kitchen adding the garlic to the marinade I'd prepared for the chicken. It was a recipe I'd gotten from one of my favorite food bloggers and had always been a crowd favorite. I don't know why it was so important that he liked my food, but I wanted it to be perfect.

"Can I help with anything?" I looked to the doorway to find Jake. He wore the same gray plaid board shorts he'd worn earlier, but now a gray T-shirt covered his chest, his hair was damp, and his face smooth.

"You shaved."

He rubbed a hand over his jaw and grinned. "Well, it's not every day a beautiful woman makes me dinner. I thought I'd clean up a bit."

I shook my head at his flattery. There it was again— him saying the perfect words to make me melt inside. I covered the chicken with plastic wrap and handed him a bottle of wine. "Can you open this?"

He nodded, and I opened the fridge to grab the veggies for my salad.

"Did you get all your paperwork done?" I asked, standing at

the sink rinsing the lettuce.

"Most of it." He pulled the cork from the bottle, then grabbed two glasses from the cupboard and filled them halfway with Chardonnay. "Tell me about your new boss?" He placed a full glass in front of me as I worked.

"He's interesting. He was named one of the top ten wedding photographers in Los Angeles, so I'm lucky for the opportunity to even work with him."

"That's great, Katie."

I nodded as I retrieved the tomatoes from the counter and continued rinsing. "I was so nervous. I'm surprised he even hired me with all my stammering. He creeped me out though. He hardly said a word, just listened to me ramble." I took a sip of wine. "But maybe that's just the artist in him. They all have a streak of weird. Like Van Gogh—I mean, who cuts off their own ear?"

Jake's mouth was set in a hard line. "How do you know this guy isn't some twisted pervert?"

I shook my head and placed all my veggies in the basket to dry. "You're paranoid." I'd worried about the same thing only hours ago, but I didn't want Jake to worry. I also didn't want to ruin this night with lectures about my boss. "I have something I want to show you," I said, hoping to distract him.

A minute later I picked up the picture of *The Gang* from my nightstand, returned to the kitchen, and handed it to him. "Remember these people?" I bit my lip as I watched his face transform to a smile.

"Where did you get this?" His eyes flashed to me, then back to the picture.

"In one of Mom's old boxes when I visited last."

"Wow, those were the days." He laughed, and then his thumb ran over the scratched image of my brother's face.

"What ever happened to Justin?" I asked, not wanting to bring down the mood with unpleasant memories.

He looked up again. "Oh, he's in Long Beach somewhere. We

go surfing together every once in a while." He shrugged. "Do you ever talk to Megan and Sarah?"

"Well, Sarah can go jump off a cliff." My tone a bit more passionate than needed. "And last I heard, Megan was living in Idaho somewhere. She's married and has twin boys."

He leaned against the counter, his lips turned in a confused smile. "Why the hostility toward Sarah? I thought you guys were friends."

I began tearing the lettuce leaves into a bowl and glanced up at him. "You know why."

The corner of his eyes creased with confusion.

"She was always competing with me. She wasn't a good friend."

"What did she compete with you about?"

"Guys mostly." Heat crept up my cheeks as I focused on slicing the tomato.

"Yeah, like there was any competition there."

I scoffed, then brushed past him to place the salad in the fridge. "Thanks, Jake."

"You've got to be kidding me." He grabbed my arm.

"What?" I looked up at him.

"You're kidding yourself if you think any guy would choose her over you."

My breath caught in my throat, and I searched his face. Did he really not remember? "Well, you sure seemed to like her."

I moved out of his grasp, placed the salad on the shelf, and retrieved the chicken before heading out to the backyard.

"What do you mean by that?" he asked, following me.

"By what?"

"By what you said about me and Sarah."

I rolled my eyes and forced a smile. "I know what happened with you guys."

"What?" His brow creased. "I have no idea what you're talking about."

"Whatever. It's okay, Jake. I really don't care."

"I *never* liked her. The only reason we tolerated her was because she was your friend," he argued, but for some reason seemed a little amused.

"Oh? So is that why I found you guys making out playing that old guitar?"

"What?" His mouth dropped open, but then recognition crossed his features. His gaze shifted to the ground, and he scratched the back of his head. "Oh, that."

"Yeah, that." I narrowed my eyes, wondering why he looked so suspicious. "What are you hiding?"

He made a weird face, then turned to walk into the house. But I would've known that guilty look anywhere.

"What are you not telling me, Jake?" I called from behind him.

"Nothing."

Oh, goodness. I knew he was hiding something now. I stepped in front of him, cutting him off. "Tell me."

"Promise not to get mad?"

"No way." I laughed.

"Okay, okay..." He shook his head and glanced up at me through dark lashes. "That was a bet."

"What?" I was appalled and elated all at the same time. "Okay, I need details."

"Dave and Justin bet me I couldn't get her to kiss me within ten minutes," he answered, scratching the back of his head again. "It only took me five."

I grabbed a dishcloth from the counter and hit him with it. "That's terrible, Jake."

"What? I was seventeen." He smiled.

I narrowed my eyes though my heart was smiling. I grabbed my wine from the kitchen counter then headed to the porch again. "Awful," I threw over my shoulder, but inside I was scream-ing, *Take that, Sarah Peterson!*

We drank wine and reminisced about old times as I watched

the chicken on the grill. Jake occasionally looked over my shoulder to make sure I wasn't burning anything, and some of the walls I'd built up over the years seemed to come crumbling down. I'm sure the wine helped, but for the first time since coming back, I was relaxed in his presence. Just like I used to be.

"Wow! Everything looks great, Kit."

"Thanks." I served us both, then sat across from him and waited for him to take his first bite.

His brows rose, and he looked at me with dramatic apprehension before popping a bite of chicken in his mouth. His tight shoulders relaxed, and he sat back against the chair. "Wow. It's actually really good."

"Oh, shut up." I smiled and took a sip of wine.

"Pancakes for breakfast, and now this? Be careful, you're going to spoil me and I'll never let you leave."

"Yeah right, a couple of weeks with me, and you'll be kicking me out the door."

"Not a chance." His eyes met mine, making my stomach flip. "How did you make this? It's amazing," he asked, taking another bite of chicken.

"If I tell you, I'll have to kill you." I smirked.

"I'd like to see you try." He raised his brows, challenging me, and I knew one kick under the table and we'd be chasing each other around the yard and playing like we used to. But that was what got us into this mess in the first place. The reason I moved away all those years ago. I cleared my throat and answered.

"It's just garlic, lemon, olive oil, and some herbs."

He nodded, his Adam's apple moving up and down as he swallowed. "And the salad dressing?"

"Just a simple balsamic vinaigrette."

"Well, it's very good, Katie. Thank you." He filled our glasses for the second time, then held his glass in the air. "To the new job." He smiled across the table, and I raised my glass to meet his.

*To the new job.*

# CHAPTER TEN

The afternoon sun was ablaze overhead, and my strides began to slow. Em sat on the steps out front, and I pulled my earbuds to my neck as I opened the front gate. "Jake's not home." The words came out on a huff of breath while my heart struggled to find its normal rhythm.

She pulled herself to stand. "Good." She grinned. "I'm here to see you."

"Oh." I laughed nervously. "What's up?" I climbed the front steps and punched in the code to open the door.

She stepped inside. "I'm going shopping and need a friend. Come with me?"

I looked down at my body covered in sweat. "I don't know, I'm a mess."

"Take a shower. I can wait." She clasped her hands together and begged. "I just don't want to go alone."

I laughed but was still a little apprehensive. We'd spent one drunken night together—okay, so that sounded bad, but it was true. Why would she want to go shopping with me?

"Come on, I'll even buy you dinner."

I shook my head and smiled. "Okay, let me just go jump in the shower." I removed my phone from my arm band and tossed it to the coffee table. "What should I wear?"

"Whatever," she replied, making herself at home on the couch.

"Thanks, Katie. I promise you won't regret this."

I rushed through my shower, towel dried my hair, and slipped on a blue cotton sundress. I had no idea where we were going but was kind of excited. I couldn't remember the last time I'd been shopping with another girl.

When I came back in the living room, Em sat up and turned off the TV. "Ready?"

I nodded, grabbed my bag by the front door, and walked out of the house. "Where are we going, anyway?"

"Dress shopping. I got suckered into going as a date to some stuffy awards banquet, and I have nothing in my closet that will work."

We approached a little black convertible parked on the curb, and she hit the key fob to unlock the doors. "Do you mind if I keep the top down?"

"No, that's fine. I've actually never been in a convertible before."

"You're kidding me?"

"Nope."

"So I get to be your first." She raised her brows suggestively, and I laughed.

"I guess so."

As we pulled away from the curb, the sun warmed my face, and my hair whipped around my shoulders. It would likely look like hell when we got there, but for the first time in months, I didn't care—it felt amazing.

"So tell me about your date?" I asked, studying Em's profile. She was so confident—like she didn't care one bit what others thought of her.

"He's just a friend I owe a favor to." She smiled.

"Any potential?"

"Oh no, he's not my type."

This was the second time I'd heard Em say this, and my curiosity got the better of me. I leaned against the door to face her, kicked off a sandal, and crossed my legs up in the seat. "What *is* your type?"

She glanced over at me. "Tattoos, piercing... You know, the kind of asshole who writes you a love song, then stomps all over your soul."

I laughed, then quickly sobered and covered my mouth. "I'm sorry. That was rude."

She gave me a little shove. "Lighten up. That was funny as hell."

I smiled back. "How do you know Jake?" I'd wondered since we first met—they seemed like such an odd pair.

"We met in a bar a couple years ago."

I cleared my throat. "Oh."

She seemed to read my mind. "Oh God, It was nothing like that. Jake's adorable, but he's not my type either." She winked. "Besides, he was hung up on someone else then."

I nodded, then turned to the window determined to change the subject. I hated hearing about Jake and other women. "So tattoos, huh? I would have never guessed."

"Why's that?" Her tone amused.

"I don't know, you look so—classic. Like a dark-haired version of Marilyn Monroe."

She threw her head back and laughed. "God, I love you."

I smiled. "Do you even have tattoos?"

"Just one." She pointed to her foot, where a small flower peeked out from her sandal.

"A daisy?" I asked.

She nodded. "They make me happy."

"Tattoos, or daisies?"

"Both. But I was talking about the daisy."

We pulled into the parking lot of a department store, and I grabbed my bag off the floor and cringed.

"What's wrong?" Em asked.

"I just forgot my phone. It's not a big deal." I shook my head and climbed out of the car.

"Let's go back and get it. It's not far."

"Nah, I'll be fine. I hate the idea of being leashed to that thing anyway."

We spent the next hour trying on loads of dresses, and I couldn't remember a time I'd laughed harder. At first we kept running back and forth between dressing rooms to be zipped, but it got old fast, and we eventually ended up in the same room.

"So what's *your* type, Katie?" Em asked as she gave me her back to zip.

"I don't know..." Jake's face popped to my mind, but I ignored it and pulled another dress from its hanger. "The kind who don't know I exist."

"Yeah, right. I find that hard to believe."

I shrugged. "It's true."

I slipped the next dress over my head and turned to face Em.

Her eyes went wide and she began to nod. "You have to buy that."

"What?"

"Just look at yourself. Shit, Katie, I'm jealous."

I turned around and looked at my reflection. It was only a strapless sheath dress, but it hugged my body perfectly, accentuated my soft curves, and worked with my imperfections. "Is it too short?" I asked, tugging on the hem that hit mid thigh. It wouldn't have been short on other women, but with my height, I couldn't help but feel a bit slutty.

"It's perfect."

"And it's not too low cut?"

"Get. It," she said to my reflection.

"I don't even have anywhere to wear something like this."

"Well, you will one day, and you'll be fucking pissed at yourself if you don't buy it. You'll never be able to find a dress that fits you like that again, and you know it."

I smiled back at her and shrugged. "What the hell!" It totally wasn't like me, but it felt good to buy something for the hell of it. To forget about responsibility and just live.

We continued trying on dresses through the afternoon, and Em eventually decided on a floor-length coral gown that made her look even more like a Hollywood starlet than she already did.

By the time we made it to the parking lot, the sun had already begun to set, and Em turned to me before she unlocked the car. "Wanna go get tattoos?"

I laughed. "No way. I hate needles."

"How about haircuts then?"

It had been over a year since I'd had a good trim, and besides, I was having fun and didn't feel like going home. "Sure."

An hour later we walked into a salon in downtown Hollywood with a bag of In-N-Out. It reminded me of a 1950s garage with polished cement floors, retro stools, and pin-up girls on every wall. Everyone seemed to know Em, and after a round of introductions, we were led to a couple of stations in the back to wait for our stylists.

"So what's your story, Katie?" Em asked, hopping into one of the chairs and handing me a burger. "Why are you swearing off men?"

"'Cause they're all jerks." I took a seat beside her, and grabbed a tray of fries.

"Ahh... this is gonna be good." She leaned forward, and even though it wasn't my favorite subject in the world, I opened up to her.

"I found out last week my boyfriend was cheating on me."

She frowned. "I'm sorry."

I cleared my throat. "That's really what brought me back here. I found myself in a position of having to start over. Jake's always been like family to me, so I ended up at his place." I took a deep breath and popped a fry in my mouth. "What about you?"

"Let's see," she said, her hand covering her full mouth as she swallowed. "I grew up in foster care, sucked at school, but understood computers. I taught myself HTML and CSS, somehow talked my way into getting my first client, and the rest is history. I've had my own business for six years, and don't answer to anyone." She flashed a smile that didn't quite meet her eyes. "I was just cheated on too. Though I was expecting it. He was the lead singer in a rock band, and sexy as hell."

"Tattoos?" My heart constricted.

"Full sleeves." She laughed.

By the time the stylist was done with us, my belly was full, and my hair resembled something off the cover of a *Vogue* magazine. The highlights were subtle, like I'd spent every day out in the sun. The long layers were blown out in full waves and smelled of candy. I couldn't stop running my fingers through the silkiness all the way home.

"Thanks for coming with me," Em said, as I grabbed my bags from the tiny back seat.

"Thanks for inviting me. I had a great time. Oh, " I said almost as an afterthought. "And thanks for dinner."

"You're welcome." She smiled. "Listen, I have this thing tomorrow," she gestured to her dress in the back seat, "but how about we work on your website Thursday?"

"I'd love that." I climbed out of the car, then ducked down to wave goodbye. "I'll see you Thursday. Have fun tomorrow."

She rolled her eyes. "I'll try."

As she pulled away from the curb, a flick of light across the street caught my attention. A man leaning against a car smoking a cigarette. He wore a hoodie so I couldn't quite make out his face, but he made me nervous. I was sure he was one of Jake's neighbors, but why was he out so late? I shook my head at my own silliness—now *I* was being paranoid. I cleared my throat and waved, barely able to make out his nod before I turned toward the house. The lights were still on in the living room, and I wondered if Jake was still up. I rushed into the house, quickly deposited my bags to my room, and went to find him.

He stood on the patio, his back to me as he looked out to the pool. Something about his stance made me wary and I cautiously moved closer. "Hey."

He glanced over his shoulder, then turned to the pool again and took a pull from his beer.

"I was out shopping with Em," I said, wondering why he was acting so weird.

"I saw." His tone held an edge to it that I didn't understand. I narrowed my eyes.

"Were you waiting up for me?"

He laughed. "Shit, Katie, I get home from work, no note, no phone call. Your car's still out front, what was I supposed to think?" He whirled around, and irritation was plastered all over his face.

"What do you mean? I'm twenty-six years old, Jake. I'm not a kid."

"Well, stop acting like one then!" He brushed past me on the way to the house, but I couldn't let this go.

"What's that supposed to mean?"

"You should've called, Katie." He tossed his bottle in the kitchen sink and continued through the house.

"I forgot my phone," I said defensively.

"I figured that out hours ago." He waved a hand at the coffee table—my phone still abandoned there after my run—and he continued on to his room.

I was so angry, frustrated, and sick of being treated like a little girl that I didn't care about boundaries and followed right behind him. I stopped at the edge of his bed and watched as he emptied the contents of his pockets to the bedside table. "I'm not sixteen anymore, Jake." My chest heaved as I spoke. "I don't need my big bad brothers watching every move I make anymore. I hated it then, and I sure as hell don't like it now.

"Regardless of what you think, I am *not* your child. I am *not* your little sister, and you don't need to take care of me. I'm a grown woman, and I won't be treated this way!" My heart was pounding so hard it was almost visible through my chest.

He turned around, his eyes blazing a molten blue. My first instinct was to back away, but I squared my shoulders and held my ground.

He stalked toward me with smooth strides that reminded me of a lion. "You're right, Katie. You're not my child," he stopped just inches from my face, "and you're certainly not my sister."

Heat radiated off his body and my breath caught.

"But you're staying in my house, and I deserved a phone call."

*My God, he was sexy.* "So you're making rules for me now?" How could I be so pissed off and turned on at the same time?

"Apparently I have to," he said, holding my gaze.

I stared straight into his eyes, not sure if I wanted to kick him in the balls or throw him on the bed and make love to him. I knew I was treading in dangerous waters—and the truth was, I didn't trust myself enough to keep my head up and not drown. "Forget this. I'm going to bed." I whirled on my heels and stormed down the hall.

"Katie, get back here," he called. "We're not done with this conversation."

"Yes. We are!" I yelled back, and slammed my bedroom door. I threw my dress over my head, stormed into the bathroom, turned on the shower, and stepped into the stream before it even had a chance to warm up.

I didn't realize before it was too late, but I completely ruined my perfect new hair.

# CHAPTER ELEVEN

His voice was low and sleepy. "Katie." My name like a caress from his lips. I rolled to face him, my heart thudding in my chest as I looked into his stormy blue eyes. He raised his hand to the side of my face, the pad of his thumb running along my cheekbone. I tilted into his soft touch, wanting to say so many things but not knowing where to start. His eyes bored into mine, asking me questions, questions I was afraid to answer.

"Katie..." his tone more urgent now, and my heart sped up. *What do you want from me, Jake?* I was afraid—afraid that if I let him in, I'd lose him forever.

"Katie...wake up."

My eyes flew open, and I pulled in a ragged breath. Jake sat on the edge of my bed, and I blinked a couple of times trying to get my bearings. *I was sleeping.*

"Sorry, I didn't mean to startle you." His voice was low, almost a whisper.

"Is everything okay?" I looked to the pitch-black window and sat up. A deep-set panic gripped my stomach as my mind raced with all that could be wrong.

"Everything's fine, Kit Kat. I just came to wake you—"

I fell back to my pillow with relief. "Oh my God, don't do that." I closed my eyes and let out a breath.

He touched my shoulder. "I'm sorry, I forgot—"

But he didn't finish; he didn't have to. He'd forgotten about my dreams. I wish I could say the same. I threw the sheet over my head and turned away. "The sun's not even up yet." I flipped over, dismissing him, but really—I didn't want him to see my face.

He let out a breath. "Come on. We need to get an early start."

I flipped over again, somewhat intrigued. "For what?"

The room was dark except for the light from the hall, but I could just make out the hint of his smile. "The beach."

A thrill shot up my spine—our home away from home—but then I remembered our argument last night, and frowned. "You can't take me to the beach and make me forget, Jake. I'm still mad at you."

He let out a breath, raked a hand through his hair, then pinched the bridge of his nose.

I was right. That was his intention. "I'm not your kid. You don't get to tell me when I come or when I go."

"I wasn't asking for that." He looked to the dark window. Our bodies only inches from touching, but I felt the wall of Alcatraz rising between us. "I was worried about you."

"I just went to the mall," I argued.

"I know." He shook his head. "I just go crazy when it comes to you. Like if—" He laughed, then scrubbed his hands over his face. "Can we just forget about last night?"

His words made my heart stop. *If ...what?* I wasn't sure if I wanted to know the answer. Something about the way he looked told me I wasn't ready. I swallowed the ball of fear in my throat and nodded.

He smiled, seeming relieved, and threw the covers from my body. "Now put your suit on." He ruffled my already messy hair. "I have coffee brewing in the kitchen."

I laughed. "What time is it, anyway?"

"Just after five."

"Are you kidding me? Why are we going so early?"

"Because that's when we'll catch the best waves."

I propped myself up on my elbows and turned on the lamp at my bedside table. "We're going surfing?"

"Yep." He grinned.

"But I don't know how." I rubbed a hand over my face, suddenly more awake.

"Well, it's about time you learned."

---

By the time I was ready, Jake was already outside loading his truck. He was dressed in board shorts, a pale blue T-shirt, and flip-flops. What used to be his uniform back in the day.

I zipped my hoodie to block out the chill and shoved my hands deep in the pockets of cut offs. "Aren't you cold?"

He glanced up, his eyes crinkling at the corners as he adjusted one of the straps around the board. "Nah." He brushed some hair from his forehead and looked so happy, I couldn't help but smile back.

I cleared my throat. "Do you need any help?"

"I think I got it." He secured the boards with black cord, then nodded toward the cab. "There's donuts in the truck."

"Geez, what time did you get up?"

He smiled again, but didn't answer.

"Are you sure you don't need any help?"

"Yeah, go get warm. We'll be ready to go in five minutes."

I climbed into the toasty cab, eyeing the pink box I knew would be filled with fresh donuts, and two insulated mugs that sat in the center console. I picked one up, blowing the too-hot coffee, and let my hands soak in some of its warmth. I kicked off my flip-flops, sat back to my heels, and selected a maple bar from the box. The donut was still warm, and the sweet icing cracked with my first bite. The buttery flavors melted in my mouth and tasted better than anything I'd had in years.

I was already on my second donut when Jake opened the door and let in a rush of cold air. "Ready?" His excitement so pure it was invigorating.

I brushed my hand over my smiling mouth to wipe away the crumbs. "When did you plan this?"

He scratched the back of his head and climbed in beside me. "After you went to bed."

*After our fight.*

He fastened his seat belt and nodded for me to do the same. "Justin's going to meet us later."

I put my feet on the floor and reached for my belt. "What? Really?"

"Yep."

"How's he doing?"

Jake backed out of the driveway and pulled onto the street. "He's getting married."

"What? Are you kidding me? Justin? The Justin who dated three girls at a time, Justin?"

He laughed. "That's what I said." He grabbed a donut as we pulled onto the main road. "He actually asked me to be one of his groomsmen."

I stared at his profile, his expression unreadable, and I wondered what he was thinking. "That's awesome, Jake. Will his fiancée be meeting us too?"

"I don't know, maybe? She may have to work."

I narrowed my eyes. "Speaking of work, how'd you get the day off?"

He shrugged. "The guys can get along without me for a day."

"Must be nice."

"Being the boss sometimes has its perks."

We spent the rest of the drive in silence, but it was perfect. Not the uncomfortable silence of strangers, but that cozy, cuddled under the same blanket kind of silence that only came when you knew someone as long as I'd known Jake.

When we arrived at the beach, the sun was just starting to peek out from the horizon, and the sky alive with vibrant hues of coral and violet. I hopped from the cab and filled my lungs with the familiar salty air I had dreams about. The air so different from any other beach I'd ever been to.

We each loaded our arms with bags and coolers, then made our way down the path I'd had memorized since childhood. The path that led to adventure, discovery, and lots and lots of laughter.

The second I reached the sand, I slipped my sandals to my fingers, and let the icy grains run between my toes. Goosebumps covered my bare legs, but I didn't care. I wanted to be as close to them as possible.

"I haven't been here since we spread Dave's ashes." I focused my attention to the sea, watching the sunrise.

"Yeah," Jake replied beside me, his voice low and hollow. It had been a day very similar to this when we said our final goodbyes to Dave. Just six days after his tragic accident, we brought him to his favorite place on earth, his final resting place—this beach. The same beach where we took my father only nine years earlier.

I looked over at Jake. He had one arm loaded like mine, a surf-board held high on the other. He'd been there both times. Holding my hand, reminding me I wasn't alone.

Just a few yards from the water, Jake set the board in the sand and turned to me. A warm glow filtered through his wild hair, and I smiled back at the man I wanted to strangle only hours earlier, but loved with all my heart. My eyes filled with tears— though this time not from sadness, but from a sense of well being I hadn't felt in years.

"Are we really going out there?" I asked, dropping my bags to the sand and wrapping my arms around my body. The waves crashed to the shore, and I could swear they were welcoming me home. "It's freezing."

He laughed. "I have an extra wetsuit, you'll be fine."

He came to stand behind me and rubbed his hands up and down my arms.

"We spent lots of days at this beach, you and I."

I only nodded, my whole body wound so tight I couldn't even breathe.

"The best days of my life."

My throat constricted. They were the best of mine too—we didn't even do anything. Just lounged around, played in the surf, ate whatever food we could scrounge together out of the cupboards, and often sat in silence similar to the one that fell over us now. Though *now* we were alone, and *now* my heart slammed a wild beat inside me.

When he turned away, I relaxed a little, and he excused himself to go get the last board from the truck. I found a large woven blanket in one of the bags and spread it over the cool sand, securing each corner with shoes and coolers.

I wished I wasn't so affected by Jake. That I could enjoy his friendship without my senses turned on hyperdrive. But it had always been that way. For him, and only him. Why was that? I plopped down in the center of the blanket, pulled my knees close to my chest, and hooked my hoodie over my legs, trying to find warmth.

Jake finally made it back to the beach, set the last board in the sand. "Are you ready for this?"

I raked my teeth over my lip, but he was so excited I couldn't help my smile.

He nodded to the yellow board over in the sand, and I hopped to my feet, following after him to where the ground became firmer.

"Okay, I'm going to show you what to do, then we'll practice a few times before getting in the water. You're going to have to take that off," he said, nodding to my sweatshirt.

I raised my brows. "No way, it's freezing."

"It will only be for a few minutes. I just need to make sure your form is okay and that's too bulky."

I let out a sigh of defeat, then tossed the hoodie toward our camp. I stood in my black halter bikini and cut off shorts, and a shiver ran through me from the cold.

When I turned to face him, he looked at me like he'd never seen me before. I narrowed my eyes, wondering why he was being so weird, then noticed my nipples were hard as rocks and crossed my arms. He smiled a little, then dropped down to the board and cleared his throat.

I closed my eyes, wanting to die, but he spoke as if nothing happened.

"You want to grip the board like this." His voice low and gruff as he lay on his stomach. He grasped the board at each side, pushing his chest up. "Your elbows should be turned out slightly, legs straight and together." His eyes were intense, and I bit my lip.

"Slide one leg forward and stand up." His motions mirrored his words, and he stood so easily it made it look like riding a bike. He stepped off the board, wiped sand from his hands to his shorts, then gestured for me to take his place.

I didn't hesitate before laying face down on the freezing board and mimicking his position. "Is this right?" I asked, my teeth already beginning to chatter as a fresh set of goosebumps traveled up my legs.

"Hands just a bit higher." He straddled the board above me and helped move my hands to the correct height. "Okay, good. Now glide one foot forward, and stand." He stepped to the side, allowing me freedom to move.

"Which foot?" I asked.

"Whichever feels natural."

Deciding on my right, I pulled it under me, shifted my weight, and awkwardly stood. It wasn't nearly as easy as he made it seem, but I managed.

"Good." He stood behind me, took my hips in each hand, and his thumb brushed against my bare skin.

"Bend your knees." His voice was low, only inches from my ear, and I had to fight the urge to lean back against him. He pushed down gently, and my knees bent under his will.

"Now hold out your arms for balance." His arms moved beneath mine, lifting them higher, and I was sure he could feel each thud of my heart as it slammed inside me. His warm breath caught my hair, and my whole body trembled.

"Are you cold?"

"Yes." I cleared my throat and moved away.

He nodded toward the camp. "I borrowed a buddy's wetsuit. It won't be perfect, but it'll be better than none." He grabbed a black duffle from the sand, pulled out a couple bodysuits and tossed them on the blanket.

"If we don't do it now, I'll forget." He shook a bottle of sunscreen at me, pulled off his shirt, then squeezed some lotion in his hand before tossing the bottle on top of a pile of towels.

I dropped to sit on the edge of the blanket, grabbed the bottle, and tried to avert my eyes from his bare skin as I applied lotion everywhere on my body I could reach. "Do you want me to do your back?" I asked, needing more time before his hands were on me again.

He nodded, and I grabbed the bottle of lotion before rising to my feet. He stood with his back to me, and my eyes ran over his gorgeously sculpted physique as I warmed the lotion between my fingers—damn he was hard not to look at. I cleared my throat, then placed one hand on the top of his shoulder. His muscles constricted from my touch, and I closed my eyes. Somehow touching him was just as arousing as him touching me. His body was firm and skin surprisingly soft and warm beneath my fingers. I worked as quickly as possible, making sure he was thoroughly covered, but not taking a second longer than necessary before turning around and offering him my back.

"Done?" he asked.

I cleared my throat again before answering, "Yes."

My nerves were like a Venus flytrap of anticipation. Each breath, each beat of my heart took an eternity, and right when I thought to turn around, he touched me. Just the tips of his fingers along my neck. Soft and lingering. Then he pushed a lock of hair over my shoulder.

My whole body became rigid as his hands settled to the top of my shoulders. The lotion was cold, but the shiver that ran over my skin had nothing to do with its temperature.

"Sorry," he muttered, as both hands gripped my shoulders, massaging them with his strong hands. "You're so tense."

I laughed nervously but said nothing.

"Relax. It's only me." His voice was low, and close to my ear.

I blew out a breath. "I know." But that was the problem. The problem was him. The problem was he had a girlfriend, and even if he didn't, our *one* kiss had been what pulled us apart. I would never let that happen again.

I forced my shoulders to relax, and his hands began to move across my upper back, then down my sides, and feather light over the sensitive skin above my shorts. "All done." He cleared his throat and began pulling on his wetsuit.

"When's Grace due home?" I asked. It was a reminder to myself more than anything. It was easier knowing he was taken—that he would never be mine.

"She'll be home sometime tonight."

"Oh." I stepped into my wetsuit. Both relief and sadness competing for attention inside my head. I wanted her home. That barrier of another person that always kept us from getting too close. But at the same time, I craved—possibly more than any other time in my life— for it to just be us. Only us.

We spent the next hour practicing on the firm sand, though this time he didn't touch me. Which should have made things easier, but the tension was so thick I had a hard time concentrating.

Eventually we both agreed I was ready, and we carried our boards toward the ocean. I was surprised by how well the suit blocked the frigid water as we began paddling out to sea. I followed behind Jake, our boards leashed to our ankles as we made our way over wave after wave. We paddled out to where the water calmed, then climbed the boards to straddle the tops—this too, was not as easy as Jake made it seem.

The sun was higher by now, not overwhelmingly so, but just enough to cast a gentle warmth over my face. The sky had matured to a vibrant blue, and the roar of the ocean set our rhythm, eased the tension, and filled me with a sense of peace. I glanced over at Jake, who looked calm and tranquil. Maybe happier than I'd ever seen before. I couldn't help but smile as I watched him. It was surprising how natural it felt to be out there with him like that. Like we'd spent a lifetime sitting side by side, taking the waves as they came. But I guessed we always had. He'd been there with me through everything.

He looked back at me then and our eyes met. "What?" he asked, but a smile lingered on the corner of his mouth.

"I don't know. I feel closer to him here."

He paused, then looked around. "Me too."

His face grew serious, and for a second I thought he might say something— though he didn't have to. We both knew what he was thinking. This was Dave's spot.

We sat in silence, gliding over wave after wave, then suddenly Jake called for me to get ready. Adrenaline pumped through my veins, and my heartbeat quickened. I positioned my body—chest up, legs straight—and began to paddle.

"Now!"

Upon Jake's signal, I pulled my leg forward, my hands braced on either side of the board, but when I pulled my foot forward, my toes caught on the edge of the board and I lost my balance. I tumbled over the side, rolled under cold water, and had to wait for a break in the water so I could surface. A moment later I came up sputtering and watched as Jake easily fell into the water from his stance on the board.

"You okay?" he yelled, as he swam back to me.

I nodded, then flashed a smile before paddling back out to sea. *Again.*

There were at least a dozen more falls, but I didn't care. If I'd been alone, I might've given up, but Jake had so much faith in me, I found myself needing to do it, if only just for him.

And then the perfect wave came, the stars aligned, and I slid my foot forward. Gripping the board with my toes, I was able to pull myself to stand. Stiff as cardboard, the wind blowing on my face, and my heart beating a mile a minute, I was surfing. I kept my balance long enough to feel the water rushing under my feet, mist on my face, and the wave carrying me to the shore. I heard Jake yell beside me, and a second later I lost my balance and crashed into the water. When I was able to stand, my first thought was to find Jake. I knew he'd be excited, and I couldn't wait to see his face. I turned around, and there he was making his way toward me. So much joy bubbled inside I thought I might explode with it.

"Did you see that?" I yelled, not sure if I wanted to laugh or cry.

A second later, he was in front of me, lifting me from the water, spinning me around in his arms. "I knew you could do it."

I held on to him, feeling giddy as I lifted my face to the sky and let the sun warm me.

He slid me to the ground, but his arms remained at my waist. "You did it."

His jaw tightened, and his eyes met mine. The mood shifted from elation to that of anticipation, and I licked the water from my lips, wanting desperately to kiss him.

He looked from my eyes to my mouth—and then a second

wave crashed over us, sweeping me off my feet and dragging both me and my board at least five feet back to shore. When I finally caught my footing, Jake was on his knees, pushing his drenched hair from his face. Our eyes locked, and we both began to laugh. "Can we go again?" I asked, not ready to acknowledge what just happened, not wanting to read into everything like I always did.

It was just after noon when we finally climbed out of the water. All my muscles aching from overuse when we finally dropped our boards in the sand and made our way to camp. I peeled the wetsuit from my body, plopped down on the sun-warmed blanket, and felt both exhausted and happier than I had in years. "I had no idea surfing was so exhilarating." I rolled to my stomach and looked up at Jake. "Why has it taken you so long to teach me?"

He shrugged. "You'd have to ask Dave about that. I think he was worried you'd mess up his game."

I laughed and flipped over on my back again, shielding my eyes from the sun. "Well, I'm glad you took me."

The beach was practically secluded, and I dug my feet into warm sand. The crashing waves roared a hypnotic rhythm, and I felt Jake sit down on the blanket beside me. He pushed something small and smooth into the palm of my hand, and I opened my eyes to see a piece of aqua blue sea glass resting there.

"How pretty." I squinted over at him, then tried to give it back.

He shook his head. "Keep it. So you never forget."

I smiled, and played with it in my hand a minute. How could I ever forget? But something in his expression made my chest ache. He looked almost sad. What had he meant by that?

Just when I was about to ask, the sun disappeared, and I heard that old familiar voice I would've recognized anywhere.

"Why if it isn't Little Katie McGregor?"

A smile tugged at my lips, and I called back, "Justin Harting—the heartbreaker."

# CHAPTER TWELVE

J ake stood, immediately giving Justin a firm hug, and I rose
to an elbow, smiling up at the face I'd always known as the
mischief maker. He was just the same—short cropped hair,
hazel eyes, and a smile designed to break hearts.

"Jake told me you were coming," I said.

Justin pulled me to stand and threw an arm over my shoulder.
"And he told me you've been back since Saturday."

I shook my head and wrinkled my nose at the sun.

"So does this mean we get to keep you? Or are you planning to
run away again?"

I cleared my throat and studied him. I didn't know he thought
of my move as running away. "Oh, shut up." I pushed playfully at
his stomach.

He laughed again and ruffled my hair. "How's life been treating
you, kid?"

I took in a deep breath and glanced over at Jake. *Had he told
him about Kevin?*

Justin eyed me warily. "What? Am I missing something?"

Jake gave me a reassuring smile, then backed toward the ocean.

"You guys catch up, I'm gonna go cool off." He picked up his board, then ran toward the waves.

"What was that about?" Justin asked.

I shook my head, knowing Jake was giving me privacy so I could tell him, but I wasn't ready for that. Justin nudged me with one shoulder, and I laughed.

"So, I hear you're getting married?"

"Yep," he replied, squinting at me against the sun, "she's not even pregnant either."

I laughed, grateful he didn't push me and because that was such a Justin thing to say. "I didn't think—"

"I know." He smiled. "But most people do. She's *it* for me, Katie."

The way he said it made me smile. There was so much adoration in that single word. *It.* That was all I've ever wanted to be. Someone's it... Jake's it... so stupid. I walked over to my shorts lying on the blanket and tucked the sea glass into its pocket before turning to face him again. "So do I get to meet her?"

"Yeah, she'll be along shortly. She's meeting me here after work."

"What's her name?"

He looked shy, something I'd never seen in him before. I bumped his shoulder.

"Kimberly. Kimberly Porter."

"Soon to be Mrs. Harting" He grinned from ear to ear, like he'd just won the lottery. "Awww...I'm so excited for you." I gave him another nudge.

He laughed. "So what's going on with you? Jake tells me you're still doing photography?"

"Yeah, weddings actually." I raised my brows.

"Oh, perfect. Kimberly keeps talking about engagement photos, do you do that too?"

I nodded.

"Well, you guys will have to set something up when she gets

here. But for now," his expression grew serious, "I want to hear more about you."

I sat back to the blanket, my stomach twisting the way it always did when I faced an uncomfortable conversation. "There's really not much to tell. I guess you could say I'm starting over," I rolled my eyes, "again."

"Nothing wrong with that." He plopped down next to me and searched my face. "Why?"

"I don't know," I hesitated, "it seems I'm an asshole magnet."

He crinkled his nose as he looked out to the ocean. "Jake mentioned something about that."

All smiles were gone now, just like I feared. "When did you talk to Jake?"

"Last night when he woke me up."

"Oh God, Justin. I'm sorry!"

He grinned, then looked out to the ocean again. "He looks happy."

I followed his line of vision and watched Jake paddle out past the breakwaters.

"He was pretty messed up after Dave died."

My throat tightened and I nodded. "We all were." I wasn't sure where he was going with this conversation, and began making circles in the sand with my finger.

"True—but he got worse after you left." There was an edge to his voice that twisted my gut.

I swallowed and looked back toward Jake. "What do you mean?" I wasn't even sure I wanted to know. I didn't like to hear about Jake hurting.

He shrugged. "I don't know. Lots of drinking—I probably shouldn't even be telling you this." He nudged me. "But that was a long time ago."

I took a deep breath and pushed down the guilt that bubbled to the surface. I'd been selfish when I left. So consumed with my own grief, with rejection, that I couldn't even see how much pain he was in. That he was hurting so badly he turned to drinking even months after Dave's death.

Justin leapt to his feet, startling me. "There's Kimberly." He jogged toward a petite brunette, whose arms were loaded with plastic bags. "Hey baby!" he called, then lifted her in his arms and kissed her firmly on the mouth. It reminded me of a love scene from a movie, and I averted my eyes to give them privacy—but the truth was, I still needed a moment to collect my thoughts.

Jake still bobbed up and down in the surf, and I couldn't stop myself from watching him. There was no use dwelling on the past, but I couldn't help feeling a little guilty about what I left behind when I moved to San Diego.

A minute later, Kimberly and Justin walked toward me, and I rose to my feet and dusted sand from my now-dry legs. She smiled and raised grocery bags of food to the air. "I hope y'all are hungry!"

Ten minutes later, all four of us sat on the blanket eating a picnic of fried chicken, potato salad, and watermelon.

"This is wonderful, Kimberly. Thank you," I said.

"Well, I love feedin' people, so get used to it."

I smiled, my eyes flashing from her to Justin. "Now it all makes sense."

"What?" He grinned, like he knew there was a catch.

"This is how you got Justin to fall in love with you."

Her face lit up when she laughed. "He does like to eat." She looked to Justin, then back to me and Jake. "Justin told me about all the trouble he used to get in with ya'll."

"Oh no." My eyes settled on Jake as nervous flutters teased my belly.

"What exactly did he tell you?" Jake asked.

"Oh, something about you boys tyin' up poor Katie at the back of the yard 'cause she kept interrupting you playin' video games."

Her eyes were full of mischief, and I couldn't contain my laughter. I elbowed Jake. "It's true. They were so mean to me."

"*We* were mean? Who was the one who ruined our comic books by coloring all over them with lipstick?" Jake protested.

"That was only because you drew mustaches on our Barbies with permanent marker!" I stuck my chest out, daring him to disagree with me.

He opened his mouth to argue, then stopped. "Okay, we were pretty mean, but you were so cute when you were angry." He winked at me. "A ball of fire, pigtails, and overalls."

Kimberly eyed us curiously. "How long have y'all been together?"

I cleared my throat and brushed some imaginary food from my mouth. "Oh, we're not together." My chest tightened, and I glanced back to Jake.

"I'm sorry, I just assumed." Kimberly looked down and her cheeks grew red.

I shook my head in an "it's nothing" kind of way, but the silence that fell over the group proved otherwise.

Jake placed his empty plate to the side of the blanket, then sat forward and rested his arm on his knee. "Did Justin ever tell you he's afraid of ghosts?" His tone was deadpan, and Justin burst into fits of laughter.

I chewed my inner cheek, then smiled, and started laughing too.

We spent the rest of the afternoon joking and playing around in the surf, and it was nearly sunset by the time we had everything packed and loaded in the truck. I dusted as much sand from my body as possible, then climbed into the cab of Jake's truck to get settled for the long drive home. Kimberly appeared at my window to ask for my number, but my eyes were locked on Justin as he pulled Jake off to the side.

"—someone's going to get hurt." Justin's voice was a forced whisper, which of course piqued my curiosity.

"I know what I'm doing," Jake replied, and I got the sinking feeling he was talking about us.

"Yeah, like you did three years ago?" It was Justin again, which didn't surprise me. He was always the one to get involved in everyone else's business.

Justin glanced up, and I looked down at Kimberly's phone pretending to punch in numbers.

His voice lowered. "You're leading her on and you know it—"

Jake pulled on his arm, and they both moved farther down the road where the sound of cars blocked their voices, and I could no longer hear what was going on.

I handed the phone back to Kimberly, whose eyes met mine, and I knew she'd overheard too.

The ride home was relatively quiet, which gave me time to consider all that was said. I was positive Justin had been talking about me—there was really no other explanation—and I knew he was right about the flirtation. It had to stop. I was treading in deep waters, and soon I wouldn't be able to hold my head up any longer. I needed to protect my heart, and I wasn't a good enough swimmer to come up for air if I were to sink again. I rested my head against the warm glass of my window, and my body sagged with defeat.

"Close your eyes, it's been a long day."

I glanced over at Jake, to the bits of sand that still lingered in his messy hair, his face bronze from spending the day in the sun, and the lips I was so tempted to kiss earlier. My heart squeezed. I couldn't let myself get close to him again. As good as it felt, our closeness was what led to all my heartache, and I couldn't survive that again.

With my head still resting against the window, and one foot tucked under me in the seat, I closed my eyes, and let my mind drift.

When we came to a stop an hour later, I opened my eyes, realizing we were already home. My face was tucked into his shoulder, my body plastered to his side, and I wiped my mouth, hoping I hadn't been drooling.

"Sorry," I muttered and moved away. *Even in my sleep I was drawn to him.*

He grinned down at me, his eyes hooded and tired. "That was nothing," he teased. "It was the snoring that was annoying."

My eyes went wide, but then his smile grew and his eyes twinkled with amusement.

"See, you *are* mean." I opened my door and climbed out. "Don't mess with me, Jake. My lipstick collection has grown, and your toys are much more expensive."

His laughter followed me as I shut my door, and my heart dropped with regret. It was so easy to play with him—but I needed to stop. We both grabbed bags from the back of the truck, and I was so loaded, I lost my footing as I walked up the front steps.

"Careful, beautiful," Jake said from behind me, grabbing my waist to hold me steady.

I closed my eyes, wanting to stay there forever, but forced myself to pull away.

Jake punched the code into front door, and I moved swiftly to the kitchen to put the remaining drinks from the ice chests in the fridge. As I watched the ice water swirl down the drain, my heart grew heavier and heavier—my thoughts consumed with Justin's words at the beach.

"Go to bed, Katie. I'll finish up."

I turned around, finding Jake leaning in the doorway. His hair messy in that way that only came from playing in the sea. He looked exhausted… and happy. God I loved him. I didn't want to, but I did. He filled my veins, consumed my thoughts, and no amount of time would ever get him out.

# CHAPTER THIRTEEN

With wet hair and a bad mood, I sat perched on the edge of my bed. My computer was in my lap, cursor hovering over the button that read *buy now with 1-click*. The wedding was only two days away, and I'd already put the purchase off too long. Twenty-one hundred dollars. I even had to pay extra for overnight shipping.

But I couldn't help the little voice in my head that told me I should forget the whole thing. It would be easier that way. If I didn't buy the lens, I'd have enough money to move out and get an apartment. I wouldn't have to torture myself daily with the man who'd never be mine. But at the same time, I'd be giving up on my dream and turning into the person I hated. The one who ran away when things got hard. Taking a deep breath, I clicked the button, then slapped my laptop closed and set it on the table.

Sleep hadn't brought me clarity; it made me grumpy.

I had no idea what I was doing, or even what possessed me to believe staying with Jake would be a good idea. I was naive, and now I'd spent practically every penny I had on a dream.

I pulled myself to stand, yanked my sandy sheets from the bed, and stormed out of the room.

If he wasn't so perfect, things would be different. If he didn't have a girlfriend, I wouldn't feel quite as bad. The truth was, I'd shut my feelings off in a heartbeat if I only knew how—but loving Jake had always been like breathing for me. I could stop, hold my breath until my face turned blue, but eventually I would gasp for air, breathing him in because my life depended on it.

I wanted to cry, to throw myself on the floor and flail like a little girl. But I pushed back the tears, threw open the garage door, and shoved the sheets in the washer. As if on cue, there was a knock at the front door, and I rolled my eyes. I didn't want to see anyone, didn't want to talk or even look at anyone either. But the knock came again, and I stalked to the front door and yanked it open.

"Whoa!" Em said, her eyes wide from the front porch. "What's his name? I'll kick his ass and be right back."

My face softened, and I actually laughed. I must have looked like a total lunatic. Shaking my head at my own misery, I stepped aside to let her in.

"What happened?" she asked as she stepped into the living room.

"Nothing...I just hate laundry." It was a lame excuse, I knew that, but I couldn't tell her the truth. Jake was her friend, and she wouldn't understand. She might even hate me for it.

"Well shit, Katie, tell me how you really feel?" She laughed, then looked down to the bag she held in her hands. "Where should we set up?"

"Oh, right." The website, I'd almost forgotten. "Kitchen?" I suggested.

We moved to the breakfast table, and Em proceeded to set up a little office. She opened her laptop, set some papers to the table, then put on a pair of cat-eyed glasses that made me smile. Everything about her was unique; everything she did exuded confidence.

She glanced up and narrowed her eyes. "Why do you look like you've just come back from a Caribbean vacation?"

I reached up to touch my pinkened cheeks. "We went to the beach yesterday."

"You and Jake?" Her brows cinched with surprise.

"Yeah, why?" Did she know? Could she see my heart on my sleeve like everyone always could? I turned toward the cupboard and busied myself making a fresh pot of coffee.

"I don't know...he's just such a workaholic. Good for him though, he needs a break from being so serious all the time."

I paused with the carafe halfway to the coffee maker. He didn't seem serious to me. He'd been playful, maybe even carefree, but not serious.

"So do you have any ideas?" Em asked, breaking me from my thoughts.

"Not really." I poured the rest of the water in the machine and forced a laugh. "I'm going to make a sandwich, you want one?"

"Sure." She glanced up, considering me, then began typing again. "We should have a barbecue tomorrow."

I pulled the ingredients for turkey sandwiches from the fridge. "Okay."

"Great." She opened up her phone and began punching out a message. "There."

I shook my head. "What?"

"The barbecue? I just asked you about it." She shook her head.

"Oh—sorry, I didn't sleep well last night. What about it?"

She laughed. "I just sent a message to Jake and John letting them know." She leaned forward and removed her glasses. "Are you sure you want to do this today? You seem off."

"I just—" I put the bread and turkey on the counter. "I had to spend a fortune on a new lens today. Money always stresses me out."

She nodded, an expression of complete understanding crossed her features, and she began typing again.

We spent the rest of the afternoon eating sandwiches and sharing ideas over a whole pot of coffee. Even though I hadn't wanted her there earlier, I was now glad for the company. It didn't change the fact that I still had no idea what I was doing, but at least I wasn't as grumpy anymore.

Em downed the rest of her coffee, then leaned back in her chair. "Well, I think I have everything I need from you. The rest is boring stuff I'll do at home."

"Thanks for doing this. I was going to try and figure something out on my own, but having a site of this quality will be amazing."

She shot me a warm smile as she began packing away her computer. "I'm glad to help."

I stood and stretched my stiff muscles. "When do you want to do your photo shoot?"

She shrugged. "What are you doing today?"

I glanced around the kitchen and put the bread clip back on the bag. "You're looking at it."

She raised her brows. "What should I wear?"

I shrugged. "Whatever you want."

"Come with me. I hate making decisions on my own."

"Sure, just let me go grab my gear."

"Shoot." Her voice made me stop, and I turned around to see her pulling at the ends of her hair. "I just remembered, I have a date tonight. Do you mind following me?" She messed up her face, and I chuckled.

"That's fine."


Fifteen minutes later, Em pushed open the rusty gate to her apartment building. It was only ten minutes from Jake's house, but the neighborhood was *so* different. I was surprised the building wasn't condemned by its appearance alone. We climbed the rickety steps to the second floor, and I swore I could feel them sway under my feet. I wasn't sure where I expected Em to live, but this wasn't it. Not that it was all bad, but she drove a sports car and wore designer dresses, for Christ's sake.

Her apartment was clean and cozy, but very small. The front room, including the kitchen, was about the size of my bedroom at Jake's. She dropped her bag on the delicate table by the door then walked to the fridge to grab a water bottle. "Want one?"

I nodded and she tossed me a bottle. "Make yourself at home. I'm just going to go get myself fixed up."

She disappeared through the only other door in the room, and I was left to look around the place. The couch was bright blue and ran along one wall, a small yellow coffee table sat in front, and a large photograph of a field of tiny daisies hung behind it.

But it was the bookcase dominating the apartment that intrigued me most. I walked closer, running my finger along the glossy white shelf as I examined the titles. *Outlander* by Diana Gabaldon, *Pride and Prejudice* by Jane Austen, and poetry by Maya Angelou. But then my eyes locked on the collection of Little Golden Books on the top shelf. More than I'd ever seen in one place. I pulled one from the collection—a copy of *The Poky Puppy* —and began flipping through the pages. For some reason it didn't surprise me. She seemed like one of those people who wasn't in a rush to grow up.

I placed it back on the shelf, looked over the other titles, then noticed a frame tucked among the bindings. It was a simple golden frame that matched the books perfectly. Behind the glass was a picture of a small child with chubby little cheeks. A boy who looked to be about two, grasping the handlebars of a red tricycle.

"What do you think?" Em asked, and I turned around to see her standing in the doorway. She wore a simple white sheath dress and black pumps. Her hair was sleek and smooth, her lips red, with a single gold bangle on her left wrist. *Classic.*

"It's perfect." I smiled at her, then noticed her eyes on the photograph. "Who's this?" I asked, handing her the frame.

The corner of her mouth turned up in a sad smile. "Just a little boy who stole my heart." She placed the frame back on the shelf, then turned to the bedroom. "I thought I could do a more casual look too? What do you think?"

"Yeah, sure." My brows furrowed. "Whatever you want."

---

We got carried away during the shoot, and when we returned to the apartment the sun had already begun to set. By the time I was finished with the bathroom, Em had already changed into a blue strapless dress and red stilettos.

"I hate to rush you out the door, but I'm supposed to be there at eight." She bit her bottom lip, then glanced at her phone and snapped it away in her small clutch.

"Don't worry about me." I grabbed my bags and hurried out the door.

The rusty gate clanged behind us as she ran across the parking lot to her car. "I'll call you in the morning about the barbecue," she said, then blew me a kiss and ducked into her convertible.

I shook my head as I hoisted my gear bag over my shoulder. Our lives couldn't have been more different. I was heading back to a house that wasn't my own, in a car that was ten years old, still dressed in my shorts and a tank top I'd thrown on after my shower. While she was off to a fancy dinner with what I imagined to be a sophisticated man. A different one than her black-tie dinner just the night before.

Maybe I should have asked her to set me up? Maybe it would help me forget...

Seated behind the wheel of my hatchback, I checked my phone to see there were no messages. I thought about calling Jake, to offer to pick something up for dinner, but quickly changed my mind. A group of men walked into the parking lot, and I decided I'd better be on my way. I turned the key in the

ignition, but it only clicked, and my heart leapt to my throat.
*Shit!*

I tried again, my hands starting to shake—but again, nothing.
*Shit. Shit. Shitty Shit!*

One hand flew to my brow, while the other reached down to
pop the hood. I stepped out of the car, spent an eternity trying to
find the stupid latch thing, then finally lifted the hood and realized I had no clue what I was looking for. I glanced up, hoping
one of the men would take pity on the poor girl with the broken
car, but the neighborhood really wasn't good, the sun was going
down fast, and the group of men didn't exactly look inviting.

I blew out a breath and climbed back into the front seat. I was
going to have to call Jake. My pride hurt, but the need for self-
preservation was stronger.

I grumbled under my breath, pulled out my phone, and
debated whether to call or text.

*Text.* I'd be able to imagine away the roll of his eyes much
easier.

ME: *Are you busy?*

His reply came a few seconds later.

JAKE: No. You OK?

I let out a sigh. Why did he always assume something's wrong?
*Maybe because the last time you called something was.*

I took a deep breath before typing again.

ME: My car won't start.

JAKE: Where are you? I'll be right there.

Twenty minutes later, Jake pulled into the space beside me. I
stepped out of my car, both grateful and embarrassed at the same
time. But when he climbed out of his seat, my heart sank. He was
dressed in gray slacks and a blue button-up shirt—he looked
amazing—and one thing was certain, he *had* been in the middle of
something.

Then the passenger door opened, and an immaculately dressed
*Grace* climbed out of the other side.

*Perfect!* Not only did I pull him away from something, I pulled him away from the something he was doing with Grace. I wanted to kick myself for feeling a little happy about that.

"You okay?" Jake asked, as he grabbed a set of jumper cables from the metal box in the bed of his truck.

I nodded. *Why did he have to be so sweet?* But I already knew the answer. He cared about me. Just in the most horrible way I could think of. Like he would a little sister.

"I hope I didn't interrupt anything important," I said to Grace. She was wearing a gray trapeze dress and navy heels—from the way she looked, I very much did.

"It's fine," she replied, but her tone did nothing to convince me.

"I must have left a light on." I chewed on my nails. Not only was it embarrassing to need Jake's help, but my appearance did me no favors tonight. I was filthy from lying on the ground during Em's photo shoot, and she was dressed like a supermodel.

Jake clamped the cables to his battery, then walked over to stand in front of my car. His brows furrowed. "Your cables are loose."

"What?" I walked to the front of my car and stood beside him.

He turned to unhook the cables from his truck, then tossed them in the back. "They're loose."

"What? How?"

"Probably because you don't take care of your car," he lectured. "Where *is* Em anyway? You shouldn't be out her alone."

"She had a date." I fidgeted with the ends of my hair.

"Great." He shut his hood. "I don't know why she stays in this dump. It's not like she doesn't have the money."

I'd thought the very same thing not long ago, but now I was defensive. "Would you stop. It's not her fault."

Grace cleared her throat. "Can you just hook up the battery so we can go? We're already late." She was leaning against the truck, and annoyed would be an understatement.

"I'm so sorry. If I'd known you guys were going somewhere—"

"It's fine," Jake replied sharply, but then his voice softened. "I'm glad you called."

In a few minutes he had the battery hooked up, then nodded for me to try the ignition. I climbed in the driver's seat, and it immediately turned over.

He closed the hood, then walked over to my window. "We'll follow you home."

His voice was soft and sweet, and a lump formed in the back of my throat. I shook my head—I'd already made him late, I wouldn't make them any later.

"I've already screwed up your evening." I glanced over at Grace. "I'm so sorry. You guys go have fun. I'll see you tomorrow at the barbecue."

She raised her brows and looked over to Jake.

*Shit! She didn't know.* "Sorry," I mouthed to Jake—wishing I had a rock to hide under—then turned on my headlights and backed out of the space.

*Way to put your foot in your mouth, Katie. Real smooth.*

# CHAPTER FOURTEEN

I decided to stop at the grocery store on the way home. It had been a while since I'd seen Jake with Grace, and even though I didn't have any right, it hurt seeing him with another woman.

I knew I shouldn't have been upset; I'd been a fool to think something had changed. He was happy and proud of me yesterday, and I was just stupid for reading into his playfulness.

I placed my basket on the counter and began scanning my items at self-checkout. Albacore sashimi, a pint of caramel gelato, and a bag of barbecue potato chips. Sure, not the best combo, but it was *my* damned pity party, and I'd eat what I wanted to.

Then my eyes locked on the copy of *Dirty Dancing* shoved on the shelf by the gum. I grabbed it, scanned it, and threw it in my bag. If I couldn't have a happy ending of my own, I wanted to watch Baby come out of the corner.

It was quarter to nine when I pulled into the driveway. The house was completely dark, which only reminded me that Jake was with *her*. Beautiful, petite, blond-haired, blue-eyed Grace. Everything I'd never be.

I quickly changed into boxers and a cami, threw my hair into a messy bun, and set myself up with a picnic in the living room.

Fresh toes always made me feel better, so I grabbed a large bowl of soapy water and my box of manicure supplies before starting the movie.

It was just after ten when I heard the gate open out front, and my stomach sank. I pulled my feet from the water, dried my toes with a nearby towel, and pretended to watch the screen as Patrick Swayze held on to Jennifer Gray's hip in the merengue.

His boots hit the deck, and my body stilled with anticipation as I waited for him to open the door.

A second later he entered, then his eyes ran from my bowl of water to my sushi picnic, and he shook his head. "I won't ask." His eyes dropped to the mail in his hand.

He was more beautiful than any man I'd seen in my life—though maybe I thought that because he was here with me, and not out with Grace. "You're home early." I ran my tongue over my suddenly very dry lips.

He shrugged. "I have to be at work early tomorrow." Then he looked up again, and the corner of his mouth lifted. "Okay, what's with the bowl?"

I laughed and glanced down at the soapy water. "I was soaking my feet."

He raised his brows, nodded his head, and gave me a look.

"Oh stop. I'm giving myself a pedicure. They're good for the soul."

"I'll take your word on that." He set the mail on the coffee table and unbuttoned the top button of his shirt.

I moistened my bottom lip again and my eyes locked on his beautiful throat. Here I was, a grown woman, drooling over a man because I could suddenly see his collarbone. "Have you really never had a pedicure before?" I grabbed a nail file out of the box.

"Nope."

"Do you want one?" The minute the words crossed my lips, I wanted them back. *What kind of sickly twisted person was I?*

"Are you offering?"

I bit my lip. *No.* "Sure." *Crap! What the hell was I doing?*

He laughed. "Let me take a shower first."

*Holy shit!* First, I couldn't believe I offered, and second, I couldn't believe he actually said yes.

As soon as he turned the corner, my head fell to my hands. But then I realized he'd be back in a minute, and I hopped to my feet, causing some of the water to slosh from the bowl. *Crap, crap, crap!*

Maybe if I told him I'd changed my mind? Said I'm too tired? But I was a horrible liar, and he'd see right through me.

I picked the bowl off the floor, carried it to the kitchen, cleaned up my picnic.

When I finally sat down, I set a new bowl of soapy water on the ground, crossed my legs high in my lap, and began to file my nails. The shower stopped running, and I took a few calming breaths. *Ridiculous. I was completely and utterly ridiculous.*

Jake walked back in the room a minute later wearing those damned sexy PJ pants. A towel hung around his neck, and he scrubbed the back of his head with one end. "Okay, what do I do?"

I wanted to tell him to go back to his room and lock the damned door, but I was still out of breath, and all I could do was stare at his broad chest and the moisture that lingered on his skin from his shower.

"Katie?"

I moved over on the couch, annoyed with myself. "Put your feet in water."

He eyed me sideways, like I'd just told him to strip, and discarded the towel to one of the chairs. "Why? I just took a shower."

*"Just do it,"* I ordered—though even to my own ears it sounded silly.

He grabbed a chair, put his feet in the soapy bowl, and I fetched my pumice stone from the box. Removing one of his feet from the water, I placed it in my lap, and began to scrub.

"Shit!" he called out, nearly jumping off the couch. "That fucking tickles!"

I laughed, feeling some of the tension fade, and yanked his foot back in place. "Don't be such a baby."

When I switched to the next foot, he was more prepared, but every time he twitched I had to bite my lip to contain my amusement. I moved quickly to his toes, pretending the whole time he was someone else, then finally finished with a dab of green tea lotion and a sigh of relief. "All done," I declared. I'd made it all the way through without doing anything stupid.

But when I glanced up and found him watching me I wasn't so sure.

"Thank you," he said, his tone strange and unreadable.

I cleared my throat. "You're welcome." Not knowing what else to do, I pulled my foot in my lap and pulled a bottle of pink polish out of the box.

He leaned forward and took the polish from my hand. "Let me."

I closed my eyes and laughed nervously. "No, I—"

But it was too late; he already had the bottle opened and the brush positioned over my toes. "Don't look so scared, it can't be much harder than painting a house, right?"

I wasn't scared, and this was *nothing* like painting a house.

He took my foot in one hand, and a glob of paint dripped from the tip of the brush before he even made it to my nail. Paint ran over my skin, and he muttered under his breath.

He glanced up at me, looking humbled, and I hid my smile as I handed him a wad of cotton balls.

"Let me just start over," he said, then hunched over and got serious.

When he pulled the brush out for the second time, he wiped one side first and looked up with a proud grin.

I nodded my approval, then sat perfectly still as the man I was in love with painted my toenails pink. At first I was enthralled. He was the guy's guy, the baseball jock, the construction worker.

But then I noticed how seriously he was taking the job, and I started to giggle. Just a little at first, a slight rumble that started in my belly. Then his pinky stuck out and his grip tightened on my foot. I couldn't stop the rumble from growing.

Eventually my legs began to shake, and he glanced up, aggravated that I was moving, and froze.

His serious eyes met mine, and I couldn't hold it in any longer. I bent over, wrapped my arms around my middle, and my whole body began to shake with amusement.

Before I knew what was happening, I was over Jake's shoulder, and we were in the kitchen. He was muttering something under his breath as he stepped outside, but I was laughing so hard I couldn't make out a word he said. The next thing I knew, he tossed me out of his arms, and I sank to the middle of the pool.

I stood up, completely shocked, and he jumped in after me, laughing as he stalked me. "You. Little. Brat."

I backed away, giggling like a schoolgirl, wanting to be caught, but knowing deep down I was playing with fire.

"I was painting your toes, and you're sitting there laughing at me?" His dimples flashed and he lunged forward.

I dove under the water, kicked off the side, and he came after me. I was able to evade him for a minute, but he was too fast, the pool too small, and he grabbed me from behind. I squirmed and kicked; I laughed and struggled—but his grasp only tightened around my waist.

Then I became aware of my thin camisole clinging to my breasts, and I stopped.

His breathing was shallow, his mouth close to my ear, and I leaned back against him. "Say uncle," he whispered.

The words hit my cheek like a caress. I stilled—my heart pounding a thousand beats per minute—but I couldn't speak.

His arms tightened and he came closer, his hands at my waist, his body millimeters from mine. If I leaned back farther our bodies would join. His chest against my back, his lips close enough to taste.

My chest began to rise and fall with each sexually charged breath, and for the first time in my life I knew it wasn't only me that felt it. It couldn't be just me.

"Say uncle," he repeated, and my body began to melt.

I was giving up, unable to resist any longer, but my throat was so tight I could barely speak. "Uncle."

We stayed like that a second—my breathing labored and heartbeat wild. But then his arms fell away, his hands trailed down my sides. When I turned around, he was already at the side of the pool, pulling his drenched form out of the water.

I took in a breath, his rejection all those years ago playing in my head like a movie, and I willed myself to wake up. My heart screamed in protest, but my voice was silent.

*No, please no.*

He never once turned around. Not even when he spoke. "I'll go get you a towel." And then he was gone, leaving me more empty and confused than I'd ever been in my whole life.

# CHAPTER FIFTEEN

It wasn't every day I came to the conclusion I was screwed. But as I stood cold, aching, and with a whole whirlwind of emotions I wasn't prepared for, it was painfully obvious. I knew I was putting myself in danger by letting him get too close, but I held a fan to the burning brush, igniting the wildfire that burned inside me. What confused me was that he didn't pull away. He held me. Maybe just a second too long, but he held me. Leaving a heaviness in my gut and an overwhelming need to flee.

But I couldn't. I had no money and needed to stay in LA for work.

Laughter from the backyard pulled me from my thoughts, and I knew I couldn't hide in here forever. The lettuce leaf I'd been rinsing was now crumpled in my hand, and I tossed it in the trash, determined not to let my emotions get the better of me. Not today. Not over a stupid fight in the pool.

My shoulders ached with anticipation of going out there. How could I pretend that seeing Jake with Grace didn't bother me? I had no right to be jealous, but I couldn't help the feelings of dread from whirling around in my belly.

Faking some sort of sickness had crossed my mind more than

once, but Jake was the one I wanted to fool, and he would see through me in an instant. *I'm such an idiot.* How could I let this happen?

The back door opened, and John entered the kitchen wearing one of his mischievous smiles. Why couldn't I have feelings for him? He was adorable, sweet, and, most importantly, available.

"I was just coming to find you." He sauntered toward me in that easy way of his, and I nervously wiped my hand on a kitchen towel.

"Just getting things ready for the burgers," I replied. *And avoiding the man I'm in love with, while he spends the day with his girlfriend.*

"Well, it's no fun out there without you, come out with us."

He had a great smile, and I couldn't help returning it as I grabbed a tomato and began slicing. Maybe I could grow to like him? Maybe if I gave him a chance... What would Jake think of that?

"Let me just finish this up," I said, grabbing an onion and removing the delicate outer layers. I knew I was delaying the inevitable—there were only so many things I could slice before raising suspicion—but I needed a few minutes to collect myself.

"Okay, Katie." The gentle way he said the words made me think he knew more than he let on. "But if you're not out in ten minutes I'm coming after you." His tone was light, but I didn't doubt for a second he was serious. He placed a beer on the counter next to me, then headed back outside.

I didn't hesitate before twisting off the cap and downing half the bottle. Drowning my sorrows with alcohol was probably not the brightest idea, but neither was spending an evening with Jake and his girlfriend sober.

Ten minutes later, with a whole tray of sliced veggies in the fridge, I took a sip of my third beer and stepped barefoot onto the back deck. The sun was just about to set, and I relished in its heat as it warmed my bare shoulders. It was my favorite time of day.

That hour when day meets night, and everything becomes more beautiful.

I watched the four of them in the outdoor kitchen. Em, John, and Grace were deep in conversation, while Jake prepared the barbecue. Such an ordinary thing, lighting coal, though Jake made it look anything but. The gray T-shirt and black shorts would have gone unnoticed on any other man, but the sight of him made it hard for me to breathe. My eyes traveled down his broad back to the bare feet I'd held in my lap only hours ago. My thoughts lingered on the intimate moment that followed and the reason I couldn't sleep last night.

I drank a good portion of my beer noticing how relaxed and happy they all seemed. Em waved her arms in the air—the center of everyone's attention. Dressed much like me in shorts and a tank top but looked like she stepped out of a magazine.

The smell of burning coal and lighter fluid drifted toward me, and I reluctantly moved closer. Squaring my shoulders, I forced a smile and listened in on Em's story. "So I finally got him backed into a corner, declared my everlasting love for him, and he puked all over my brand new red boots!"

Everyone laughed, and I joined in. Even though I wasn't quite sure what the story was about.

"What about you, Katie?" John asked, throwing an arm over my shoulder. I knew he was trying to include me, but all I wanted was to blend into the background and hide.

"What's that?" I took another pull of my beer, trying not to notice how adorable Grace looked in her pale yellow sundress. Cute as a button. Damn her!

"Who was your first crush?"

The question startled me, and I glanced over at Jake. "I can't really think of anyone."

I caught Grace staring at me, and heat rose to my cheeks. John didn't seem to catch on to the tension and continued his interrogation. "Come on, everyone has someone." He squeezed my shoulder, and I could sense Jake's eyes on me. I was suddenly pissed off. He knew how I felt then—still knew. How could he not? I was practically trembling in his arms last night.

I took another long drink of my beer before answering. "Well, there was this one guy. But he turned out to be an *asshole*."

Jake choked on his beer, and Em began pounding him on the back, but I couldn't look at him. I moved from John's embrace toward the table and popped a blueberry from the tray into my mouth.

"What about you, John?" I asked, turning around to lean against the table. The beers had already given me a slight buzz, and I decided that flirting with John might be best way to survive this night.

"What about me, sweetheart?" he replied, walking toward me with that devilish grin.

"Who was your first crush?"

"Well, I was eight, and I threw a handful of mud at a little cutie named Penelope Sanders. If fact, that's how I got this scar." He reached up to touch his chin, and I smiled, wondering if he was telling the truth.

"Katie, are the burgers ready?" There was an edge to Jake's voice, but I pretended not to notice.

"Yes, they're in the fridge," I replied sweetly, just like a nineteen-fifties housewife.

"Can you come show me?"

I rolled my eyes and followed Jake inside. From the forceful way he walked, I could tell he was already annoyed with me. Good.

I brushed past him when we got to the kitchen, yanked open the fridge, pulled out the tray of burgers and set them firmly on the center island. "There you go," I said, then, not wanting to stick around, I turned back to the door.

"Are you mad at me?" His gruff voice halted me.

I spun around, intending to give him a piece of my mind, but stopped. The expression on his face made my throat tighten. "No, why would I be mad?" *Because you held me like I was the most precious thing on earth, when you knew nothing would ever come of it?*

"You've been avoiding me since I got home."

What he said was true, but nothing I could say would make things better. I was close to baring it all, to walking out the door and telling him to leave me alone.

"Katie—"

The torture in his voice was measurable, and I had no doubt he was sorry. Just like he was three years ago. But I didn't want sorry. The last thing I wanted was for him to say he was sorry. I closed my eyes, knowing I couldn't bear to hear his excuses. All the reasons he would never think of me the way I wanted him to.

"Everything okay?"

I turned to face the girl who'd won him. The girl he wanted. Grace.

"Yep. Need a drink? I know I could use another."

She shook her head, and I grabbed another beer and stormed outside.

Em blocked me at the door, and I could tell she was curious about what transpired. For someone who'd known me such a short amount of time, she read me so well.

"You okay?" she whispered, and I nodded, trying for a reassuring smile.

When I joined John back at the table, Jake's unspoken words haunted me. I knew he was upset, but I couldn't let myself think about that now. Dwelling on last night was the last thing I needed.

Jake and Grace walked out after me, carrying the platters of veggies and burgers with them, and I forced myself to take a deep breath. My dislike of her wasn't fair. I knew that. She saw me as a threat, and if I put myself in her shoes, I wouldn't like me either—but I was too pissed to care about being reasonable. Determined not to obsess any longer, I turned to John.

"So, tell me more about this Penelope?" I twisted the cap off my beer.

He leaned back in his chair and didn't disappoint me. "Not much came of Penelope. She moved away that summer and broke my heart. I'll always remember her spark though." He touched his scar again with one finger.

"You know, I could have sworn you told me you got that scar in a bar fight," Em called from behind me, and I laughed.

"You must be mistaken, this mark is definitely from an eight-year-old vixen." He winked, then changed the subject. "But if you want to know about my first love, well that was Tabetha Swanson." A far-off look crossed his features, and I knew I was in for a good story. "I was fourteen, and she was my buddy's older sister. God, she was a good teacher."

I laughed and leaned forward. "What did she teach you?"

He raised his eyebrows suggestively. "I can show you if you want?"

The way he looked at me made me blush, and I shook my head. "But you were so young."

He took a pull of his beer and shrugged. "I wasn't *that* young."

"Fourteen? You were a baby. How old was she?"

"Seventeen."

"If she was just a year older she'd be in jail," I teased, amazed by how easy he was to flirt with.

He chuckled. "Well, it's a good thing no one ever found out then."

I glanced up, and Em flashed a smile, taking a seat next to me.

"So how old were you?" John asked, resting forward on his knees.

"How old was I when what?" There was no doubt what he was asking, and I squirmed a little.

He seemed amused, and I knew I must have been blushing again. "Yes, Katie. How old were you? You know, when you lost it?"

I chewed on my lip, then downed the rest of my beer. "I'm not answering that."

"Holy shit, this must be a good story." His enthusiasm drew the attention of the others, and I had to resist the urge to crawl under the table and hide.

"Leave her alone, John, don't you know a lady never talks about such things." Em nodded to me, but John wasn't put off.

"Wait…are you still?" His eyes went big, and he leaned even closer.

"John!" Em scolded, but I cut her off.

"It's okay." I shook my head. Sure I'd never been more embarrassed in my life. "I was twenty-three." *There, I said it. Nothing to be ashamed of. It was what it was.*

But the whole world went silent, like I just said I was pregnant. My eyes betrayed me by wandering over to Jake. He was resting against the stone next to the barbecue, and he didn't hide the fact he was watching me.

*Yes, Jake, I was a virgin that night, and I would have given myself to you body and soul. I still would, if only you wanted me.*

I let out the breath and turned back to the table. "Geez, John, stop looking at me like I have two heads."

"I just don't know what to say. How is that possible?" He ran his eyes up and down my body. "If I'd known you then, I would've made it my mission to tempt you over to the dark side."

I laughed and shook my head, wishing I could see Jake's reaction but not daring to look.

"It's true, Katie. I'm really good with a Lightsaber. I'd be happy to give you lessons any time. Just say the word."

Heat rose to my cheeks, and I rolled my eyes at him. "I need a beer. Anyone else?"

John and Em nodded, and I headed back into the kitchen.

Knowing I'd need a few more before the night was over, I retrieved the red tub from a low cupboard and began filling it with ice. The back door opened, and my body stiffened. I knew it was Jake even before I turned around.

"I need cheese for the burgers," he muttered, then opened the fridge beside me and pulled a package from the deli drawer.

I stepped aside, careful not to touch as I continued filling the bucket with ice. He closed the door but didn't move away. "What are you doing?"

My heart constricted, but I pretended I wasn't affected by him. "I'm filling this bucket with ice," I said snarkily. My hands were frozen, and I tried to focus on their numb tips, instead of the flutters in my stomach or the crazy beat of my heart.

"That's not what I'm talking about."

I closed the freezer, then placed the heavy bucket on the center island. "Oh?"

"John's a player. He's with a new girl every month."

"So?" I brushed him aside, opened the fridge, and began transferring beer into the bucket of ice.

"I really don't think it's a good idea. He's not what you need right now."

"How do you know? Maybe he's exactly what I need." I couldn't look at him. He'd know. He'd see the hurt under my icy surface.

"You're not that kind of girl."

My blood turned hot, and I grabbed beers two at a time, shoving them into the ice. "What kind of girl am I, Jake?" Even if I wanted to, I couldn't hide my anger any longer.

"You're the type that wears your heart on your sleeve, and keeps your virginity until twenty-three." His voice softened, and I felt something solid in my throat, making it difficult to swallow.

"I'm not that girl anymore."

"I think you are."

"Well, you're wrong." I closed the fridge and turned around. "Thanks for the warning." Grabbing the bucket with both arms, I made it to the back door before realizing I had no hands to open it with.

"Can you help me?" I asked, squeezing my eyes shut.

He came from behind me, one hand resting on the wall, the other on the knob, caging me in. "I don't want to see you hurt."

*The only one who can hurt me is you.* "I'm a big girl, I'll be fine."

Seconds went by, and my heart slammed in my chest. "Okay, Katie," he said, breaking the silence. Then pushed the door open, setting me free. "If that's what you want."

# CHAPTER SIXTEEN

B y the time dinner was ready, the sun was completely gone, and my mood had changed from bad to worse. I knew I needed to shake it off, to stop thinking so much, but Jake's words kept playing in my head. Was that what I wanted? To bury my feelings in another man? To pretend, like I had with Kevin?

Em's voice pulled me from my thoughts. "What are you going to do while Jake's out of town?"

"What was that?" I'd heard her, just needed a few more minutes to comprehend.

"When Jake's gone. Do you have any plans?" she repeated.

Confused, I glanced over to Jake, noticing for the first time how tired he seemed. Like he hadn't slept in days.

"Sorry, I forgot to mention it. I'll be gone next week. Leave Saturday night."

My stomach twisted, and I looked over at Grace.

"I have a conference. Renewable energy," he explained.

"You better get rest while you're gone," Grace cooed. "I want you to have plenty of energy for your party when you get home."

His party. Jake's birthday, I'd almost forgotten.

She leaned into his lap, speaking in that comfortable, flirtatious way of lovers, and bile rose in the back of my throat. She spoke of champagne, appetizers, and all the guests who would be in attendance.

My brows creased. Is that what he wanted? Champagne and big parties? Parties like his parents had, that drove him to knock on our door, looking for an escape?

John leaned over my shoulder and whispered in my ear, "Don't worry, Katie. I'll keep you busy while he's gone."

The alcohol was making him exceptionally flirty, and I knew he wasn't serious, but I secretly hoped Jake saw, or even better heard what he'd said.

"I have a shoot Thursday," I answered Em, my mind reeling and lonely. "Someone actually found me from my website."

She looked confused, and I realized it had been a while since she asked the question. "When Jake's gone, I mean."

Her face lit up and she leaned forward. "That's amazing, Katie."

"It's just an engagement session, but I'm hoping to turn it into more."

"What time is the wedding tomorrow?" Jake asked, his voice hollow as he took in the empty beer bottles in front of me.

"Afternoon." I didn't mention that I had to leave by nine in the morning, or the fact that I was nervous as hell. It would have only prompted more questions, and I didn't want to talk to him.

The truth was the wedding would be a lot of work, and the responsible thing would be to stop drinking and go to bed. But I'd already had too many to care.

I fished another bottle from the tub and sat back in my seat.

"You should eat something," Jake suggested, and I looked up to see him watching me.

"I'm sure Katie can take care of herself, Jake," Grace replied.

She climbed up into his lap, and I twisted off the cap and drank a good portion, ignoring them both.

The food was good, but my stomach was twisted in knots. The

alcohol began to slowly work its magic, and if I closed my eyes, I could almost pretend everything was fine.

By the time dinner was over, I was on my eighth beer and hadn't been this drunk since college. Em put on some music, then pulled me to the middle of the patio and started to dance. I knew what she was trying to do. Get me out of the funk I'd been in all through dinner. Grace sat on Jake's lap, but I periodically caught him glancing at me. I knew he disapproved of how drunk I was, but in that moment, I didn't care.

"So, do you like John?" Em asked me, her hands in the air as she moved her hips to the beat. "You guys have been pretty flirty."

"Maybe," I said, but my eyes flashed to Jake to see if he still watched me, and I didn't sound very convincing. He wasn't. He was talking to John, and I wondered if he was giving him the same warning he'd given me in the kitchen.

"Hey, John!" I yelled, beckoning him to me with my finger. "Come dance with us." If Jake thought he was going to butt into my life, he was wrong.

A slow grin spread across John's face as he sauntered across the deck toward us. I draped my arms around his neck and danced a little closer than I normally would, but I had a point to prove. Even with him pressed so close, there was no flutter. Maybe I was just too drunk to notice, but deep down I knew it was something else. I wanted to look up. To see Jake's reaction, but that would be pointless. He made it clear he disapproved, and trying to make more out of his words would lead to heartache. He was only being protective.

When the second song ended, I headed inside, needing to pee. I swayed entering my room but caught myself with the wall. I checked my email on my laptop, replied to a message from Rick about directions, and read it over three times before pressing send.

On my way back through the kitchen, I grabbed another beer

from the fridge, and when I closed the door, Jake leaned against the counter.

"Don't you think you've had enough?"

"No." I cleared my throat, then tried to brush past him, but he blocked me.

"How many have you had?"

"I don't remember."

"By my count, you've had at least eight."

By my count, it was nine, or maybe even eleven. "You've been counting?" I slammed the bottle on the counter then stepped toward him. The tension and frustration I held inside was too big to control any longer. "I don't need you, Jake."

He stepped closer, and we were so close we almost touched. "Don't do this because you're mad at me."

It was hard to breathe, and my throat constricted. "I'm not mad at you." But the words came on a whisper.

"You could have fooled me." His breathing was just as ragged as mine, and my gaze traveled from his intense eyes to his beautiful mouth.

"I'll go find her!" Em's voice called from the backyard, just a second before she barged into the kitchen.

I grabbed my beer off the counter and moved around him, but I could tell by Em's expression I wasn't fast enough. She saw.

"Sorry, I just needed another beer." I held up my bottle and smiled, but when I got outside, Em didn't immediately follow. Part of me was glad about that. I didn't want to have to explain what just happened. I didn't understand it myself.

John sat at the table with Grace, while a whirl of feelings stirred inside me for a man whose girlfriend sat only ten yards away.

I decided trying to like John might be the best thing for everyone. I opened my beer, slowly walked toward him, and sat on his lap.

"How'd I get so lucky?" John asked, wrapping his arms around my waist.

"You look comfortable, and I'm cold." It was a total lie, but what was I supposed to say? I'm using you to help me forget? To help everyone forget. To move on from something I knew would only hurt me.

"Well, in that case, let me warm you up." He pulled me closer at the same time Em appeared beside me. She eyed me up and down, then arched a brow to ask if I was okay. I gave her a quick nod and took a pull of my beer.

"Who wants to play cards?" she asked, just as Jake stepped out of the kitchen.

John took the cards out of the box, and I moved to my own seat, pulling in a much-needed breath.

"Blackjack. Deuces wild. Everyone know the rules?"

Silence confirmed that we did, and he continued. "What are the stakes? He looked around the table, but no one answered.

"Well, I'm broke, so don't look at me," I said.

"Okay, let's play for clothes then." His eyes twinkled as he looked between me, Em, and Grace.

I bit my nails and shook my head.

"Where's your sense of adventure?" he teased.

Then Grace, who hadn't said anything to us all night, chimed in from the other side of the table. "I'm in."

Everyone turned in her direction, but she looked right at me. "I've got nothing to hide."

I took a deep breath, sure she was challenging me in some way. Did she think *I* had something to hide? I turned back to John, mentally calculating my four articles of clothing. "Okay, I'm in."

"Why the hell not," Em muttered, pulling her seat closer to the table. My jaw fell open in shock, and she shrugged. "It's on my bucket list."

Her answer sent me into a fit of manic giggles, and she elbowed me under the table.

"We're not playing strip poker." Jake's voice cut through the night, and I turned to face him.

He stared at me, his eyes pleaded with me to stop.

"You don't have to play if you don't want to." I wasn't sure about the game a second ago, but in that moment there was nothing that could've pulled me away.

"Come on, Jake. Don't be such a buzz kill," John said, shuffling the deck.

He seemed to consider it for a moment, then finally agreed. "Fine. Deal me in."

The first round, I was dealt a six of hearts and a five of diamonds. Eleven. I was supposed to do something with that, but my head was too foggy to remember. I hit twice and busted.

Grace won the round with twenty and earned the shirt from everyone at the table. I'd forgotten about the other side of the game. The fact that I would soon see Jake completely nude.

I only had three articles of clothing left. My bra, panties, and shorts. This made me even with Em and John. Though I was pretty sure John was cheating because he was the only one still wearing shoes. And Grace would have been ahead, but she'd made the mistake of wearing a dress that night, so we were even too. But Jake—he was at a greater disadvantage; at best he had only two losses left. This was going to be a quick game.

"Damn!" John exclaimed. "I need another beer. Anyone else?" The red bucket was now empty, so he walked backward toward the house, waiting for a reply.

"I'll take one," I answered, even though I knew it was a bad idea.

A minute later John handed me another bottle then dealt the next hand.

I took a long drink and peeked at my cards. Sixteen. I couldn't remember—hit or stay? Crap! "Hit."

Three of diamonds. Good. "Stay."

Jake won the round with twenty-one, and I began taking off my shorts.

"Keep them on."

I pretended not to hear him and stood to slip them down my legs. On pure luck I'd put on my good underwear that day, and inwardly smiled as I tossed my shorts over. There was no doubt in my mind he was mad at me now. The heat coming from his eyes could've melted steel.

I glared at him. "If you don't want to see, turn around."

"Now, kids…" Em warned, shaking her finger at us.

I started to take another drink, but my head began to spin, and I set the bottle back to the table. I looked at my next cards. Seven of spades and six of clubs. *Twelve. No wait, thirteen.* "Hit me." I placed both feet on the ground in an attempt to make the world stop spinning.

*Three of hearts.* "Hit."

*Queen.* "Crap."

John won, and I debated whether I should give him my panties or bra.

"Okay, that's enough." Jake stood beside me. "Time for bed."

Deciding on my bra, I began to fumble with the clasp.

"Keep it on, Katie." Jake's voice was quiet as he spoke only to me.

"Don't tell me what to do," I replied, finally working it free and throwing it to John.

The next thing I knew, Jake covered me with a towel and tossed me over his shoulder. I wanted to scream, but bile crept up my throat and I thought I might be sick. "Put me down," I whispered through clenched teeth.

"No." He stormed through the backyard, into the kitchen, and everything began to spin like a carnival ride.

When he finally put me on my feet we were in my bedroom, the bile had climbed higher, and I couldn't hold it in any longer. I stumbled to the bathroom and barely made it to the toilet before my whole body began to convulse.

"It's okay, baby," Jake said from behind me. "Just let it out." He held my hair with one hand and stroked my back with the other. I vaguely heard someone knocking and Grace's muffled voice, but Jake didn't answer. He pressed a cool washcloth to my head, and I squeezed my eyes shut. Even in my drunken state, I was mortified. There I was, wearing nothing but white lace panties, puking my guts out, while the one man I never wanted to see me like this held back my hair.

When I had nothing left, Jake grabbed my robe and draped it over my shoulders.

A cool glass was pressed into my hand, and I sat down to the tile floor. "Drink this," Jake whispered, and for the first time that night, I didn't argue.

He filled the glass again and handed me a couple pills. I vaguely heard the shower running as I tossed them back and took another drink.

He lifted me to stand, pulled my robe around my shoulders, and held me close. His strong hand stroked my back, and I wondered how I could ever be mad at him. All he was trying to do was stop me from making a fool of myself.

"Why don't you take a shower. I'll find you something to wear."

But I didn't want him to leave me. It felt so good standing there like that. In the morning I knew things would be different. I wouldn't be able to say I was drunk, to hold on to him as tightly as I did now.

He turned me toward the shower and left the room. I stepped under the warm water, allowing the tears I'd been holding in all day to run down my cheeks. I rested my head against the cool tile, frustrated I'd let myself get so out of control. *This wasn't me.*

I washed my hair and scrubbed my face, letting my tears rinse down the drain with the bubbles. When I stepped out of the shower, I saw my pink cami and boxers sitting on the counter. I brushed my teeth, quickly dressed, then found Jake sitting on the edge of my bed. Waiting.

He stood when I entered the room and fresh tears blurred my vision. "I'm so sorry," I whispered.

He shook his head, and my heart squeezed from the look on his face. He looked tired, tormented—sad. "Let's not talk about this now. Get some sleep." He pulled back my covers, and I climbed into my bed.

"Thank you, Jake," I said softly, then rested my head on my pillow and closed my eyes.

He pulled the sheet over my shoulders, and the mattress shifted under his weight as he sat beside me. His hand ran over my cheek, smoothing the hair from my face, and I felt like I did every other time he was near me—safe. He would never let anything bad happen to me. Or if it did, he'd be right by my side, holding my hand. I wouldn't let myself think beyond that. Right now I just wanted to enjoy his closeness.

A few minutes passed and I began to relax. My breath turning shallow, and sleep threatened to take over. I felt Jake lean closer, and I inhaled the earthy scent of his skin.

"I'm sorry, Katie." His soft lips pressed against my forehead, lingering for just a second before he stood.

I wanted to ask him what he was sorry about, but sleep was too close, and I finally let it take me.

# CHAPTER SEVENTEEN

My eyes cracked open, and even with the soft light of morning the room was too bright. Em sat on the side of my bed, her short hair illuminated by the sun like a halo, and my chest filled with panic. "What time is it?" I croaked, my throat so hoarse it felt like I'd gargled sand.

"Quarter to eight," Em replied.

I willed myself to sit, then pinched the bridge of my nose as my head threatened to split in two. "The wedding is today."

She nodded and handed me a glass of frothy orange liquid and a couple of Tylenol. "Are you going to be okay?"

I laughed a little. "I don't have a choice." Which was the truth. I needed this job. I threw the pills to the back of my throat, then downed them with a drink that tasted of tangerines. "What is that?"

She only shook her head and took the glass. "It'll help with your hangover. Get in the shower. I'll make you something to eat."

A minute later, warm water ran over me as clips of last night played in my head. What the hell was I thinking? That wasn't me; I didn't get drunk the night before an important job. I was responsible! I chose the *blue* pill... didn't I? What would've happened had

Em not awoken me? Rick made it clear I had one chance, and the opportunity almost washed down the drain because of my decision to act like a sulky idiot. Like the idiot girl who made a fool of herself at every turn. That's what I was doing. Making myself look like a fool.

Visions of Jake stroking my naked back and the way he took care of me consumed my thoughts. He'd called me baby. An endearment he'd never used before. He'd said he was sorry, but why? I let out a defeated sigh and quickly scrubbed my face. Normally a shower was rejuvenating, but not today. Today, I was so embarrassed I wanted to cry. But I didn't have time to wallow in tears. I didn't even have time to wash my hair.

When I entered the kitchen ten minutes later, Em stood at the sink, and a plate of scrambled eggs waited for me on the counter. "Thanks," I said hoarsely.

"No problem." She loaded a dish into the washer and smiled.

"How do I look?"

She dried her hands, then tucked a wayward tag into the neck of my blouse and scanned from my messy ponytail to my black slacks. "Like you just spent the night with your head in your toilet." Her eyes crinkled. "But in the cutest possible way, of course."

I don't know why, but even with the mood I was in, her honesty made me laugh. "Of course."

I made myself a cup of coffee, then rested a hip against the counter and tested my stomach with a bite of egg. "Is Jake still sleeping?"

She shook her head, and the expression on her face made my stomach drop. "He woke me up before leaving and told me to take care of you."

I cringed. *Take care of me.* It was always that. "What happened after—" But I stopped. So many questions lingering on my tongue, but I couldn't ask any of them. I didn't have time for answers, and I wasn't sure I wanted them anyway.

"You mean after Jake threw you over his shoulder like a caveman?" Her brows were creased, and she shook her head. "The game ended. Grace left…"

I took a deep breath as guilt threatened to send me over the edge. I hadn't thought about Grace, or how my childish behavior could affect their relationship. As jealous as I was, I didn't want to be the reason for that.

"Is that where Jake went this morning?" I knew the answer, but I needed the confirmation. He took care of me last night because that was what he did. But today, he went to smooth over the conflict I created for him and Grace. She was his girlfriend; I was the girl he took care of out of obligation.

"Yeah, I'm pretty sure…" Her eyes filled with sympathy, and I nodded, stuffing more egg in my mouth as an excuse not to speak.

It was hard to believe someone like Em would ever be in a situation like mine. In love with a man I was destined never to hold. But the way she looked at me, in spite of her beauty, made me think she understood.

After eating all my stomach would allow, I downed the rest of my coffee and set my plate in the kitchen sink. "Thanks again for everything. I don't know what I'd do without you."

"Don't worry about it." She bumped me with her shoulder. "I expect payback one of these days. With interest."

"I promise." And it was a promise I was determined not to break.

The crunch of gravel mixed with my rapid pulse were the only sounds heard as I pulled in front of Rick's house. It was different than I'd imagined. Not new and state of the art but old, rustic, and covered with brick and ivy. My shoulders began to relax—I made it in time—but then I spotted Rick leaning against the back of his SUV. He stood in perfect stillness, his expression hard and unamused. We made eye contact; then he pushed from the shiny black surface and climbed into the driver's seat.

I glanced at my phone in the center console—I was five minutes early. Why did he look so pissed? My mind flashed to the message I sent last night. Had I said something that pissed him off?

I'd put every penny I had into this opportunity—if I screwed this up…but I wouldn't let my mind go there. That was a slippery slope I didn't have the strength for right now. I squared my shoulders, took a deep breath, and got out of the car.

When I climbed into the passenger seat beside him, the silence in the cab was suffocating.

"Good morning," I said, my voice harsh, and not my own.

He eyed me up and down. "Morning."

I cleared my throat and reached for my seatbelt. "Where are we headed?"

"Downtown." He shifted the car into drive, and we were on our way.

An hour later I stood breathless in front of the St. Dominic's Catholic Church in downtown Los Angeles. It was beautiful. The entrance perfection all on its own. Weathered stone sculpted with ornate sophistication, a door that must have been twenty feet high and carved into a masterpiece of geometric shapes. It was humbling to stand in the presence of such art—let alone hold a camera in a place as magnificent as this.

Rick went over my instructions once again, and adrenaline pulsed through my veins. My job would be to spend the morning with the bride and her bridesmaids. He explained they'd feel more comfortable with a woman, that I'd be able to take more unguarded shots, but he looked so angry I wondered why he was giving me so much responsibility.

He rattled off a list of "must have" details, "…gown, flowers, ring, garter, shoes." Then he turned to me and eyed me up and down once again. "Don't screw this up, Katie."

Details were my thing, the part of photography I loved most. I wasn't worried about that, but Rick's warning terrified me.

A minute later, I followed the wedding coordinator down a dark hall to the bride's quarters and tried to push all the episodes of *Bridezilla* from my thoughts. This wasn't my first wedding, but somehow working under Rick's scrutiny made me feel as though it was. I took a deep breath and braced myself as the coordinator pushed open the door. A bride wearing a white satin robe stood in the center of the room. She looked over her shoulder, smiled, and her shoulders visibly relaxed. I knew in that moment everything would be fine.

I spent a few hours with the girls, listening to nervous chatter, as everyone got ready. Then later that afternoon, I left the bridal chambers to meet Rick in the sanctuary. Deep mahogany pews were surrounded by stained glass windows, and stone pillars framed the scarlet aisle that would lead the bride to her groom. A gasp of pleasure escaped my throat.

Fifty rows back, a staircase led to an upper-level balcony. I knew this was where I was supposed to be, so I climbed to the very top. There were no seats above, just a mahogany banister that extended across the width of the sanctuary. I took a couple of practice shots and began to panic at the vast absence of light.

"Is there a problem, Ms. McGregor?"

Rick's cool voice startled me, and I whipped around to face my boss. "I—I just didn't realize there would be so little light."

His jaw tightened, and he roughly set his equipment to the ground before stalking toward me. "Fuck. I thought you knew what you were doing."

All I could do was blink. What could I even say to that?

"Give me your camera," he barked.

I handed it over and watched in stunned silence as he adjusted the settings, then gave it back to me.

"You can't be serious. That shutter speed is way too low." *1/50, way too low for the lens I was working with.*

"Take a shot," he commanded in a low voice.

I flung the camera strap around my neck and turned. My hands gripped at my sides as I gritted my teeth. I wanted to tell him he was an idiot—a jerk, but I did neither.

I felt him move behind me as I got into position. Then one of his hands snaked around my middle, while the other took the arm that held my camera and pressed it close to my body. My gut twisted. He was demonstrating how to make my body strong and still, like a human tripod. Something I'd known since I was thirteen.

"Take a deep breath, Katie," he whispered in my ear. "That's right. Now take the shot." His voice was demanding, urgent, and I did as he said.

A second later, he moved away, and exhaled. *What the hell was that?*

"Five shots in rapid succession," he ordered. "Exactly like that, and you'll be fine." He didn't wait for me to answer, or even look at my camera before he picked up his gear and heading back down the stairs. The shots were perfection.

The rest of the ceremony and reception went off without a hitch, and I began to question whether my uneasiness on the balcony was an overreaction. Rick was gruff and demanding, but he knew what he was doing. His ways weren't what I was used to, but this was different than any other job I'd ever had. He wasn't an office with human resources and a break room. I was working for an artist, one who was brilliant and looked up to by his peers. Did it really matter that he barked orders and crossed boundaries? I had the opportunity to learn from him, and I needed to shut up and deal with it.

We made it back to Rick's house at just after eleven, and I was completely exhausted. A wedding would do that regardless, but I hadn't started the day in the best shape in the first place. He invited me inside while he backed up my images, but I told him I needed to make a phone call, and sat in my car. The truth was, even though I resolved to work with him, the thought of being alone with him in his house made my stomach turn.

"You did good today, Ms. McGregor," he said, as he handed me my camera through my car door.

"Thank you. I had a lot of fun." Which was the truth. I was able to escape from my own life for a moment, and nothing could've been better than that today.

"Good, because I'll have another job for you in two weeks."

"Yes—yes of course." A thrill ran through me, and I sat straight up in my seat.

"It's a weekend job, and will pay double the thousand I'm paying you tonight. We leave Friday afternoon, and won't come back until Sunday. Does that work for you?"

My pulse quickened. This was great news, though I couldn't help but worry about being alone with him for that long. "Yes, of course," I stammered out.

"Good." He handed me a manila envelope I could feel was thick with cash. "I'll be in touch."

A thousand dollars? We'd never talked about money, but this was double what I was expecting. When I pulled away from the curb, I realized that in two weeks' time I would have enough money to move out of Jake's house, to live on my own, and finally get settled. I wouldn't be a burden to anyone; I'd have no one to call when I'd be home late or to yell at me when I forgot. Jake would have his life back, and I would no longer be a burden. The thought should've made me happy, but the feeling that settled inside me was anything but.

When I pulled in front of the house, the lights were still on, and a lump formed in my throat. Jake was home and waiting for me. I wanted to see him, but didn't want to at the same time. I wished we could just forget about last night and go back to how things were at the beach. But life was never easy like that, and I knew I had to face him.

After depositing my gear in my room, I slipped off my shoes

and found him on the back deck. The small lights that streamed across the patio reminded me of fireflies in the darkness, and a hint of chlorine and freshly cut grass lingered in the air. It felt like the hot summer nights we spent under the stars, lying on the concrete cooled by the night's sky, and dreaming of all the things we'd do when we grew up.

Jake sat on a stool by the bar, his back to me as he strummed his old guitar. I recognized the song he played. "Stand by Me," the anthem of my teen years. The song we sang around campfires after Dad passed, a vow between Dave, Jake, and me that we'd always be there for one another—even if no one else was.

Then Jake began to sing. The deep baritone I hadn't heard in years. The lyrics of pain, sorrow, and hope—so quiet I had to strain to hear. I wanted to move closer, to see his face, but I didn't want to ruin the moment. I didn't know why, but I needed this.

I leaned against the door, closed my eyes, and let it all soak in. The peacefulness of the yard, the cool breeze that swept away the long day, and the sound of Jake's voice. A sinking feeling settled inside. This was one of the last days I'd be alone with him. In two weeks I'd be gone—it wouldn't be the same.

When I opened my eyes a minute later, Jake was watching me, and the music stopped.

My heart clenched, but I didn't move. Neither did he. He just sat there, his eyes penetrating mine as I searched for something to say.

He placed his guitar to the ground, stood, and shoved his hands in his pockets. "My shuttle will be here in a few minutes." His voice was deep, his eyes intense, and I nodded. I'd forgotten he was leaving. I didn't want him to.

Then he swallowed, and took a step closer. "I've been thinking a lot the last couple days…" Something about the way he looked at me made it difficult to breathe. "We've been through a lot together, you and I."

Emotions stirred in my belly and I chewed my bottom lip. It was true. We'd been through *so* much.

He stepped forward and searched my face. "You're a huge part of who I am, Katie, I want to you know that."

My throat tightened and I couldn't speak.

"When you came home—" He stopped, his eyes drifting to his feet before his next words. "You're one of the only people who've ever mattered to me in my life."

My eyes were locked on him, but I remained silent. Not wanting to interrupt, not knowing what to say if I did.

"When Dave and I landed our first construction job, you were the only one who was proud of me. I can still remember you jumping up and down in that old house." He laughed under his breath. "Your opinion was all I cared about. Not my parents, not my buddies at the office..."

He looked up, and his hand gripped the back of his neck. "After Dave died—you were the only reason I was able to hold myself together."

I covered my mouth, and his eyes flickered with the twinkling lights.

"But there's something I've been wanting—needing to tell you." He looked to his feet and swallowed—hard. "Katie...I was supposed to meet the inspector that morning. Dave covered for me because my car wouldn't start." His brows were furrowed and his voice strained. "I tried to tell you so many times, but I couldn't stand the thought of you looking at me differently. Knowing that if it wasn't for me—"

I stepped closer. "Jake, don't."

He shook his head and visions of him on his knees in our old living room flooded me.

"Is that why your Mustang isn't here? Did you sell it?"

He nodded, and I pushed myself forward, slowly moving closer. I stopped when I stood in front of him, my throat so tight it practically strangled me.

He placed a hand along my neck and trailed a thumb across my jaw.

"It wasn't your fault, Jake." I grabbed his wrist and looked into his eyes, needing for him to believe me. "I would have never thought that. You could have told me."

He nodded. "I know I haven't been the easiest guy to live with the last few days, but you coming back hasn't been easy. "

My stomach twisted and I turned my head. Here it was. He'd tell me how complicated I'd made his life. That I needed to find another place to stay. Coming home hadn't been easy for me either, but the thought of hearing the words from his mouth made all the air expel from my throat. "Rick hired me again." I stepped away. "In two weeks I'll be able to move out, you'll have your place back. Your life back."

His brows furrowed, the lines in his forehead deepened. "Katie, that's not what I meant."

"It's time." Even as the words flowed from my mouth, I wanted him to tell me differently. I wanted him to hold on to the girl who was scared to death of losing yet another man she loved.

He searched my face. "Where is this coming from?"

I ran my teeth over my bottom lip in an attempt not to cry. "I know I haven't made things easy for you. For Grace—"

"We're over, Katie." He cut me off.

My heart leapt to my throat. "What?"

"That's where I was this morning." His eyes bored into mine and he stepped toward me. His strong hand settled on the small of my back, urging me closer. I shook my head, wondering if I was in the middle of a dream. "I'm sorry I hurt you." His voice was low, almost a whisper as he spoke. My left hand settled on the smooth cotton of his shoulder, and we began to sway. I didn't know what was happening between us, but in that moment I didn't care. I didn't care about our past, or that if he pulled away, I would break.

His thigh brushed mine as we danced. Our bodies so close I

could feel his heat. He took my right hand and laced it around his neck, tipped my chin with one finger, and ran his thumb over my bottom lip. "I missed you."

I looked up at him, and his eyes shifted to my mouth. I wasn't sure if he was talking about tonight, of if he meant the three years I'd been gone, but I couldn't make a sound. My breath caught, and his hands settled on my hips. The scent of male skin, warm with sunshine, filled my senses, and his lips settled on mine. My mouth parted in an instant, opening to give him access to every part of me. I held nothing back, my heart and every vulnerability was there for the taking. His lips slanted over mine, devouring every-thing I offered, giving me all of him in return. Exerting pressure on the back of his neck I urged his mouth closer. His silky tongue touched mine and was so much sweeter than I remembered. Every inch of my body on fire from his touch.

I was consumed by the kiss, unaware we'd moved backward until we hit the wall by the kitchen. My hands traveled from his neck, down his corded arms, exploring smooth skin and hard muscle. He touched the side of my neck, his fingers gently urging our kiss deeper. I opened to him, drawing him in, needing him… needing *this*.

His large hand traveled up my spine, sending a shiver all the way to my toes, and I arched my back, trying to get closer. Then the doorbell rang, and our kiss broke. He pressed his forehead to mine, his breath coming in labored puffs. "My shuttle."

My body stiffened, and panic replaced my desire. The last time we kissed he pushed me away, and now he was leaving again. Leaving me confused, in the dark, and scared out of my mind.

"Katie, don't." He caressed my face, his thumb brushing gently over my swollen lips, and I relaxed a little in his arms.

"I'll be back late Friday. We'll talk then, okay?" His voice was low and sexy—his eyes as wild as I felt.

I trusted him. I had no idea what was going on, but there was a promise in his expression, and he wasn't pushing me away.

He pulled me closer, groaned deep in the back of his throat, and buried his face in my hair. "Don't give up on me, don't ever give up on me."

Tears blurred my vision, and I nodded into his chest. I didn't know what he meant, but there was no doubt in my mind—I could never give up on Jake.

He cupped my face and kissed me once more. "I'll see you next week." He whispered the words against my mouth, then walked away. The sounds of the door closing behind him signaled I was alone, and my mind began to flood with thoughts.

His confession, his words...our kiss. After all those years of wanting, it was hard to believe it was real. That Jake meant the words he spoke. That such an unguarded and passionate moment hadn't been a dream. But I could still feel the warmth of his body pressed against mine, and the scent of his skin still lingered on my clothes.

In a fog of euphoria and confusion, I somehow made it back into the living room. He'd been gone less than five minutes, yet the house was already different. Knowing he slept in the other room filled me with a sense of security, and for the next six nights I'd be alone. Every sound became magnified. The creak of the floors, leaves rustling outside—I could even hear cars driving by out front. I rushed to the door and slammed the chain on the lock. I knew it was probably silly, that I was being paranoid, but it calmed me nevertheless.

When I entered my room, I pulled the comforter down from my bed, and a yellow paper fluttered to the floor—one from the same pad I'd seen Jake scribbling notes on a hundred times. I bit back a smile and dropped down to pick it up.

*Katie,*

*I wasn't sure what time you'd be home, and didn't want to leave without saying goodbye.*

*Please keep all your lipstick to yourself. I like my stuff, and expect to have it unmarked when I get home.*

*If you catch anything on fire, call John. He's not good for much, but he'll be there if you need anything.*

*Be good,*

*Jake*

*P.S. Can't wait to hear about the wedding.*

A whirl of happiness grew inside me and I grabbed my phone, programmed John's number, then typed a message to Jake.

ME: Where do you keep the fire extinguisher?

The phone chimed with a quick reply.

JAKE: Under the sink. Are you okay?

I sat on the bed as I typed again.

ME: I was thinking about making popcorn while you were gone.

JAKE: Don't!

I laughed.

ME: Don't worry, I know what I'm doing this time.

JAKE: Careful, Katie, I'm not opposed to hiring a babysitter.

ME: Have a safe flight.

A minute passed, then another text.

JAKE: I miss you already.

My heart squeezed.

ME: I miss you too.

I stripped off my clothes and threw a nightshirt on over my head. When I climbed into bed, the sheets were cool and soft against my bare skin, and I replayed every detail of our kiss. I had no idea what my future held; all I knew was that everything was about to change, and I couldn't wait.

# CHAPTER EIGHTEEN

I didn't realize the burden I'd been carrying until it was lifted, but as I hung up the phone that Thursday afternoon, the chain that attached me to Kevin was finally cut. A clean bill of health meant I never had to think about him again. That his infidelity affected no more than the past, and I could finally move toward my future. The future I hoped would include Jake.

I pulled myself from the couch, made my way into the kitchen, and gathered all the ingredients for chocolate cake. Jake's favorite. In twenty-four hours he'd be home. He'd walk through the door and we'd talk. I'd ask him about everything. What our kiss meant. What happened with Grace. What he saw in our future. Yes, I'd sworn off men only a couple weeks before, but the truth was, the rules didn't apply to Jake. They never had.

But what if I didn't like his answers? What would I do then? He wasn't with Grace anymore, but that didn't change the fact he didn't do serious. In fact, he confirmed it when he broke up with her. Would I be okay with that? Could I have a non-serious, non-committed relationship? I thought so—I just didn't know if I could have one with Jake.

I cracked the eggs into the bottom of the bowl—my mind

swarmed with confusion and *what ifs*—and began to whisk my frustrations into the form of a birthday cake. The one thing I had perfected since the age of ten. The only thing I could give Jake that he didn't already have.

Hours later, I added dark chocolate shavings to the top of the homemade coconut pecan frosting, licked my fingers, and tossed the last bowl in the sink to soak.

The doorbell rang, and I looked down at my flour-dusted clothes. It was probably Em or John. It had become the norm for one of them to stop by after work. They would say they were in the neighborhood, but I had a hunch Jake was having them check up on me. We'd order in food and watch a movie—I'd had more pizza in the last week than I cared to admit. But tonight I'd already decided on Chinese. Egg drop soup.

"Coming!" I shouted, as I made my way to the living room. I wiped my hands on a kitchen rag, removed the chain, and yanked open the door.

Grace stood on the front porch, and my breath caught in my throat. She smiled sweetly, scanning over my dusty cut off shorts to my equally messy shirt. A woman carrying a digital tablet stood next to her, and all I could do was stand there in shocked silence.

"Katie." Grace nodded to me. "This is my party planner, Gigi."

Their perfectly groomed hair matched their perfectly pressed suits. I must've looked like Pig Pen in comparison.

"May we come in?" Grace asked, blinking at me expectantly.

I moved aside. "Yes, sorry. Please come in."

*What was Grace doing here? And why did she have a party planner with her?* My mind grasped at a memory of Grace talking to Jake about a party last Friday. But they'd broken up. Breakups voided out birthday parties—didn't they?

"We're just here to run over the plans for Saturday." She flashed me a sweet smile again and walked inside. "Jake deserves nothing but the best. Don't you agree, Katie?"

"Yes, of course." My hands fidgeted with the towel, and I

gestured toward the kitchen. "Sorry I'm such a mess, Jake didn't tell me to expect company."

"Didn't he?" She smiled again, then turned to the party planner. "Gigi, Katie has known Jake since they were practically babies. She's staying here until she gets her feet on the ground. Poor thing was cheated on by her fiancé."

They both turned to me, a look of pity on Gigi's face, and the same fake smile on Grace's. Her words weren't exactly true. First of all, I'd met Jake when I was six. Practically my whole life, but I was hardly a baby. And second, Kevin was never my fiancé.

"Can I get you ladies something to drink?" I asked, my mind reeling with what to do. "Water? Or I just made some sun tea. It might still be warm, but I can add ice?"

"No thanks, we're fine," Grace replied.

I looked to Gigi—even though Grace had rudely answered for her—and she shook her head.

"We were just at dinner discussing Jake's party, and Gigi wanted to come by and look over the backyard."

"Do you mind?" Gigi asked.

"Oh, not at all." Because what was I supposed to say? I had no idea what was going on, and I wasn't about to have it out with Grace, with Gigi as a witness.

"I assume you'll be working Saturday?" Grace asked.

"Working?"

She raised her brows. "Yes, don't you do that on weekends? Or are you finding it difficult to find a job?" Her tone syrupy sweet and slightly amused.

*Bitch.* "Work is awesome. I'll actually be shooting for one of the top wedding photographers in Los Angeles next weekend." I looked into her eyes. "But no, I'll be there on Saturday. It's Jake's birthday."

She was quiet for a second but then nodded to Gigi, and they made their way to the kitchen. "Come with us, Katie," she called over her shoulder. "We'd love another opinion."

For the next hour, Grace and Gigi talked about all their plans. "Only the best," they kept saying, as they ticked off various wines, beer, and the contents of the fully stocked bar. I barely recognized any of the brands they spoke of, and Jake wouldn't either. He was a Sam Adams kind of guy. All the other stuff wouldn't matter.

Grace spoke of all the important people who would be at the party: her friends, high-profile clients, her boss. The longer she went on, the more I wondered what had brought them together in the first place. How this was a party for Jake at all? But then I remembered about their work connection. Maybe that was what this was about?

White lanterns would be hung outside and cocktail tables arranged around the deck. They even planned to take down Jake's twinkling lights—the ones that reminded me of fireflies—because they didn't fit with the "vibe" they were trying to create. A catering service would pass out hot appetizers, and a valet would park cars out front. It was enough to make my head spin. To make me reconsider everything.

Grace reminded me of his parents. Her designer clothes, the way she talked—all the fake materialism he grew up with. But maybe that was it? Maybe that was what he saw in her? Maybe deep down a part of him craved that life? If things were over between them, why would she be doing all this? If they were still together, then why had he kissed me?

By the time they'd left, my gut was twisted in knots. Jake had said they were "over" but hadn't said they broke up. How could I have let this happen? How could Jake do this to me? Put me in the position of becoming the other women when he knew how much I'd been tortured by Kevin's infidelity.

Regardless of what I thought about Grace, this wasn't who I was. I didn't want to be that person, and I wouldn't. I sat on the couch and began to rub slow circles at my temples.

I wanted to trust Jake. To believe that he'd never do anything like this. But the last time I trusted someone—but Jake wasn't

Kevin. He was a good man, and he'd never lied to me before. He'd asked me not to give up on him, and even though I knew it was stupid, I didn't want to. I wanted to believe that he'd never do anything like this. Maybe it was that tiny part of me that still believed in magic, in love at first sight, and the little fortunes that came inside of cookies, but I wasn't ready to give up—not yet.

In exasperation, I threw myself back on the couch and smothered a scream into the pillow. Jake would be home tomorrow night, and I had no idea what was going on. I wanted to trust him, but the uncertainty was enough to make me eat a whole batch of chocolate chip cookies.

I glanced at my cell on the coffee table as hundreds of questions ran through my mind. The most obvious being Grace. Had they broken up after the barbecue? Or what I feared most…had I become the very thing that ended my relationship with Kevin?

Crap! I needed to know. I picked up my phone and began to type.

ME: Hey, are you busy?

My thumb hovered over *send* knowing he probably was in a meeting. That he wouldn't have time to answer. Screw it! I hit the button and held my breath.

JAKE: I'm on break, what's up?

*Exhale.* I'd sent a dozen messages while he'd been gone—all of them silly. None as important as this.

ME: Did you break up with Grace?

*Straight to the point. Rip it off like a Band-Aid.* My heart was in my throat as I looked down at the message. Could I really have this conversation over text? Without seeing his face or hearing his voice?

Delete. Delete. Delete!

ME: Do you want me to pick you up tomorrow?

Maybe I was a coward, but a part of me wasn't ready to know.

I sent the message, my head in my hand, my heart on my sleeve, and my whole world up in the air.

JAKE: The shuttle's already scheduled, don't worry about it.
ME: Okay.
JAKE: Everything good?
ME: Of course.

*Liar.*

After a hot shower and a pep talk about not giving up, I felt a little better and ordered my Chinese. Enough for Em and John in case they showed. I did the dishes, tidied up the kitchen, then put my camera batteries to charge for the next day's engagement shoot. Anything to keep my mind from wandering to things I had no control over. Just as I sat down on the couch to check email, there was a knock at the door.

"Just a sec!" I retrieved my wallet from the nightstand and began fishing out my credit card on the way to the front door.

I twisted the deadbolt, and the door thrust toward me. My breath halted as the chain strained against its anchor. Adrenaline shot through me, my muscles tightened, and I pushed back. An arm covered in black wedged through the gap, a knee and a scruffy face shadowed by a dark hood.

My heartbeat slammed in my ears, the chain so taut the screws began to give, and I threw all my weight against the door. Screams and ragged breath echoed in my consciousness—some of which I recognized as my own—then suddenly the door slammed shut, jolting my body with it. I bolted the lock, my whole body trembling as I slid to the floor, pushing back on my heels until I made it to the coffee table.

I grabbed my cell and hit John's number. *Please pick up. Please pick up.*

It rang three times before he answered. "There's someone here," I said, my voice a ragged whisper.

"Katie? I can barely hear you. Are you okay?"

"I don't know." I shivered and I hugged my knees into my chest. My teeth chattering.

"I'll be right there!"

The line went silent and I dialed nine-one-one.

The woman's voice came high pitched on the first ring. "Nine-one-one what's your emergency?"

I replayed the event in my mind, unable to form an answer.

"Hello?"

" I...I just don't know..."

"Ma'am, are you hurt?"

I scanned over my body. "I don't think so. There was a man at the door... I..."

"Is he still there?"

"No, no... I think he's gone."

My eyes were glued to the front door as the operator continued to ask me questions. I went to the back patio—to Jake's room to check the locks, then gave her my address. She stayed on the line talking to me, reassuring me an officer was on his way. But her words did nothing to comfort me, and I began rocking back and forth on the couch as I watched the door.

Another knock came too soon, and I froze.

"Ma'am, are you okay?" the operator asked, but I couldn't answer—couldn't move. Seconds passed, and the knock came more insistent. "Chinese! Hello? I need a signature." There was a muffled exchange, followed by John calling through the door. "Katie, it's me."

I stumbled to my feet, unlocked the door, and threw myself at John's chest.

He set the bag of food on the floor and enveloped me in strong arms. "What happened? Are you okay? Are you hurt?"

My body shook as I recounted the details. We waited for the cops which seemed to take hours, but in reality only took fifteen minutes.

"I'm Officer Peterson, and this is Officer Gomez. Do you mind if we look around?"

I shook my head, and Officer Peterson began inspecting the broken chain, while Gomez went to check the yard.

John sat with me while I gave my statement. They rattled off questions, and I struggled to give clear answers. I thought he was Caucasian, but he wore glasses and a hood. The only other thing I saw was his hand. Big and strong, but covered in a black glove. I'd never experienced anything like this before. Never been in a fight, never even played any contact sports. The closest thing would've been wrestling with my brother or Jake. But they never wanted to hurt me, and when I was behind that door, I knew I was fighting for my life.

"There've been some home invasions in the neighborhood, and we think you were their next victim. You're very lucky, Ms. McGregor."

*Their victim. More than one.* I nodded, my mind consumed with fear. What would have happened had I not started chaining the door when Jake left? What would they have done had they gotten inside?

Officer Gomez must have sensed my anxiety, because he leaned forward and spoke directly to me. "We're taking this very seriously, Ms. McGregor. We have two cars patrolling the area, and that won't stop until these men are caught."

John stayed with me that night. We watched TV, but I couldn't focus. My eyes kept shifting to the door and the chain that was practically ripped from the wall. He eventually turned the channel to some old black-and-white cowboy movie he declared to be the best story ever told. The music was soft, the absence of color oddly comforting, and not ten minutes later, I fell asleep.

When I opened my eyes again, John sat on the edge of the couch pulling on his boots. I shifted to sit and stared at the light streaming under the door and through the cracks of the shutters.

John looked at me as he gathered his cell phone and keys off the coffee table. "Em will be here any minute. I'd stay, but I'm the only one holding down the fort while Jake's away."

He looked tired. *Had he slept at all?* "I'll be fine. Don't worry about me." I tried for a reassuring smile, but he didn't look convinced.

"Lock the door behind me, don't open it until Em gets here. I've checked all the windows and doors—"

"John. Go. I'll be fine."

My phone chirped at the table, and I picked it up. "It's Jake."

His brows furrowed. "He's not going to be happy about this. I don't envy you."

I took a deep breath. "I know."

# CHAPTER NINETEEN

"I'm not leaving you," John insisted, before the electric drill fired again.

Em spent the whole day with me. She even came to the engagement shoot at Griffith Park. But when we got back to Jake's, I told her to go home. That I'd be fine. That Jake would be home soon, and he'd take over as security guard. I needed to talk to him alone. I had the perfect opportunity to tell him about the break when he called that morning, but I didn't take it. I knew once I told him, he'd flip out, and my questions about Grace would be put on the back burner. So yeah, there would be lots of talking tonight, and I didn't want to have that kind of conversation with an audience.

Em was completely understanding. She handed me a keychain of pepper spray and made me promise to call if I heard anything suspicious. John, on the other hand, wasn't so easily swayed. He came by to install a new chain lock and security hardware on all the windows. It was obvious he wasn't planning to leave me alone anytime soon.

"I really just want some time to myself. It's been a long twenty-four hours, and I need some rest."

He looked up, his eyes crinkling in the corners with amusement. "Sweetheart, I know you're gorgeous, but I think I can control myself for one evening. I just want you to be safe, that's all."

I rolled my eyes at the typical John innuendo, but I knew I'd scared him last night. I could see it on his face. "I *will* be safe. There are two cars patrolling the neighborhood tonight, and the officers said it wasn't their MO—they're not coming back."

"I don't care what they said, Katie. I'm not leaving you alone when there's some sick fuck out there attacking women!" The drill blared to life again, anchoring another screw into the wall.

John was a protector, and he'd taken me under his wing. I was thankful for that, but I needed to be alone. "Jake's coming home tonight," I blurted out, "and I really need to talk to him...alone..." My words trailed off as my eyes shifted to the floor. I could feel him watching me even before I looked up.

"What's going on between you guys?" But I heard the silent question—*and what about Grace?*

All I could do was shake my head. That was the problem. I had no idea.

He grabbed his bag of hardware, and I followed after him as he moved to my bedroom to install the next lock. It wasn't like I'd be alone long. Jake was due home in less than an hour, but if John was still here, he'd tell Jake about the break-in—our talk about Grace wouldn't happen.

"Shit, Katie. I don't like it." He drilled the next hole, then blew out a long breath. "Call me if you hear *anything,* chain the lock when I go. Don't answer for anyone."

As I waited for Jake, anxiety wrapped around me and squeezed like a python to its prey. I couldn't shake the feeling that the conversation ahead of me would be life changing. In the end, I would either have Jake in my life, or I wouldn't.

I had a dream that he'd walk in the door, his hair a mess from the long flight, looking tired and disheveled. He'd smile at me.

That smile that lifted only half his mouth. The one that made butterflies migrate to all the private places inside me. He'd drop his bags, and I'd run into his open arms...and that was where my fantasy stopped. He'd been gone for six days, I'd run endless scenarios through my mind, but in the end of each make-believe conversation, I was filled with a sense of dread. Because what if he hadn't broken up with Grace? Or what if he never intended to leave her at all?

I'd promised myself that if that was the case, I'd leave. Get a hotel, find a room to rent, do whatever I had to...but I wouldn't stay. I couldn't let myself be the other woman. As much as I didn't like to admit it, I knew I wasn't strong enough to resist the temptation of Jake. But another reason lingered in my subconscious. If Jake could do that to Grace, what would prevent him from doing the same to me? And if that was the reality, Jake wasn't the person I thought I knew all my life.

Determined to push the conversation from my mind, I decided to torture myself in a different kind of way. I stalked to my bedroom, opened the closet, and stared at the pile of laundry mounted high in the corner. *I really hated laundry.*

As I threw the first dry load onto the couch, my phone chimed to life with a new text.

JAKE: Missed my flight. Taking the red eye. Don't wait up.

ME: What happened?

But there was no reply. A twinge of fear tickled the back of my neck. I'd sent everyone away, and now Jake wouldn't be home for hours.

I continued to wash and fold laundry, the pepper spray within reach as I watched infomercials about some new kind of shampoo and a workout that would give me a perfectly sculpted ass.

By the time I finished the laundry, it was already past two in the morning. My eyes grew heavy, and I curled up on the edge of the couch—the pepper spray in hand—as I watched old reruns of *I*

*Love Lucy* episodes. I wanted to stay awake, but exhaustion consumed me, and I eventually drifted off to sleep.

When I opened my eyes again it was ten in the morning, and a blanket covered me on the couch. Jake's luggage sat in the middle of the living room floor, and my heart squeezed knowing he was home. I climbed off the couch, wrapped the blanket around my shoulders, and walked down the hall to Jake's room.

The door was left open a crack, and I let myself in. He lay on his stomach in the center of the king-sized bed. His exposed back a beautiful contrast to the dark sheets thrown over his hips. All the shutters were closed, but the room was filled with the soft light of morning, giving his skin a velvety glow that took my breath away. He hugged a pillow to his chest, reminding me of a little boy, and I had to resist the urge to climb in next to him. To run my fingers across his muscles and feel his skin against mine. But it had been past two in the morning when I finally fell asleep, and he hadn't been home yet. I knew he must've been exhausted, and I couldn't bear the thought of waking him up just yet. Maybe I was procrastinating... Or maybe I didn't want whatever was brewing between us to come to end. Because until I knew for certain, I could hold on to the fantasy where Jake loved me, and everything was one big misunderstanding.

Today was his thirtieth birthday, and although I knew I wouldn't be able to relax until everything was out in the open, I didn't want to start the day with a fight. I went back to my room, splashed the sleep from my still-tired eyes, brushed my teeth, and threw on cut offs and a T-shirt. As I was just about to pull away from the curb to go to the store, a patrol car drove past me. I needed to tell him—and I would. Soon.

When I got home, he was still asleep, and I slipped into the kitchen to mix up the batter for crepes. It was a recipe from one of my favorite food bloggers, and I'd been saving it for a special occasion. I didn't know if this was to be our first of many breakfasts together, or our last. But either way, I wanted to remember it.

The crepes were paper thin with hints of caramelization around the edges. They smelled of browned butter, freshly baked pastries, and sweet vanilla. I piped a filling of lightly sweetened cream infused with lemon zest in the center, then finished the plate with a dusting of confectioners' sugar and sun-ripened berries. It was a dish made in heaven, but my stomach was turned in knots.

Jake stirred as I sat on the edge of the bed, the plate of crepes on the verge of snapping under my vise-like grip. His eyes cracked open, and a slow, sleepy smile transformed his face as he rolled to his back.

"Morning." His voice was deep with gravel and flirtation.

My stomach squeezed with an awareness so strong I nearly lost my balance on the edge of the bed. "It's not morning. It's almost noon. What time did you get home?"

"I don't know. Four maybe?" His eyes shifted to the plate in my hands. "Is that for me?"

My skin pricked as the scent of warm skin and pure male drifted toward me. It was more than I could take sitting so close to him like that. His naked chest practically begged to be touched, and my mind ran with naughty images of what he wore beneath the sheet. "Happy birthday."

He smiled, then sat up. The blankets strained under my bottom, effectively pulling me closer. He cut a forkful of crepe and shoveled it into his mouth. The groan that followed was almost my undoing, and I was thankful he closed his eyes so he couldn't see my face. A hint of cream lingered at the corner of his mouth, and I had to fight the urge to lick it off.

"This is amazing. Have you tried any yet?"

I shook my head, suddenly parched.

"Here." He cut another piece and slipped it into my mouth.

I was mesmerized as the taste of cream and berries exploded.

I'd never been fed like that before. Let alone by a practically naked man, in an empty house, in the middle of a king-sized bed.

His tongue darted out to catch the cream I'd wanted to lick, and he cut another bite.

I couldn't stay there like that. He did things to me. Things that were primal and urgent, and I simply didn't trust myself. I stood, and thrust the plate toward him. "There's fresh coffee in the kitchen when you're ready," I blurted, then turned around and left the room, not allowing him a chance to speak.

As I fixed another plate in the kitchen, I heard Jake enter behind me.

"Any more of that?" he asked.

"Sure." I turned around and locked eyes with the hard wall of his chest.

He took the plate with one hand and lifted my chin with the other. His thumb trailed over my lower cheek as he smiled down at me. "Flour."

"What? Oh." I began wiping at my face with both hands. Had it been there the whole time?

"Don't worry, I got it." He winked, then grabbed a cup of coffee on his way to the table.

I turned to the counter to fix myself another plate, my heart behaving like I just got back from running a five-K. "How was your trip?"

"It was good. Hectic, but I'm glad I went…"

He continued to talk, but all I could think about were the questions that hammered for release inside my head. My plan was to wait until after breakfast. To enjoy our last moments before everything fell apart. But I wasn't sure I could. I was teetering between jumping him like a sex-crazed lunatic and having a nervous breakdown.

With a plate full of crepes my stomach would barely allow, I sat down.

His brows wrinkled with concern as he looked at me. "Are you okay? You look like you're going to be sick."

The questions were eating me alive, and I couldn't take it any longer. "Jake..." I took a cleansing breath, then blew it out before I continued. "We need to talk."

He set his mug on the table, the words of doom floating between us, and leaned back in his chair. His brows came together, and he looked confused.

The knock which came next surprised us both, and his eyes bored into mine, silently telling me not to move as he rose from his seat to answer it.

My hands raked over my face when he disappeared. There was no going back now. In a few minutes, I would have answers. Answers I both wanted and didn't want all at the same time.

When he came back into the room his forehead was creased with concern. "There's an officer here to see you."

I swallowed the bile that rose in the back of my throat, and brushed past him to the front door.

Officer Peterson stood in the middle of the room and nodded to me as I entered. "Ms. McGregor."

I wrapped my arms around my middle, and Jake came to stand by my side. "Is everything okay?"

The officer looked from me to Jake. "There was another attack last night. A few miles from here. We think we got them this time."

I could feel Jake's eyes focused on me as I stared at Officer Peterson.

"We'd like you to come down to the station to ID them in a line-up."

Jake turned to me, a scowl of concern replacing any shred of the smile he wore earlier. "Katie, what's going on?"

My eyes focused at nothing as I looked out the window on the way to the station. Jake hadn't said a word since Officer Peterson told him about the attempted break-in, the women who were attacked, and the fact that I was almost a victim. He needed time. It was obvious the news upset him. I could practically see the adrenaline pumping through his veins. But more than that; he seemed hurt.

When we got out of the car, he grabbed my hand as we crossed the parking lot, and sat with me as I filled out more paperwork. Eventually we were escorted to a small room where a detective sat in the corner and explained the identification process to me.

The room was bare except for a couple of seats and a curtain I knew covered a one-way mirror. Jake's arm wrapped around me as I stood waiting to face the man who tried to attack me two nights earlier.

Eventually the detective opened the curtains, and eight men walked into the room on the other side of the glass. They stood in a single-file line, while I looked into their faces. The room was warm and stuffy, and it was almost impossible to breathe the thick, fear-laden air. I began to tremble as I scanned from one man to another. Their faces smug and terrifying—all strangers. Jake held me close, bending down to kiss the top of my head every few minutes. But this job was mine, and I continued to stare into the eyes of all the men. They were all big and strong, the right size, but I realized any one of them could've been my attacker. I turned to the detective, my voice shaking. "I...I just don't know."

"Are you sure, Ms. McGregor?" he asked.

"Yes. It was dark. I just don't know."

The curtains closed and Officer Peterson entered the room. I started to cry. "I'm so sorry. I wanted it to be one of them, but it was just so dark."

"Ms. McGregor, you did great. We have a positive ID from two other women. We have a case with or without your identification."

He continued to give us information about what would happen next. The assailants would be taken into custody, arraigned; then a date would be set for their trial. I was told to prepare myself for the possibility of having to testify, but due to the fact I couldn't make a positive ID, it might not be necessary.

When we made it back to Jake's house it was nearly six, and a catering truck was parked in the driveway.

Jake's shoulders sank as he pulled along the curb. "Shit."

"Your party..." I said in a low, distant voice.

He hopped out of the truck and walked around to open my door. "We're canceling it."

As much as I wanted that, it wouldn't be possible. "People will be showing up in two hours. There's no way you could contact them all in time." I climbed out of the car and began to make my way to the front gate.

He grabbed my arm and spun me around. "Why didn't you call me, Katie?" His voice was deep with emotion, his eyes hard and searching.

"It all happened so fast... I didn't want to bother you."

"You didn't want to bother me? You were attacked in my home, and you didn't want to bother me?"

"Jake—"

A man dressed in a culinary jacket and carrying a clipboard approached us. "I'm sorry to interrupt, but are you Katie McGregor? I'm from Banquet Catering, and we're supposed to be setting up."

I looked back at Jake, seeing all the questions in his eyes, having a million of my own, but knowing that soon the house would be swarmed with people. I couldn't do this now. Not like this.

I turned to the caterer and nodded. "Please, right this way."

# CHAPTER TWENTY

By the time I'd shown the caterer where to set up, the decorating company was at the front door. At least ten men began trampling back and forth to the backyard, carrying large poles and fabric, shouting orders, and all I kept wondering was where Grace and Gigi were.

"Can you sign here, ma'am?" one said, shoving a digital pad in front of me.

"What's this?" I asked.

"The contract for the tent. We need a signature before we can begin installation."

"A tent?" Grace said nothing about a tent.

"Yes. Because of the rain."

He pointed to the sky with the stylus, and for the first time that day, I noticed the ominous clouds. Even the weather had sensed my doom and decided to watch the show.

As soon as I signed the little box, the man began barking orders to his crew, and in just over an hour the tent ran from the back door all the way to the pool. White organza cascaded from the ceiling in a swag, then down the sides fastened in bundles of elegant, draping fabric. The lanterns Grace spoke of were hung across the ceiling and reminded me of something you'd see at a wedding, not a man's thirtieth birthday party.

Chairs and cocktail tables were brought in, arranged around the edges of the tent, and covered in dark cloth. I spun around in a daze, seeing but not really observing my surroundings—with the exception of one thing. Jake was nowhere to be found. A part of me ached to know what he thought of all this, to know if he was still upset with me about not telling him about the break-in, but the other part was thankful he couldn't see my face. The ordeal at the station had shaken me, and I didn't have the strength for such a serious conversation now.

Questions pulled me from one direction to the other. Questions I didn't know the answers to. Where the hell was Grace? And why had she left me in charge of this?

"Hey," John called to me as I finished up with the caterer. "Why aren't you dressed?"

"What?" I spun around, glancing down at my cut offs and T-shirt. "What time is it?"

"Quarter to eight."

"Shit. I don't even know what I'm going to wear."

I tried to brush past him, but his voice stopped me. "Did you talk to Jake?"

I shook my head.

"I passed him in the garage. Go talk to him. Before people start showing up."

"I can't." My throat thickened.

"Why?"

I could feel his stare, but I wouldn't look at him. "Because hearing things out loud makes them real." He had no idea what I was talking about, probably thought I was nuts, but I didn't wait for a response—I crossed the short distance to the house and almost ran to the seclusion of my bathroom.

With a heavy heart, I braced myself against the vanity and stared at my reflection in the bathroom mirror. I was a mess. My hair had fallen from the ponytail, my eyes were puffy and tired. A knock came at my bedroom door but I ignored it. I needed to pull myself together and tame the emotions that threatened to spill over the edge. I turned on the faucet and splashed cold water on my face over and over hoping for clarity.

I heard the clamor of happy voices a few minutes later and realized guests had already begun to arrive. I wasn't ready for this. I couldn't face all these people I didn't know and pretend I wasn't on the verge of cardiac arrest. Jake was right; I wasn't that good of an actress. I wore my heart on my sleeve, and right now it was held together by fragile silk thread.

There was another knock, followed by Em's voice. "Katie, are you in there?"

With one last glance at my lifeless reflection, I pushed myself off the counter, wiped my face with a towel, and unlocked the door.

Em slid through the opening, her hair sleek and smooth, looking perfectly elegant wearing a black cocktail gown. "Why aren't you dressed?" she asked, taking me in.

"I'm not going out there. I don't even know those people."

"Don't be ridiculous. Here." She handed me her glass of wine, nodded for me to drink, and opened my closet.

"What happened?" She eyed me curiously before continuing her search for something suitable for me to wear.

"A really long day." A really long week. A really long life.

"Want to talk about it?"

Could I tell her? Confide in her about Jake, our kiss, Grace, my failure at the station, and the fact Jake was mad I hadn't told him about the break-in? I knew that if I started, the fragile wall I'd built around myself would begin to crumble, and it would only take one little stone to shift for everything inside to fall apart.

I threw back the contents of the wine glass. "No."

She laughed, then pulled out the little black dress I'd purchased the day we went shopping. The perfect one. The one for a day I wanted to remember—not tonight.

I shook my head, and her brows furrowed, but she shrugged it off and grabbed another. A strapless coral empire dress I'd once worn to a wedding.

"Put that on," she said, tossing it to the foot of my bed.

Within a few minutes I was dressed in the coral fabric that draped to mid thigh. Em did my makeup, flat-ironed my hair so it hung straight down the middle of my back, and I slipped a gold bangle onto my wrist. It was a simple dress, but it made me feel feminine and beautiful. I needed that if I was going to go out there tonight.

Em gripped my shoulders. "You look amazing. Who cares about those people? You stick with me, and we'll have a good time."

A smile turned my lips, not quite meeting my eyes, and I nodded.

"Come find me when you're ready."

When she left the room, I sat on the edge of my bed and slipped on a pair of gold flats. It wasn't "all those people" I was worried about. In fact, I was only worried about one of them. I just needed the evening to end so I could talk to him.

When I made it to the backyard, it was just past eight thirty, and at least fifty people already filled the tent. Music came from the speakers, mixed with the sounds of rainfall and people having a good time. I scanned over the guests chatting happily around cocktail tables, drinks in every hand, and caterers passing out appetizers from silver platters. My eyes immediately locked on Jake—as if they didn't have a choice. My whole existence was drawn to him. My body, soul, and mind hunted him, craved him as though he was crucial for my survival. He stood with a group of people toward the back, wearing black slacks that hugged his muscular thighs and a white linen shirt left open at the throat. I wasn't used to seeing him like that. Clean-shaven, hair tamed…the sight of him took my breath away.

Then Grace approached him in a skintight red dress. The kind that molded to every curve, showed every flaw, but Grace didn't have any. Her stomach was completely flat, her hips adding the perfect amount of flair, breasts full and halfway exposed. She stopped when she reached his side, and ran a hand seductively down his arm.

I closed my eyes. She only touched his arm. That didn't mean anything. I swallowed back the bitter taste in my throat and turned to find a waiter standing behind me offering some kind of dumpling. I shook him off and shuffled my way through the crowd, finding Em and John standing in line at the bar.

John was laughing at something Em said and did a double take as I approached. "Holy shit, Katie. You look gorgeous." He eyed me up and down and grinned.

"Thank you." I forced a smile and joined them in line. "Do you know many of these people?"

He shook his head. "No. Though it doesn't surprise me. I think this was more a ploy for Grace to impress her boss more than anything."

Em hit him in the arm. "Shh. Someone will hear you." She turned to me. "Katie, what do you want to drink?"

"Chardonnay," I replied.

"Two glasses of Chardonnay, a Sam Adams, and three shots of Patron," Em said to the bartender, then turned and raised her brows at me and John.

"Oh no, I can't," I interjected.

"Sure you can," she responded with a wink.

"Jake told me about your time at the station today," John said, his forehead wrinkled with what I knew was disapproval. I was supposed to tell Jake about the break-in yesterday. "He was pretty upset."

"Wait, what happened?" Em asked.

The attack was the last thing on my mind. I didn't want to talk about it, but Em looked concerned, and I tried to conjure up an answer.

"They caught Katie's attackers," Jake said from behind me, and my whole body stiffened at the sound of his voice. His arm brushed mine, and I let out a breath.

"Wow, Katie. No wonder you were on edge earlier," Em replied.

"So was I the only one who didn't know?" Jake raised his eyebrows then looked from Em to John.

"Hey man, happy birthday," John replied, and smacked him on the back. "How was the conference?"

"Conference went well," Jake muttered, then spoke quietly in my ear. "But had I known you were in danger in any way, I would have caught the first flight home."

His words left me breathless, and I had to fight against turning into his arms. I needed him, we needed to talk—

"Jake, what do you want to drink?" Em asked.

He stared at me a beat before answering. "Sam Adams."

I swallowed.

His arm brushed mine again. A soft sigh of a touch that would've gone unnoticed from anyone else. But my whole body was aware of him in a way I'd never felt with another man. Had it been deliberate? Did he crave my touch as much as I did his?

He stood so close I could see the smooth texture of his shaven face, and I wanted so badly to run my fingers across his cheek. To feel its warmth under my fingertips. The faint smell of his spicy aftershave filled my nose, causing a sweet ache to settle between my hips. I don't know what it was about him, but I wanted to bury myself in his neck and inhale until I was lost.

Suddenly Grace approached with a whole group of people I didn't know. She stopped on his other side and laced her arm possessively through his. "Happy birthday, baby."

At that moment, Em handed me the shot of tequila, and what seemed like a bad idea just a moment ago now felt like Superman had swooped down to save me. I tossed the drink to the back of my throat and swallowed the whole thing in one gulp.

I needed air. I grabbed my glass of wine off the bar and made my way to the edge of the tent where I spotted an open table.

I climbed on one of the high seats and crossed my legs. What was I even doing? I was holding on by a thread of hope, and if I wasn't careful, I'd have to enroll in AA. My finger ran along the bowl of my wineglass, transfixed by the play of light the lanterns cast through its translucent surface.

When the light disappeared, I looked up to see a man standing in front of me. "Oh, sorry. I didn't know this table was taken." I hopped from the stool and grabbed my glass.

"Don't go," he said in a rush. Then pinched the bridge of his nose and smiled. "I've just been trying to work up the nerve to come talk to you, and I finally found you alone."

I grinned in spite of myself and glanced over at Jake. Grace still stood by his side by the bar, but his back was to me, and I couldn't see his face.

He followed my gaze. "Can I get you something to drink?"

"Oh no, I'm fine." I held up my full wineglass, then took a small sip.

His shoulders relaxed. "I'm Chris."

I nodded. "Katie."

"How do you know the birthday boy?" he asked, swirling a glass of brown alcohol.

"We grew up together." But that wasn't all he was to me. The description didn't even come close to what he was to me. He was the man I loved with all my heart. The only person in my life besides Mom who remembered Dad and my brother. There was something so comforting about that. Knowing you held the same memories as someone else—the thought of losing him split my heart in two.

Chris went on to say something about Grace and real estate, but I wasn't really listening. He was attractive enough. Well-dressed, dark hair, and a nice build. I had no doubt women found him appealing, but my eyes kept traveling over to Jake, and I wondered how much more of this I'd be able to endure.

I took another sip of wine and focused in on what Chris was saying. "...flip houses. It's a gamble, but it's paid off so far. What do you do, Katie?"

"Photography." I glanced over at Jake again, this time to find him watching. My heart squeezed, and I looked back at Chris. "I'm just getting into the wedding market here in LA," I said, clearing my throat.

"Oh, really? My sister's getting married next spring. I should get your information."

He gave me his phone, and as I was entering in my information, John came to stand by my side. "Katie, can I borrow you for a second?"

My brows furrowed, and I excused myself, following John to the other side of the tent.

"Is everything okay?" I asked when we were alone.

"Yeah, I just thought Jake was going to lose it," he said, taking a pull from his beer.

"What?" But I understood all too well. It was because I was talking to Chris. I looked over at Jake a few feet away, and our eyes met. It was okay for me to have to watch Grace on his arm all night, but the minute another man talked to me, his friend was sent to run interference.

I turned away to see Grace walking in our direction. A man with salt-and-pepper hair by her side.

"Jake, you remember my boss, Peter. Peter, this is my *boyfriend*, Jake."

All the air pushed painfully from my lungs. Jake shook the man's hand, then scanned from Peter's eyes to mine. Time stopped as my suspicions were finally confirmed, and his ocean-blue eyes penetrated my soul.

I shifted my eyes to the floor, trying to pull in a breath as everything around me began to echo. I couldn't stay here. Placing my drink on a nearby table, I began to push my way through hordes of people, waving off caterers with trays of food.

John caught up with me and grabbed my hand. "Are you okay?" He turned me around and lifted my face. "If Jake doesn't see what's in front of him, he's an idiot."

I nodded, but then a warm hand came around to cup my elbow. "Can I talk to you?" Jake's breath caught my cheek, and my senses were filled only with him.

But I couldn't do it. Not like this. Not with Grace under the same roof. Not when everything I thought I knew was ripped from under me with a single jerk. "I can't."

"Katie." His tortured voice gripped that part of me deep down, and twisted.

A group of people appeared at the door. They called to Jake, wished him a happy birthday, then pulled him toward the bar.

I turned back to John, shaking my head while my eyes burned with unshed tears. I was weak. I couldn't do this. I made it the few yards to the kitchen and didn't stop until I was in the front yard.

Toeing off my shoes, I filled my lungs with the sweet taste of a summer storm, and with one foot in front of the other, I pushed through the gate, passed the valet, and began to run. I had no idea where I was going or what I would do when I got there. All I knew was that I needed to get away. I needed to put distance between myself and the source of my betrayal.

Huge drops of rain began to fall, mixed with the salt of bitter tears. Tears of anguish, hurt, and unrequited love.

Fat, hard pelts hit my face as though the sky wept along with me, and my feet slammed hard against the pavement again and again. I didn't stop, didn't even slow until I made it to the park a few blocks away.

I crumpled to my knees on the wet lawn, sucking in air like I'd held my breath the whole way, and let the rain wash over me. I didn't want to think, didn't want to feel. I just wanted to be. To exist for a moment, and let some of my tension disappear into the ground with the rain.

# CHAPTER TWENTY-ONE

The storm had settled to a delicate drizzle by the time I made it back to the house. From the sidewalk I could see that everyone had gone. The street that an hour ago was littered with cars was now completely empty, and the sound of the party no longer filtered into the night air. I took a deep breath and walked up the driveway.

Jake sat on the front steps and my heart stopped. His white shirt was plastered to his muscular form, his brown hair dripping and face intense. He leaned forward on his knees, watching me, and I forced myself to unlatch the gate.

"I've been looking for you..." His voice came low and raw and took my breath. "Everywhere..."

Sadness rushed to the pit of my stomach and I knew this was it. There would be no more running away, no more excuses or interruptions. I had to leave—even if it meant abandoning my own heart.

He stood, and my hands flew to my mouth. I wanted the ground to open up and consume me. To shield me from the over-whelming emotions that stirred inside. My throat thickened with the words I came to say, and in one breathless crack, I let them out. "I'm leaving, Jake."

"Katie—"

He took a step closer, but I held up my hand to stop him. "Let me finish!" My tone was desperate, aching with the all the tension and confusion collected since I'd come home.

He stood with his hands fisted at his sides, waiting for me to speak, but the word wouldn't come. I'd recited every syllable at the park. Said them over and over until they were perfect, but standing in front of him now, my clothes soaking wet and heart ripped out of my chest, I couldn't think of any of them.

"You were *home* to me," I said in a torn whisper.

He ran his hand through his drenched hair and gripped his skull.

"You were my protector."

"I know what it looked like—" His voice came thick and tortured.

"I trusted you!" I cut him off. "And you let me become the other woman."

He rushed toward me and grabbed my arms, urging me to look up. "Grace and I are *over*." His face was intense, his eyes pleading for me to believe him. "I broke up with her before I left for the damned conference."

I searched his face and swallowed back tears that threatened to choke me. "Then why all this?" My voice trembling.

He shook his head and squeezed his eyes shut. "Because she'd been planning it for months—because working together made things complicated—because she begged me to play along..." His grip loosened, but he didn't move away.

My head began to spin, my breath swallowed. "Why didn't you tell me?"

"I planned to... " He looked me in the eyes. "I tried to..."

*But I wouldn't talk to him.*

His rough hands traveled up my arms, and even though they

were soaking wet, they generated a heat that sent goosebumps over my cold skin.

"I never meant to hurt you." His voice was soft and heavy with emotion. "It's fucking killing me that I did."

One hand moved along my neck, the pad of his calloused thumb grazed my jaw, and my whole body trembled with conflicting urges. I wanted to pull him closer and push him away all at the same time.

Molten blue eyes penetrated my soul, while my heart begged me to run. "What do you want, Jake?"

"For you to trust me. For you to stop telling me you're leaving me. And to kiss you until you no longer hurt."

A tear slipped down my cheek and my eyes shifted to his lips—I wanted that too. More than anything in my life, I wanted that.

His solid frame took mine, enveloped me like I was meant to be there, and he lifted me to my toes. His hips to mine, our hearts pounding as one. "I would never do that to you, Katie. Never."

His whispered words brushed against my mouth, and I claimed fists full of his sodden shirt crushing my mouth to his. Urgent, gentle, both loving and passionate at the same time.

His lips moved against mine, like a thousand promises never to hurt me, to protect me forever, and I took each one. Needing them more than anything. Needing them more than air.

I slipped my hand under his shirt, and his kiss deepened. He lifted my thigh, causing my dress to bunch at my hip, and he cradled me against him. The bulge of his erection grinding against my belly.

He pressed his forehead to mine, his breaths coming in hard, ragged pants. "We should slow down." But his fingers contradicted his words as they twisted in the wet fabric of my dress, gathering it higher until his palm brushed against my exposed side.

"Jake." I dug my hips deeper, wanting more of him. Desperate for his touch. Drunk with lust and desire. "Please don't stop."

His jaw flexed and he searched my face. All that we'd been through flashed through my mind in an instant. All the times he pulled away, all the rejection that scarred my heart. Then the backs of his fingers caressed my cheeks, and without words he lifted me and cradled me in his arms. He didn't move at first, just looked at me with an intense heat that made my insides clench and my breath slow.

He carried me through the house, kicking his bedroom door open to crash against the wall, then lowered me to my feet beside the bed. Somehow the intimacy of his room was more intense than what we'd shared outside, and I looked down to his chest.

His hands moved over my arms, then up to lift my chin. He stepped closer, his hand along my throat, cupping my breast through drenched fabric, and he took my bottom lip in his mouth. I sucked in a breath, and my fingers shook as I fumbled over the buttons of his shirt. I'd never wanted anything more in my whole life, yet I was terrified. What if I wasn't enough? What if I didn't satisfy him?

Jake's hands traveled down the front of me until they reached the edge of my dress. In one easy motion he lifted it over my head and discarded it to the floor, leaving me nude except for my panties.

I was exposed, completely vulnerable as his gaze slowly took me in. My lips, my breasts, the thin, white cotton that covered my most intimate parts. My heart was in my throat, my breath heavy as I resisted the urge to shield myself. I didn't have the body he was used to. All my insecurities rushed to the surface, and I began to tremble with them.

"What's the matter, Katie?" His voice low and hoarse.

I shook my head. "I'm no good at this."

His hands enveloped mine. "You could have fooled me." His mouth covered mine, and he pushed me back until my thighs hit the edge of the mattress. His hands brushed up my sides, and he gently lowered me to the soft sheets. He removed what was left of his clothes and joined me on the bed. His biceps flexing as he suspended himself above me.

My need for him burned; every nerve in my body was on fire. His fingers moved from my collarbone, down my breasts, all the way to the edge of my panties. Then they slipped under the edge and found the slick heat of my core.

"Fuck, Katie."

His lips ran over my jaw, my neck, and his fingers began to move in slow circles adding the perfect amount of pressure where I needed it most. One finger slipped inside, then another, and I arched against his hand. His skilled fingers working magic as they curled inside me. I grasped his back with both hands and shamelessly began to press myself against his hand as a sweet ache ran the length of my body.

"Jake, please," I breathed.

He lifted my hips and pulled my panties down my thighs. Abandoning them to the floor with my dress. He threw me back on the pillows, and my pulse quickened. This was really happening. I was naked in Jake's bed, and he was going to make love to me.

His mouth came down on mine, and my hands found his back, exploring every inch of muscle. He moved lower, placing featherlight kisses along my neck, my chest, until his mouth covered the hard peak of my nipple. Tugging, sucking, sending a surge of deep pleasure to resonate through me. This was not Kevin. This was Jake, and he owned me.

He moved to the bedside table, and I heard a rip seconds before he settled between my thighs. I knew he was ready, and I opened wider, welcoming him.

His eyes met mine and he swallowed. "Do you want me?"

I looked up at his handsome face, his jaw flexed with concentration, eyes smoldering with his own desire. I'd never wanted anything more in my life. "Yes."

In one swift movement he entered me, filling me with the

width of his erection. I grasped his smooth flesh. My teeth grazed his shoulder, and I rolled my hips, taking every inch of him I could. He moved slowly at first. A tortuous rhythm as he propped himself on his elbows. My breaths came hard and heavy, and he picked up speed. Asking, taking, demanding, and I wrapped my legs around his waist, lifting my hips higher, matching him thrust after thrust.

His pace increased, pushing me farther, and I selfishly took every bit of him. A delicious tension built inside as he pushed me to the edge of my sanity. My legs began to shake as the pressure grew with unbearable intensity, and my whole body clenched around him. Jake's mouth smothered my cry as I shattered into a million tiny pieces. His pace slowed and he kissed me thorough and deep. His hips grinding with achingly slow movements as wave after wave of my orgasm rushed over me.

With one last, powerful thrust his jaw flexed, and he found his own release. The weight of him sank into me. I ran my fingers through his hair as a deep sense of satisfaction settled inside.

"Am I too heavy?" he asked through puffs of breath.

"No. I like the way you feel."

He propped himself to his elbows and traced fingertips over my jaw. "You're so beautiful."

His thumb ran over my bottom lip, and I kissed the pad of it, sure that in any moment I'd wake up. His lips came to mine, nibbling soft kisses across my parted mouth, and I never wanted him to stop, never wanted him to leave. I just wanted to spend the rest of my life with him on top of me, our bodies joined. We fit perfectly, like two pieces of a puzzle.

His cock twitched inside me, and I clenched around him, already wanting more. He rolled to the side and got out of bed. My body shivered with the cold of his absence, and I heard the static sound of the shower. He was back by my side a second later, pulling me with both hands.

He stood in front of me and walked me backward until I felt the cool tile floor beneath my feet.

"I never should have let you move to San Diego."

His words caught me off guard, and my heart picked up speed. "Why didn't you stop me?"

"Because it's what you said you wanted." He guided me into the shower, and warm water ran over my body.

My throat tightened with raw emotion, but I forced out the words. "All I've ever wanted was you."

His head fell to my shoulder, and I ran my hands down his back. "I don't deserve you. I don't know what I ever did to make you want me."

He didn't know? Without him I would have been lost. "You were everything."

His fingers ran through my wet hair, and he looked at me with an intensity that made my knees weak. "Don't ever leave me again." His mouth covered mine, and he pushed me against the tile. His arms and body caged me in as he trailed soft kisses down my neck. I sucked in lungs full of steamy air, and my head fell back against the wall. Surrendering my body to his gentle touch.

He squeezed body wash into his hand, and the scent of clean spice filled my nose. Rough fingers settled on my shoulders, then ran gently down my body from breasts, to abdomen, all the way to the juncture of my thighs. I was brazen with my desire for him, my legs parting on their own accord as his thumb found my slick folds.

When he turned me toward the water I grabbed the body wash and began an exploration of my own. Even after our lovemaking, I still felt timid as my hands coasted from his shoulders to his back. He let out a low groan of encouragement as his muscles flexed under my slippery hands. My fingers ran down his corded arms to his hard abdomen, then lower.

When I reached his erection, I pressed my body against him

and tiny whimpers escaped my lips. I just had him less than ten minutes ago, and I was already a quivering mess.

He moved with me under the stream of water, rinsing us both, then pushed farther until I was up against the wall again. The shower was full of hot steam, and the cool tile against my back sent shivers up my spine. His hands traveled downward, over my bottom, until he gripped both thighs and lifted. I straddled him, my legs wrapped around his waist.

"Damn, Katie."

My breath came in heavy pants, and my hand went between our bodies. I gripped him in my palm, and I tried to shift myself on top of him. "I'm on the pill," I whispered against his mouth.

He froze, and my invitation lingered between us in the air. I suddenly felt stupid and naive, and a rush of heat crept up my neck. "I'm sorry—I just—I've been tested— we don't have to—"

He pressed me deep into the wall, one arm supporting my weight, as the other silenced me with a finger to my lips. "Hush."

His intense stare left me immobilized. The sweltering heat of it turned my insides to liquid. "I've never not used a condom before."

Now I was speechless. Jake was a grown man, one who'd had many partners, yet he'd never been with a woman while unprotected.

He shifted me lower, his eyes never leaving mine, and I felt him between my thighs. My throat thickened with emotion as I realized the significance of what was about to transpire. He was giving himself over. Whole, uncovered, and without question. And then he entered me.

# CHAPTER TWENTY-TWO

I awoke in a tangle of limbs, too warm with my face buried in the crook of Jake's neck. I had no idea what time we'd fallen asleep, but my muscles already ached in protest of the things I'd made them do. A good ache. One that reminded me of each word, each kiss, each touch.

His arms and legs covered me like a blanket. An electric one—turned on to night-sweats mode. How the hell had I fallen asleep like this, I didn't know. I was the needs-a-king-sized-bed-so-we-don't-touch kind of girl. I couldn't even stand Kevin's feet touching mine, and here I was completely surrounded by Jake. I smiled against the warmth of his skin. This was so surreal. Like at any moment the alarm would beep and I'd be startled out of a dream. But this wasn't a dream, and every moment, every touch, was burned into my brain forever. My leg began to tingle under the weight of his thigh, and I stretched a little to see the clock.

3:04 a.m.

Jake was as hot as a sauna, but I wanted to stay like this forever. Skin against skin, each breath coming in unison. I'd never been touched like he touched me. Cherished in the arms of a man who could so easily break me. I arched my back, hoping to free up a little more room to breathe, but he pulled me closer and burrowed in like I was one of his pillows. Not that I minded. I'd actually pay good money to be his pillow, fantasized about it for years actually. But the last time I'd eaten was the bite of crepe he fed me yesterday morning, and even though the sun had yet to rise, I was suddenly ravenous—and trapped. Not the best combination. But sleeping with someone you've known your whole life gives certain advantages. Like knowing the fact he slept like the dead, and he was also very ticklish. I poked him in the ribs, causing him to stir, and took the opportunity to roll away.

The light was still on in the hall, and I could just make out Jake's black T-shirt that hung on the foot of the bed. I grabbed it and pulled it over my head. It smelled of him. The smell I'd longed to be closer to since I was a girl now clung to me like smoke from a fire. My whole world had changed in an instant. I'd gone from thinking I was losing him forever to holding him naked in my arms. Life was funny that way. Just when you think you have it all figured out... I buried my nose into the soft cotton at my shoulder and inhaled the earthy spice that was so unmistakably *Jake*.

He'd been such a giving lover. I wasn't sure what I'd expected, but it was so much more than anything I'd ever had with Kevin. No. Anything I had shared with *anyone*. He'd been as affected as I was. There was no doubt in my mind. I was swept away. Not just my body, but my soul. I glanced down at the bed. His muscular back, well defined even in the relaxed state of sleep, his sun-bronzed skin so kissable it made me question my need for food. Could it really be this easy? Did he really want me? All of me?

For how long? These were all things I should have thought about before falling into bed with him. Before falling in *love* with him... But in the heat of a moment, I wasn't thinking about our future. In fact, I wasn't thinking about anything at all. And whether he wanted it or not, every piece of my bruised and battered heart was his. I just had to trust that he'd hold it tight. And not let it fall apart.

I scooped up our still soggy clothes and deposited them into the laundry basket on the way to the kitchen. The house that was filled with the commotion of guests just hours before was now replaced with quiet. The counters were wiped clean and all evidence of the party was gone. But a quick peek to the backyard revealed the tent and tables still remained. *What had happened when I'd run?*

My stomach let out a loud gurgle, and I opened the fridge to find Jake's untouched birthday cake on the bottom shelf. Should I? It's not like he'd care. Plus, the only other things in there were the appetizers purchased by Grace.

I pulled out the cake, placed it on the counter, and just when I was ready to cut a large slice, warm hands snaked around me from behind. "Hey," Jake said in my ear, his voice low.

I leaned back against his firm chest and smiled. How would I ever get used to this. To be able to touch him whenever I wanted. "Did you sleep well?"

His arms tightened around my waist. "I did. Until I realized you were gone." He nibbled kisses along the side of my neck. "Finding you barefoot in the kitchen wearing only my shirt may have made up for it though." The curve of his lips brushed against my neck. "Is that for me?"

I nodded, and the rough bristle of his whiskers rubbed against my cheek. "Want some?"

"Yes. Among other things." His hand moved up the back of my bare thigh, then cupped a handful of my naked bottom.

Oh God, I wanted other things too. "Stop distracting me and make a wish." I pulled a candle and lighter out of the drawer, put it in the center of the cake, and lit it.

"Hmmm... My wish? It involves you, this cake, and nothing else."

I bit my smiling mouth closed. "Blow out your candle." My voice alarmingly breathy. "I'm hungry, and if I don't eat I'll pass out."

"When's the last time you ate?" He moved to lean a hip against the counter. He wore only his black PJ pants, and his dark brows furrowed.

"Yesterday morning."

"Shit, Katie." He blew out the candle, and without bothering to cut a slice, took a ample forkful and fed it to me.

"I can feed myself, you know." My hand covered a mouthful of rich chocolate cake.

"Obviously not." He smirked. "Otherwise you would have done so before now."

I swallowed. "Well, I was a bit distracted." I flicked my eyes to the backyard. "What happened last night?"

"I told John to get rid of everyone." He cut another piece and put it in my mouth. "Went after you."

He said it like it was nothing. He asked over a hundred people to leave so he could find me. Friends, colleagues... My stomach dropped. "What happened with Grace?"

He cleared his throat and looked me in the eye. "I'm sure she's pissed." He shook his head. "That doesn't matter now."

But it did matter. To me it mattered. I had so many questions, but only one wouldn't go away. "Why did you play along?"

He set the fork down, his jaw tense as he looked at me. "I meant to tell you as soon as I got home, to explain the situation, but then the damned cops were at the door, and I was hearing you were attacked."

"What about later?"

"I tried to." His eyes met mine and he raked a hand through his hair. "When she asked me it seemed like a reasonable request. Everyone was already invited. Her friends, clients...her boss. I thought it would make for a clean break. No hard feelings."

I nodded, then turned to the cake and took another bite. I hated my own insecurity. All I wanted was to enjoy the here and now. To stop thinking about the past or future, but I couldn't help it. I'd lost people through illness and tragedy. Had my self-esteem crushed by infidelity. But if Jake rejected me...

He grabbed my shoulders and turned me to face him. "I'd do it all differently if I could."

I nodded again, focusing on his bare chest as I tried to swallow the burning lump of emotion that settled in my throat. I didn't want to cry again. This should have been a time of new beginnings, but all I could think about was how it would end. Endings were what I knew best, and as morbid as the thought might have been, beginnings were only an opportunity for more of them.

"I'm not perfect, and I never claimed to be." His voice was low, and the backs of his fingers touched my cheek. "I made a mistake. A big one. I wish I could take it back, to say it will be the last—but I'd never do anything to intentionally hurt you..."

His hands moved up and down my arms as if to warm me. "Why won't you look at me?"

My eyes brimmed with tears, and I squeezed them shut. Why was I acting this way? Everything about last night said he wanted me. Why couldn't I shake this uneasy feeling? It was all happening so fast. Just yesterday I thought he was still with Grace. Two weeks ago I was seeing him for the first time in years. I inhaled a shaky breath and forced my eyes up.

His hair was a shaggy mess. The creases in his forehead deep with worry, and a dark shadow of whiskers covered his set jaw. He looked tortured, and his eyes burned into mine with such raw emotion that my knees went weak with the intensity of it.

I crushed myself against his chest, wrapped my arms around his waist, and his heartbeat pounded against my ear. "I don't know what's wrong with me. I'm just scared, I think."

"Don't be scared, Katie. You can be angry, or pissed off, or a whole lot of other things, but please don't be scared of me."

His voice rumbled against my cheek, and I looked up at him. "I'm not scared of you. I've never been scared of you." I swallowed.

"I'm scared about what this is. I'm scared about our past, and our future—"

His lips silenced me, crushing mine with an urgency I wasn't prepared for. A kiss of passion, want, and need. Telling me to trust him. Not asking, but demanding that I believe in him. In us. He lifted me up and set me on the counter, his hands braced on either side. "Forget about our past." His nose trailed along my neck, his voice husky and soft. "I'm not the same man I was then. I know what it's like to live without you, and I never want to live that way again."

Then he gripped the back of my neck and looked me in the eye. "Our future is whatever you want it to be. Just tell me what you want, and I'll make it happen."

Tears ran down my face, and my whole body began to tremble. I opened my legs wider and wrapped my arms around him, needing the feel of his skin against mine.

"What's the matter, baby?"

"I've never felt this way before." It was as if every emotion filled me all at once. Happiness, fear, hurt, sadness, love. All bubbling to the surface at the same time. So powerful I shook with it. But I wasn't scared, and I wasn't sad, I was happy. In love. His mouth covered mine again but this time soft and gentle. Worshiping lips that made me forget about my fears, forget about everything.

"What do you want, Katie?"

*For you to love me.* But I couldn't say that. I couldn't even hope for that. It was too soon, and I was still too fragile to handle that type of rejection. "Make love to me."

He lifted me off the counter, and I wrapped my legs around his waist. "As you wish," he said, then grabbed the cake and carried me down the hall to his bedroom.

"Was Kevin really your first?"

Jake's whispered question startled me, causing my heart to jump. Where had that come from? We'd just had mind-blowing sex, I was practically comatose in his arms, and he wanted to talk about Kevin? Maybe I should just pretend I didn't hear him? But the question would torment me if I didn't answer.

"Yes," I replied, frozen with my head resting on his chest.

"Do you mind explaining to me how that's possible?"

I could hear the smile in his voice and my body relaxed a bit. "What do you mean?" I asked, thankful to be having this conversation in the dark.

"You had boyfriends. I hated all of them."

"You did?"

"You couldn't tell?"

"Well yeah, Dave hated them too—"

"I didn't hate them like Dave."

My heart constricted at his confession. "What do you mean?"

He chuckled. "Because I was jealous."

I pushed up on his chest so I could examine his face. I couldn't see much in the darkness, but I knew he was smiling. "You were?"

"Very." He ran his thumb over my bottom lip, his voice rich with amusement. "So, can you explain to me how it's possible?"

"Well… It's not like we didn't do stuff. I just wouldn't let it go all the way."

"Why?"

"Why is this so important to you?"

"It just is." His fingers continued to trace from my chin, up my jaw, to the top of my ear.

"Because I always measured them up against you." I swallowed before continuing. "You always won."

He flipped me to my back and rested on his forearms above me. "What the hell did I ever do to deserve you?"

"I can't even imagine my life had you not been there." My

throat was thick as I looked up at him. "You were with me through everything."

"I wasn't there after Dave..." His voice was serious and ragged.

We'd never talked about it before. What happened after our kiss. In fact, all talking pretty much stopped after that. Maybe it was just too heavy a subject after the loss of Dave, but he wasn't the only one to blame. Maybe if I'd stayed... "I wasn't there for you either."

Silence fell over the room as he stared down at me. "You're unbelievable, you know that?"

His words were only a whisper but made my heart ache. I shook my head against the sheets. I didn't know what to say. He was the one who was unbelievable. I was just me.

"What are you doing Tuesday night?"

My brows knit together. "I have an engagement shoot with Justin and Kimberly, why?"

"What about after?"

"Nothing."

"Will you go out to dinner with me?"

I laughed. That wasn't what I was expecting. "Are you asking me out on a date?"

He smiled down at me. "Katie McGregor, will you please have dinner with me Tuesday night?"

"Isn't that a work night—"

"Just answer the damned question."

I giggled. "Yes, Jake Johnson. I'll have dinner with you."

# CHAPTER TWENTY-THREE

"Did you get any good shots?" Justin asked, as we walked back to the parking lot from the ravine.

"Lots. You guys are adorable." I placed my gear bag in the front seat of my car then turned to see Justin throw his arm around Kimberly's shoulders.

The warm afternoon breeze played with the lock of my hair that escaped from my ponytail, and I tucked it securely behind my ear. Today had been a workout but well worth it. The resulting images would be beautiful—a timeless keepsake of the boy and girl who fell in love.

Kimberly's cheeks were still flushed from our hike, so I grabbed a bottle of water from my front seat and tossed it to her. "Here. It looks like you could use this."

"Thanks." She smiled.

The western sun gleamed on my face and I shielded my eyes. Their shoot had been perfection. They'd moved, laughed, and fit together so naturally it almost made my job too easy. I'd read an article in a photography magazine once. It said you could predict the success of a marriage by how difficult an engagement shoot was. If the author's words held any merit, Justin and Kimberly would grow old and gray together. The thought made me happy.

But it was still weird seeing Justin like that. Doting over a girl like a lovesick puppy. I'd known him since junior high, and ever since, women have been in and out of his life faster than a fast food restaurant. Just like...Jake.

"Actually, we wanted to ask you about your packages? We'd love to have you shoot our wedding."

I cleared my throat and focused on Kimberly's question. I wouldn't let myself think about Jake and his revolving door—people changed. I smiled. "I'd be honored."

"We've set the date. May twenty-first of next year. Hopefully you don't have anything booked?"

I laughed a little, knowing she was only being kind. "The day's all yours. I can send you over the price breakdown when I get home."

Kimberly grabbed on to Justin's arm and beamed at me. "We're going to have an early dinner at that new seafood buffet down the road. Want to join us? We could chat about the wedding?"

I shook my head and bit my lip. "I wish I could, but I already have plans." I fetched the keys from the front seat, then shut the passenger door.

"A hot date?" Kimberly asked, a hopeful expression on her face.

Heat rushed to my cheeks, and I looked down at my hands. I was hoping to avoid any questions about Jake—last I'd seen them, he had a girlfriend. How could I explain what was going on between us? Especially after overhearing Justin's warning to Jake on the beach. I cleared my throat again. "Nah, just a friend." But when I glanced up, Justin's eyes were focused on me, and he gave me a knowing grin. He wasn't buying it.

"How does Jake feel about your *friend*?" Justin asked, his suspicious tone making me uncomfortable.

I swallowed.

"Oh come on, Katie. Who do you think you're fooling?" He smirked.

"I'm not trying to fool anyone." But my voice hitched a little. *Damn, I'm such a bad liar!* I walked around to the driver's side and unlocked the door. Justin followed.

"Do you know what you're doing?" His voice was low. Laced with concern and disapproval.

I whipped around and looked him dead in the eye. "Why does every man in my life want to fill Dave's shoes?" It might have been harsh, but I didn't want his lectures. I didn't want another big brother.

"You're going to get hurt."

"I'll be fine."

"Katie..." He looked to the sky and his voice softened. "He cares about you. Don't get me wrong. But I know Jake. You guys don't want the same things."

It was on the tip of my tongue to tell him to go to hell, that Jake and I wanted exactly the same things. But the truth was, I didn't know what Jake wanted. Sure, he wanted me now. He would probably even want me a few months from now. But in a few years? Would he want me then? Would he want me big and swollen with his baby in my womb? Would he look at me the way Justin did with Kimberly? Would *we* grow old and gray together? I pushed the thoughts aside.

"How do you know? People change. Don't you think?" I flicked my eyes over to Kimberly to prove my point.

"Look, we both know I was just as wild as Jake, but the difference was I always wanted a family. I was just looking for the right girl. Jake's never wanted that. And if you're honest with yourself, you know it's true."

I grabbed the door handle and counted to ten. What he said hurt. Yes, Jake had been very vocal about not wanting to settle down. Not wanting to recreate the family life he'd grown up with...but that was years ago. He was just a kid.

"He's playing Superman, Katie. That can only last so long."

My eyes narrowed. "What's that supposed to mean?" I squared my shoulders. "You think he's saving me?"

Silence.

"I don't need saving!" I yanked the door open and glanced back at him. "I know how to take care of myself."

He held his hands up in a silent surrender and retreated back a step. "I just care about you. I don't want to see you hurt, that's all."

I blew out a breath and took in another calming one. "Justin..." I glanced over at Kimberly, who was twisting the water bottle in her hands. I hated that she witnessed me like that. Justin had always been intrusive. Prone to spilling his thoughts and getting involved in everyone's business. But he always meant well. I gave Kimberly a reassuring smile, then turned back to Justin with a bit more composure. "I'll be fine. Really. I know I won't be able to convince you, but things will be okay."

*Right?*

---

We parted ways, and I drove home in complete silence, but my mind screamed at me. This morning I was floating on a cloud of happiness, but Justin had to go and ruin it. Well, I wasn't going to let him. He didn't know what was going on with Jake and me. He didn't feel the almost out of body experience every time we touched. There was something special between us. There always had been.

The house was empty when I dropped my gear bag on the living room floor, and even though I missed Jake something fierce, I let out a sigh of relief. I didn't want him to see me before I was ready. And if I was honest with myself, I needed time to let Justin's comments settle to the back of my mind. I kicked off my shoes, and sat crisscross on the edge of the couch. My stomach ached with regret for the way I'd left things with Justin. Even if he *was* being a complete and utter ass, I knew he was doing so because he cared. I grabbed my laptop off the coffee table and typed out an email.

*Hey Jus,*

    *I feel horrible about how we left things. Please send Kimberly my apologies. She looked so stressed when we argued, and I feel awful. I know you can't help yourself from being a pain in the ass, and I know you're just looking out for me, but I've never been happier in my life. Please don't worry. And please don't say anything to Jake about you knowing. He should be the one to tell you himself.*

    *I'm attaching a price list with my friends and family rates. If you would still like me to shoot your wedding, I'd be honored.*

    *XOXO,*

    *Katie*

As I hit send, the heaviness I'd been carrying the whole ride home lifted. I snapped my laptop closed, and leapt from the couch. When I opened the door to my room, a waft of fragrant strawberries filled my nose. There on the nightstand stood a huge bouquet of fruit. Large ripe berries, some dipped in chocolate, some not. Pineapple cut in the shape of flowers, and various slices of melon, oranges, and grapes. My hand flew to my mouth, and I let out a gasp. Closing the door behind me, I walked slowly toward the arrangement like if I moved too fast, it would disappear. A white envelope was nestled between the fruit, and my heart pounded as I opened it.

*I was going to send flowers, but I thought something naturally sweet and covered with chocolate was more appropriate. Just like my Kit Kat. See you at 7.*

*Jake*

My eyes brimmed with tears, and I started to giggle. I was torn between the need to both laugh and cry. I plucked a stem of pineapple from the arrangement and jumped on my bed to read the note again—just like a silly teenager. A slow grin spread across my face and I began to laugh. Not because it was funny, but because never in my life did I expect to be here. To be in a relationship with Jake, with him sending me chocolate-covered fruit and sweet messages. I might not have been able to say the words to him just yet, but they bubbled inside me begging for release. "I love you, Jake Johnson! I love you, I love you, I love you!"

---

Two hours later, I stood in the bathroom wearing the new black lace bra and panties I'd purchased just for tonight and watched the spider I'd just smashed swirl in the porcelain bowl until it disappeared. Justin was wrong. I didn't need saving. I could take care of myself.

I took a deep breath and studied my reflection. My long hair was curled in perfect waves, my eyes smoky and vibrant courtesy of YouTube tutorials, and I felt sexy, powerful, for the first time in my whole life, worthy.

With my bottom lip held firmly between my teeth, I entered my bedroom and pulled the little black dress out of the closet. The one that was too short, too low cut, and made me look like a total sexpot. Butterflies swarmed in the pit of my stomach as I considered the short length of fabric held by strings on the hanger.

For a moment I hesitated, but then swallowed my nerves and quickly slipped it over my head. The fabric clung to my body perfectly, hugging every curve like it was made only for me. I stepped into four-inch heels as nervous energy coursed through me. Tonight was special. An official date with Jake, and no matter what happened in the future, I never wanted to forget this moment. I took a cleansing breath, plopped my lip gloss into my little black clutch, and snapped it shut. I was ready.

At five after seven, the doorbell rang. It had only been a few days since the break-in, and my heart hammered as I looked out the peephole.

Jake stood at the door wearing dark jeans, a black button-up shirt, and a brown suede jacket that accentuated the broadness of his shoulders. Little curls flipped up at his nape, and the way his hips narrowed to that perfect v made me want to skip dinner and explore every inch of him in bed.

My heart skipped a beat, and I gripped the door handle. "No fidgeting," I whispered to myself, then took a deep breath and yanked the door open.

He didn't speak at first, but his eyes darkened, and his expression wavered between desire and something deeper.

"Hi," I said, as my insides melted under his smoldering gaze.

He stepped inside but remained silent. We stood only inches apart, practically nose to nose with me in my four-inch heels. My body already aching with sexual desire.

"Aren't you going to say anything?" I asked, fighting the urge to bite my lip—or his—or—

He smiled and laced his hand around the small of my back, pulling me closer.

"I may be too jealous to take you out looking like that."

My chest tightened and I smiled.

"You look stunning." His lips brushed softly against mine. "Are you ready to go?"

"Yes," I whispered, trying to pull myself together. "Let me just get my things."

Forty-five minutes later, we walked into the foyer of *The Patio*. A beautiful five-star restaurant nestled in the hills of Malibu. The decor was simple, modern, with bleached hardwood floors, crisp white linens, and flickering candlelight. Jake gave his name to the maître d', and we were escorted to a table for two at the edge of the uncovered deck. The view was spectacular, and the only thing separating us from being able to step on the beach was a banister that stood three feet high, made of crystal clear glass. I inhaled the salty air and looked over at Jake.

"This is amazing."

"I thought you'd like it."

The maître d' helped me into my seat, and I paid extra attention to the skirt of my dress to be sure everything was where it should be. I opened the menu to make my selection, but as I scanned each page, my stomach dropped. There were no prices. I'd been to a place like this with Kevin and some co-workers once. Everything was fine until we got home, and he scolded me for ordering the lobster. "Do you think I'm made of money, Katie?" he'd asked, and no matter how hard I tried to explain that I didn't realize, he wouldn't be appeased until I wrote him a check for my portion of the bill.

"There aren't prices," I whispered across the table to Jake.

He smiled and shook his head. "Don't worry about it."

"I don't know what to order. I only brought forty dollars with me." My hands began to fidget with my napkin. This night meant too much for it to get messed up over what I chose for dinner.

His brows furrowed, and he set down his menu. "Order want you want. I'm paying."

"Jake—"

"I'm paying." He cut me off, then brushed my foot with his under the table.

I smiled a little and shook my head. "Okay."

When the waiter arrived a short time later, I ordered the seared albacore salad and a glass of Sauvignon Blanc, even though my stomach still twisted in knots about the money. Once again, I had to remind myself I was dealing with a different man. This was Jake, the man who gave up his profitable career as a lawyer to work in construction with no guarantees. Money didn't matter to him.

Jake ordered an appetizer of seared scallops in browned butter sauce, herb-crusted rib-eye, and a beer. Even dressed in designer jeans, looking like something you'd see on a billboard, he was still a simple guy. Easygoing, comfortable, perfect. The waiter collected our menus, then left us alone with the sound of waves crashing on the shore.

"So what do you want to do this weekend?" he asked, taking one of my cold hands in his warm one.

"I have the wedding with Rick, remember?"

"Damn." He stroked my palm with his thumb. "I really don't like you spending the weekend with that guy. You hardly know him."

"He's not a guy, he's my boss. And I'm not spending the weekend with him, I'm working."

He chuckled. "When will you be back?"

"We'll be covering the family brunch after the wedding on Sunday, so I'm guessing the evening sometime? Six, maybe seven?"

"I just wish I could meet this Rick. Make sure he can be trusted."

"Jake." I shot him a warning look across the table. "I'll be fine."

The waiter placed our drinks and appetizer on the table, and I used the interruption as an excuse to change the subject. "Tell me something I don't already know about you."

"I think you know everything about me," he replied seriously.

"Come on, there has to be something. A place you want to go? Things you want to do before you die?"

"I don't know." He shook his head and took a pull of his beer. "Go to Australia, wrestle a crocodile?"

I laughed. "You're such a guy."

He shrugged. "What about you, Kit Kat?" His grin so devilish it caused moisture to pool between my legs.

I shifted in my seat. "I want to ride in a hot air balloon."

"Such a girl." He winked. "Where?"

I smiled and finished my bite of scallop. "I've never thought that far. I guess it could be anywhere. But it has to be a rainbow one."

"Of course."

I cleared my throat and tried to contain my silly grin. "Tell me something else."

"Like what?"

"I don't know, a secret?"

His eyes twinkled, and he set down his beer. "Okay. When I was six I thought my penis was a tail."

I choked on air and covered my resulting cough with a napkin. "What?"

He shrugged again.

"What did your parents say?"

"I don't think I ever told them. Don't worry though, I figured out what it was really for." He raised one brow. "Though I guess you already know that."

Heat rose to my cheeks, and I took a long sip of wine.

"Your turn," he said.

"Okay." I cleared my throat and sat a little straighter. "Do you remember Dave's Steve Garvey baseball that went missing?"

"Yes..."

"Well, I took it out to the field on the cul de sac, and lost it." My face scrunched in anticipation of his reaction, but he only smiled with mischief that made me nervous. "What?"

"Dave and I microwaved your 'N Sync CD."

My eyes widened, and I half rose out of my chair. "I knew it!"

"Yeah, well... We knew you had something to do with that baseball."

I glared at him. God, he was gorgeous. So relaxed, happy, and playful. This was the Jake I knew. The Jake I'd loved my whole life.

"Your turn," he said after a pause.

I leaned back in my seat and downed a gulp of wine. "Okay." I bit my lip as I contemplated the secret I swore I'd never tell another living soul. "You were the first man I ever saw naked."

"What?" Now he was choking.

"I was fourteen, I think? You came into Dave's room to change after a shower, and I just happened to be in the closet looking for a lost CD." I raised my eyebrows.

"And you watched me?" His eyes widened with amusement.

"Yes." I could barely contain my laughter. "And afterwards you just happened to—you know." My eyes ran down his body suggestively.

"What? No I didn't." His eyes widened.

I was laughing so hard it took a second before I could pull in a breath. I shook my head. "Kidding—Dave came in, and you did some stupid boy crap and I was stuck in the closet for hours."

He leaned back in his chair, his eyes narrowed, but his smile infectious. "Serves you right."

"Meh." I shrugged. "It was worth it."

"So what did you think?" he asked, leaning forward again.

"You know darned well what I thought."

"Enlighten me."

"Okay... I thought, 'Is that all?'"

He coughed and moved his foot away from mine under the table.

I laughed. "Kidding, kidding."

He glared at me.

"I thought..." I kicked off my shoe and slipped my toe under the hem of his jeans. "I thought it was just as perfect as the rest of you."

Our meal continued with sexual banter and flirtation, which had me aching to find an empty coat closet. Everything was amazing. The food, the atmosphere, and the company. Even though I had only a glass and a half of wine, I felt drunk and giddy with happiness when I excused myself to the ladies' room.

The bathroom was tiled in shades of sparkling blue in a pattern that reminded me of a mermaid's tail, and the stall doors were a solid wood that went all the way to the ground. I couldn't help my naughty thoughts from wandering. On impulse I slipped my panties off, folded them in a little bundle, and shoved them in my purse.

I'd never done anything so brazen before, and when I returned to Jake a moment later, my heart was racing. A slice of flourless chocolate cake sat between us, and I didn't hesitate before diving into it with one of the two spoons.

"What's wrong?" Jake asked, eyeing me warily.

My face burned with my new secret, and I swallowed my cake before leaning forward. "I have something for you," I whispered, throwing a glance over my shoulder to see if anyone was around. When I saw no one watching, I slipped the folded-up lace under the table, and adjusted my skirt to make sure I was fully covered.

He narrowed his eyes, then shifted his gaze to his lap. At first he was confused, but when his eyes darkened, I knew he understood. "Damn," he said, looking over his shoulder. "Where's the waiter when you need him?"

I laughed and took another bite of rich chocolate cake.

He shifted in his seat. "I actually have something for you too."

"Oh yeah?" I ran my heeled foot up his leg until I reached the only thing I could think of at the moment.

He groaned. "That's already yours, sweetheart." He then reached into his pocket and pulled out a little brown box. It was a slightly smaller than my phone, with a blue ribbon tied in a perfect bow.

I sat up in my seat and took the little package from his outstretched hand.

My chest grew heavy and I took a breath. The box weighed practically nothing, but the way he watched me told me it was so much more than nothing. I untied the little bow, removed the top, and stared down at the face of a 1955 Mickey Mantle baseball card.

"What's this?" I asked, even though I knew exactly what it was. Dave's baseball cards. The ones I'd sold to get away from Kevin.

"They're all there." He smiled, but a sinking feeling continued to grow inside.

Without even looking at the others, I put the lid back and slid the box across the table. "You should return them."

"What? What are you talking about?"

"It's too much, Jake. Return them." I sold them for four thousand dollars. Common sense told me he'd paid way more than that to get them back.

"That's crazy. They're yours."

"I don't want them." I stood up from my chair, and he followed suit. "I don't want you to *save* me."

He shook his head and his forehead creased with bewilderment. "What are you talking about? It's a gift, Katie. I don't see why it's such a big deal."

"You don't give gifts that cost thousands of dollars, Jake."

"I don't care about the money."

"Well, I do. Take them back."

He braced his hands on the table, and I suddenly became aware of the scene we were creating.

"No." His tone was final, and completely infuriating. I huffed in a breath and balled my fists at my sides.

"Then give me back my panties," I said between my teeth.

He smirked. Heat rose to my chest, and anger twisted my belly just like the time he cut my Barbie's hair. I narrowed my eyes and glared at him. "Give them back."

"Nope."

"Fine then," I said in a forced whisper, turned on my heels, and headed for the back exit.

"Katie! Where are you going?"

# CHAPTER TWENTY-FOUR

The black ocean beckoned me as the storm of frustration cluttered my mind. I knew I was overreacting about the cards, but I couldn't help it. The stubborn look on Jake's face made me want to scream. How could I accept them when Justin's words still haunted me?

My bare feet sank deep into the icy sand with each step, and I tried to focus on the sound of the waves instead of the chill that washed over me. It was cold. Colder that I wanted to admit, but the goosebumps that covered my arms and legs made it impossible to deny. I cringed. Jake still had my damned panties, and the cool breeze that blew between my thighs made it painfully obvious.

*The bastard.*

But he wasn't a bastard. Deep down I knew that. I was frustrated and confused about so many things. Angry with Justin for the things he'd said, angry with myself for being the type of person someone wanted to save.

I had no idea where I was going. All I knew was that I needed to walk. To cool off, clear my head, and let go of some of my irritation.

I only made it past the first lifeguard station before he called to me. "Katie, wait!"

My heart constricted at his voice and I slowed. I was annoyed, but I wouldn't make him chase after me.

"You can't just run away every time I do something that pisses you off."

I could sense his irritation but wasn't calm enough to really care. "Well, stop pissing me off then."

"Not gonna happen."

He was probably right. He'd been doing it since I was six. Why would he stop now?

"Why won't you just return them, Jake?" I stopped and gripped my shoes tighter in my hands.

"Because they're yours." His voice grew serious and hit me in the pit of my stomach.

"They're not mine. I sold them." I turned around to face him.

"They're yours." His hands were shoved deep in his pockets, his face serious as shadows played on his chiseled features. Damn, he was hard to stay mad at.

"What the hell did I do wrong?" He looked confused.

I rolled my eyes and scoffed. "Contrary to what everyone seems to believe, I'm a strong woman. I know how to take care of myself, and I know how to kill my own spiders." Even to my own ears it sounded silly, but when he started to smile, I glared at him. "What's so funny?"

He covered his mouth with his hand and took a step closer. "Nothing."

He stopped in front of me, his face composed. "Don't you think I know that?" He began again. "Don't you think I know how strong you are? What I don't understand is what baseball cards have to do with it." His voice was soft but his expression hardened.

I let out a breath and looked out to the ocean. "Because it was *my* shitty situation, and I got myself out of it. Because I don't need you saving me." I turned around to start walking again, but in a second he was there, his hands holding my arms secure.

We stood still a moment, frozen by the electric charge that shot through me every time we touched. His body was stiff behind me, and I closed my eyes, torn between wanting him to let me go so I could run, or throw me to the sand and make love to me.

His hands loosened, and he bent down until his mouth brushed my ear. "I know you're a strong woman, Katie. The strongest woman I've ever known."

I closed my eyes and relished in his warmth.

"I know you don't need me. I know you can take care of yourself." His lips trailed along my jaw. "Kill your own spiders. But all that has nothing to do with those cards."

I leaned back in his arms knowing I couldn't possibly resist him any longer and let my high heels drop from my fingers to the sand. "It's too much."

"Don't you know I want to give you everything?" His arms wrapped around my waist and his chin rested on my shoulder.

Why did it mean so much to him? Why did he have to be so stubborn?

"I—" He started to speak but stopped.

Something reminiscent of fear gathered deep in the pit of my belly. "What is it, Jake?"

He took in a breath, and his grip tightened around me. "I can't give you Dave back." His voice low, and filled with an emotion that twisted the deepest part of me. "But I can give you his cards."

I turned around and placed my hand on either side of his face. The strong man who still tortured himself with the loss of his best friend stared down at me. "Jake."

His brows were gathered in that way that left creases in his forehead, and my heart ached. "It's not your job to give me anything."

He shook his head but didn't speak.

I narrowed my eyes at him. "You remind me of him sometimes."

One brow lifted, and his lips twitched. "I do?"

I nodded. "Usually when you're frustrated with me."

His grinned. "Must happen a lot."

I bit back a laugh, and he wrapped his arms around me and pressed his lips into my hair.

"It's been so long since I've talked to anyone who remembers him. I know it's silly, but I felt him slipping away from me in San Diego. I couldn't hear his voice anymore...it scared me."

"He'd never leave you, Katie." His voice was deep and gravely, but I kept my eyes on the waves.

"Do you think he's happy we're together?"

He took my icy fingers between his hands and played with them a minute before answering. "I think he'd hate the fact that I have your panties in my pocket... But yeah... I think he's happy we're together."

I laughed, then nodded against his chest, somehow finding comfort in his words. I knew he was right. Even though Dave had been more protective of me than a mama grizzly to her cubs, he trusted Jake more than anyone in the world.

"I'm so stupid, Jake."

He pulled back and looked at me with confusion.

"You were so sweet to give me those cards, and I don't know what I was thinking. I'm just stupid, and stubborn, and hot-headed sometimes."

He shook his head and smirked. "You're not stupid, Katie."

I smiled at the fact that he stopped at stupid, and looked into his eyes. I was lost in the moment. Alone with Jake under the stars. The cool breeze softly lifted my hair, and he pressed his forehead against mine. "Katie?"

"Yes?"

"Thank you."

Such simple words that were spoken every day, but the way he said them took my breath. "For what?" I whispered.

"For tonight."

My throat thickened. How could he possibly thank me? If anything, I'd ruined our first date. My fingers moved along his jaw, then dipped into the sexy indent of his chin. "I'm sorry I had a tantrum."

He pulled back, raised his brows, and smiled at me. "I like your tantrums," he said seriously.

I shook my head. "You're crazy."

"Crazy about you."

It was the first time he'd said something like that, and excitement pulsed in my belly. I took his hand and walked backward until I led him under the lifeguard station. "I don't want to talk anymore." I placed his hand on my thigh and ran it up until it came to the hem of my dress.

His fingers brushed the fabric higher, and I smothered a moan in the crook of his neck. When he reached the juncture of my thighs, he groaned, then stripped off his coat and laid it on the sand. With his hand on the small of my back, he lowered me to the soft suede, then knelt in the sand between my legs.

My hands flew to his waistband, but he grabbed my wrists and moved them slowly away until he held them above my head.

"I want you," I protested.

"And I've wanted to taste you ever since I knew you were naked under that dress."

With one hand holding both of mine secure, he yanked the front of my dress and bra down, exposing my breasts. "God, you're beautiful."

His open mouth covered mine, silencing further protests and making me forget everything except his lips, his tongue, and my drenched center aching for his touch. Lazy kisses traveled down my neck, his tongue teasing a trail along my collarbone until his mouth covered the rock-hard bud of one of my nipples.

I arched against his mouth, my hands straining from his grip. "I want to touch you."

He smiled down at me, then guided my hands until they gripped the beam of the lifeguard station above my head. "Trust me."

My eyes fluttered and my head fell back in the sand as he continued his descent down my abdomen. When he reached the bottom of my dress my breath came in quick pants. And when his teeth grazed along my inner thigh, my legs began to tremble.

He gripped my bottom with both hands and lifted me. My heels dug deep in the sand in anticipation of his mouth, and I squirmed with excitement. His warm breath met my clit, sending shivers down my spine, cooling my sweltering heat, and causing all my muscles to clench with sheer pleasure.

When his tongue found my aching nub, I gripped the beam tighter, and bucked against him. Long fingers plunged into my center, curling and stretching inside me, massaging me and driving me crazy.

Between each kiss he spoke to me, urging me on, telling me to let go, to trust him, that he would take care of me.

"Jake, I—"

But I couldn't finish. His fingers and tongue moved in a torturous rhythm that made my toes curl and every nerve in my body to come alive. *Yes, yes!*

In one swift motion his mouth was on mine, and I tasted my sticky arousal on his lips. He plunged inside me, filling me with the thick, hard length of his erection, and I wrapped my legs around his hips. My hands flew to his back, gripping his shirt as he pushed me higher, my whole body rocking as he pounded into me over and over. Every time he entered, my body clung around him, needing what I knew only he could provide. And then I slipped over the edge, gripping him tighter as rippling waves of my orgasm surged through every part of me. Jake stole my shredded cry with his mouth and drove inside me one last time.

His breath caught. He groaned deep in the back of his throat and collapsed on top of me—his weight anchoring me deep into the ground. Without it, I was sure I would have floated off to heaven.

Minutes went by before either of us spoke, his face buried in the crook of my neck as I traced the lines of his muscles through his thin shirt.

"I've never had sex outside before," I said, smiling into the darkness. "Or with a man who was fully clothed either."

He grinned down at me, his hair ruffled and disorderly. "Yeah, well, you didn't seem to mind a minute ago."

"I didn't say I minded." I took one of the curls at his nape and played with it between my fingers.

His face sobered and his features etched with devotion. He rolled off of me, helped me adjust my dress, and pulled me to sit between his thighs.

I leaned back against his chest and burrowed into his warmth. It was so peaceful here. Not a soul in sight, the only light cast by the stars and the few buildings off in the distance. The ocean played its love song, and I knew I would never forget this night, this moment, not for all eternity.

We stayed like that for another half hour. Me nestled between Jake's thighs as we watched the tide roll in and erase the day. But when I heard his yawn for the third time, I rose to my feet and pulled him to stand. We dusted each other off the best we could, then walked hand in hand back to his car.

"Have you talked to Em or John?" I asked, stopping at a bench and putting on my shoes.

He scratched his head, and I couldn't help but wonder what he was thinking.

"John yes, but only at work."

Under the light of the nearby parking lot, I noticed more sand on my dress and busied myself brushing it off as an excuse not to look at him. "Em called me today and left a message. I didn't call her back—I didn't know what to say."

He went silent for a second. "What do you mean you didn't know what to say?"

I shrugged. "I didn't know what to tell her about us."

"What do you want to tell her?"

I shrugged again.

He took my hands and lifted me from the bench. "Tell her I've had you tied in my bedroom as a love slave."

I rolled my eyes and smiled, even though my stomach was full of tangled yarn. "We should make plans with them. Em and John, I mean. It's been a while."

"Sure, whatever you want."

"How about tomorrow?"

He ran his hand through his hair, then gripped the bridge of his nose. "I can't tomorrow. I'm behind on paperwork, and the inspector is coming on Thursday."

"What time does the inspector come? Maybe after?"

He nodded. "Sounds perfect." Then he kissed my lips, grabbed my hand, and we walked back to his waiting truck.

# CHAPTER TWENTY-FIVE

"Wow." Em wrapped me in a long hug at the front door. "You look amazing."

I glanced down at the draping fabric and my bare feet. "Do you think it's too much?" I found the dress in the back of my closet with the tags still on. A light peach linen with tiny delicate straps that crossed in the back. I changed three times before she arrived, and only settled on this when I heard the knock.

Em shook her head and smiled. "No, you look great."

I gave a small nod, then turned to my room and beckoned her to follow. "Where did you say we're going again?" Even to my own ears I sounded strange. High-pitched and off-key. Last I'd seen her, Jake was still with Grace, and after my interaction with Justin, I didn't know what to expect anymore. Would she disapprove? Would she warn me off, or think I wasn't good enough?

For so long, every look, every word had been guarded to make sure no one knew my secret. Now it was time to hold Jake's hand —the hand that had been in another's only a week ago—and make this thing between us real.

"Donovan's," she answered. "It's a little pub owned by John's uncle. I can't believe we haven't taken you yet." Em tilted her head and eyed me suspiciously. "There's something different about you."

Heat flushed my cheeks, and I pulled open my closet. "You're just used to seeing me in shorts," I joked, then gestured to my laptop on the nightstand. "Plus my eyes are still glazed over from editing photos all day."

She laughed and plopped down on my bed. "Ahhh... So is that what you've been up to?"

"Pretty much," I lied. "Which reminds me..." I opened my dresser and took out the little box that contained the flash drive with all the proofs from her session and tossed it to her. "Go ahead and plug it in."

She caught it in the air and plugged it into my computer on the nightstand while I searched my closet for a pair of shoes. I'd hoped Jake would've been home before anyone arrived, but he'd been stressed from work and said he'd be home as soon as he could. Actually I hadn't seen him much since our date. The night before I'd tried to wait up for him but ended up falling asleep on the couch. He awoke me with kisses and carried me to bed. It felt so natural. Like I'd waited all my life, knowing that eventually we would end up together.

"Boots or flip-flops?" I asked, holding up a pair of brown distressed cowboy boots and gold sandals.

She glanced from the screen. "Boots," she answered, then her eyes immediately locked back on the monitor. "These are stunning."

I smiled and sat next to her on the bed so I could see which one she was looking at. "That's my favorite." I pointed to a candid shot from a moment when the wind picked up and blew her hair in front of her face. She wasn't looking at the camera, and her eyes were half covered by wisps of her dark hair, but there was something there that intrigued me. A woman who held many secrets.

A loud knock sounded at the front door and I jumped. Em

raised her eyebrows but smiled with understanding—I hadn't quite gotten back to my old self after the attack. She hopped from the bed to answer it. "I'm sure that's John. I'll go get it."

I quickly pulled on my boots, ejected the flash drive, and joined them in the living room. "Hey stranger," I called to John as I walked into the room.

"Hey gorgeous," he replied, then knocked my chin softly with his fist. "Jake out back?"

"I was hoping he'd be with you." An uneasy feeling settled in my stomach. Where was he?

He made a face and shrugged. "Got anything to drink?" he asked, brushing past me on his way to the kitchen.

"There's some beer in the fridge," I called, but something about his expression made me wary. "Didn't you just get off work?"

He came back into the room with a bottle and twisted the top with his bare hand. "A couple hours ago."

The garage door opened, and Jake entered the room still dressed in his jeans and work shirt. He nodded to Em and John, but his eyes met mine, and one side of his mouth lifted in an adorable smile. He dropped his bag as he strode toward me and my heart flip-flopped in my chest. I was vaguely aware of Em and John watching, but didn't care. He stopped just inches away then scanned me from head to toe. "I like your boots," he said softly.

I bit my lip and smiled. "Thanks."

He lifted me off my feet, a small gasp escaped my parted mouth, and he kissed me. A kiss that claimed me as his, that left no question as to what had been going on the last few days. I heard Em take in a sharp breath, and John let out a low whistle before Jake slowly lowered me to the floor.

"I'm going to go take a shower," he said in my ear, and a part of me wished we were alone so I could join him. Instead, he left me in the living room, my face flaming red as I turned to face our audience.

"I knew it!" Em announced when Jake rounded the corner. "Tell me everything."

I didn't tell her everything, but we talked about the party, about Grace, and our first date—minus the intimate details—and the longer I spoke, the more at ease I became. She wasn't there to judge me, to warn me against Jake, or tell me we wanted different things. She was actually giddy with excitement and eager for every word. John seemed happy too but didn't offer much except a few pats on Jake's shoulder when he came back in the room.

We arrived at the pub thirty minutes later, and Jake held my hand as we all walked from the parking lot to the front entrance. It was only a few blocks away from his house. I'd driven past at least a dozen times but never once noticed it. The front of the building was painted black and reminded me of an old grocery store. Gold lettering over the double-door entrance read "Donovan's Irish Pub. Est. 1963."

For a Thursday night, the bar was pretty lively, and I held on to Jake's hand as we made our way to the bar. A group of drunk girls sang an out of tune rendition of "Hotel California" on the stage in the far corner, while the whole pub came alive with hoots and hollers cheering them on. One of the three bartenders raised a hand to John as we approached, then gestured for us to keep going. We walked past a couple of pool tables crowded with people and settled in the last four stools at the end of the bar.

Another man nodded to John, then came over to clear the empty bottles and wipe down the counter in front of us. "I was beginning to think you forgot about me," he said to Em.

"Not a chance, Colin." She flashed him a charming grin, then hopped up on a stool next to John.

"Who's your friend?" he asked her, throwing me a smile that was guaranteed to break hearts.

"Her name's Katie, and she's with me," Jake said, wrapping his arms around me from behind.

Colin laughed, and shook his head. "Story of my life. What can I get you guys?"

"Round of Harp," John replied.

Colin nodded, wiped his hands again, and left to fill four mugs with the pale lager.

"Do you sing?" Em asked loudly over the chaos of the bar.

"Only in the shower," I replied.

"Oh come on. You can't be as bad as them." She gestured a thumb toward the stage and I laughed.

"Katie has an amazing voice," Jake said, taking a seat on the stool beside me.

I turned to face him. "How do you know?"

His brows rose in a *who do you think you're talking to kind of way*. And then I remembered. All the recitals, all the plays he attended when we were young. Sure, Mom had probably threatened his and Dave's lives to make them come—but he was always there. One time he even brought me flowers. Just a few simple stems of Gerbera daisies I'd recognized from Mom's garden. I'll never forget the furious flutters that beat inside me when I saw him walking toward the stage. All the girls at school knew who he was, and he was coming to talk to *me*. "You did great, Kit Kat," he'd said, then bent down and pressed his seventeen-year-old lips to my freshman cheek. I almost fainted then and there. I never thought he was really listening—I guess I was wrong.

Colin returned with our beer and a basket of fish and chips he said were "extras," and placed them in front of us. "Anything else?"

John shook his head. "Thanks, we're good."

I grabbed a fry out of the basket, then looked past Em, who was flipping through the Karaoke catalog, and spoke to John. "I didn't know you were Irish."

"I'm not," he said, downing a long swallow of beer.

Jake chuckled next to me, and I raised my brows.

"I thought this was your uncle's place," I clarified.

John shook his head and smirked. "It is, but he's not Irish. He just always wanted to own an Irish pub." He popped a fry in his mouth and smiled at me.

I laughed. "Did he buy it like this?"

"No... We actually helped build the place," he said, waving a finger between him and Jake.

I narrowed my eyes, then turned to the entrance. "But...what about the sign?" *Donovan's Irish pub, Est. 1963.*

John shrugged and everyone laughed.

"He comes from a family full of liars, Katie," Em said, elbowing John playfully in the ribs. "Makes me wonder if his name's really John."

He threw his head back with laughter, and I twisted out of my seat. "Where's the restroom?" I asked Em. She gestured to the hall behind us, and I leaned over and gave Jake a quick kiss before excusing myself.

There was a line at the ladies' room—of course—but I entertained myself by listening in on a conversation between two drunk girls about lost panties. I'd only lost my panties once—though I guess that fact could be argued. I knew exactly who had them. The thought made me smile.

I did my business, applied some Chapstick, then headed back out to the hall. Large hands gripped me from behind and I startled. Then Jake's voice whispered in my ear and his rough jaw grazed my cheek. "I was beginning to get worried." His arm snaked around my belly. "What do you girls do in there anyway?"

I grinned and leaned back against his chest. "Talk about missing panties."

I felt his smile brush the side of my face, then he grabbed my hand and pulled me to the back of the hall. "You and your panties," he groaned.

He pushed me into the alcove, and my back hit the hard surface of a door. He leaned forward, his masculine form caging me in.

"I didn't say they were *my* panties," I clarified, but couldn't help smiling as I looked from his beautiful eyes to his sexy mouth.

His knee wedged between my thighs, and he grinned at me. "Why are we here? I want you home," he whispered, "in my bed." His hand found my thigh and lifted my skirt to my hip. "Naked."

Breathless, my hand went to his jaw, and I pushed my thumb firmly over his lips. "I want that too," I whispered between my teeth.

Just then the door opened behind me, and Jake yanked me forward against the wall of his chest.

"Get a room, Jake," I heard Colin say behind me, and I smothered a giggle into the crook of Jake's neck.

Colin continued down the hall, and Jake looked down at me, *want* in his eyes but a smile on his mouth. "I've always hated that guy."

We reluctantly went back to the bar with a plan to stay only another hour, then finish what we started in the hall. I loved Em and John, but my desire for Jake was insatiable.

"How about 'Oops!... I Did It Again'?" Em asked when I returned to my seat.

"Uhh... no," I replied without hesitation.

"Come on, you have to sing *something*."

"Fine." I bent over to look at the book, and we eventually agreed upon "One Way or Another" by Blondie.

Em scribbled our name on the little sheet, then hopped from her seat to give it to the DJ. "We'll be up quick. I think the DJ likes me."

Jake leaned over and whispered in my ear, "Should I be worried?"

There was amusement in his voice and I smiled. "About Em?" I asked.

He shook his head. "You're singing the ultimate stalker song."

I smirked and leaned into his shoulder to nip his earlobe. "You'll be fine as long as you never try to leave me."

He laughed, then pulled me off my seat and into his lap. "Not a chance, Kit Kat."

Em came back, her forehead creased and jaw tight.

"What's wrong?" I asked.

She didn't say anything, just threw a chin in the direction of the stage. I felt Jake tense behind me before I turned around. Grace stood on stage with a microphone in her hand. She wore a skintight black dress, her blond hair curly and wild—she looked sluttier than Olivia Newton-John in *Grease*.

I whipped back to the bar and shifted to my seat. "Shit. Should we go?"

"Fuck, no"—John laughed—"and miss the show?"

Then the music started, and she began to sing "You Oughta Know" by Alanis Morissette.

"What's she doing?" I whispered to Em.

"Fucking the microphone with her mouth."

I glanced back over my shoulder and found her looking right at Jake. "I don't think it's me you have to worry about," I whispered in his direction.

"If you're uncomfortable, we can go." He tucked a lock of hair behind my ear, and his searching eyes met mine. My throat tightened—why was I so scared? We were doing nothing wrong, but all I wanted was to run away and avoid the whole situation. But I couldn't run away from every conflict that presented itself to me. I grabbed Jake's hand under the bar and squeezed. "I'm okay," I mouthed, then turned to the bar and ate another fry.

A couple of minutes after the song ended, Grace walked toward us with the same man she'd introduced Jake to at the party.

"Jake, you remember Peter?"

Jake nodded, his jaw tight, and shook Peter's hand.

Grace examined him from head to toe, stopping at our joined hands in his lap. Her eyes flashed to mine, and she smiled a wicked smile that had me adjusting in my seat.

"Let's give a round of applause for Em and Katie!" the DJ announced over the speaker, and I panicked. I didn't want to leave Jake alone with Grace, but Em was grabbing my arm and pulling me to the back of the pub. We climbed the steps to the stage, the cheers so loud I couldn't even hear myself think. We each grabbed a mic from the stand, and we both turned around just in time to see Grace give Jake a hug.

My head was in a fog, my eyes locked on Jake, forgetting to sing until Em elbowed me. Grace turned toward the stage, laughed, and looped her arm through Peter's before heading for the exit. I sang the words as if on autopilot, glancing between the monitor and Jake, who watched us from the bar. A moment later he answered his phone, and I watched him cover one ear, straining to hear over the music. Then he walked outside, through the same door Grace used not two minutes earlier.

Alarm bells went off in my head, and my voice tapered to a stop. Em threw her arm around me, singing louder to make up for my absence, but all I could do was stand there, staring at the door and willing Jake to come back.

Just as Em and I were hanging up our mics, Jake walked inside. He tilted his head toward me, his smile bright and relaxed, and I let out a small, breathy laugh.

*This was Jake*, I reminded myself. I walked down the steps—ignoring all the cheers and hoots from the group of college boys sitting at the bar—and threw my arms around his neck. "Why was Grace here?" I asked close to his ear.

He pulled back, looked me in my eyes, assessing me. "Just her way of letting me know we still work together."

"Oh." I'd forgotten about that.

I looked down to my feet, but he lifted my chin back up with a finger. "What's wrong?"

I swallowed, but knew it was pointless to pretend with Jake. "Who called?"

His lips lifted in a half smile, and he shook his head a little. "Have you always been this suspicious?"

I grinned a little in spite of the nervous flutters. "Yes."

He leaned in close to my ear, his body perfectly molded to mine. "You'll find out soon enough." Then his lips moved to hover over mine. "Until then, you'll just have to trust me." Our mouths met, and his tongue swept inside, filling me with his sweet taste. I no longer cared about Grace, about phone calls, about anything but leaving that *damned* bar.

# CHAPTER TWENTY-SIX

When I pulled in front of Rick's house the next morning, I did a quick check of the time before putting the car in park.

8:50

Ten minutes early and no boss waiting for me outside. My shoulders relaxed, and I pushed my head back into the seat.

That morning Jake had crawled out of bed before dawn. I'd watched with hooded eyes as he walked naked into the shower. Steam clouded the mottled glass, but his hard male form was still obvious as hot water slid down his body.

For three days I would be without him, and my heart ached with that fact. I threw the covers from my body, walked barefoot to the shower, and stepped inside without saying a word. I wrapped my arms around his waist, pressed my cheek to his muscular back, and took in a shaky breath. I don't know why I was emotional, but I felt like a little girl leaving home for the first time. "I'm going to miss you."

He turned around to face me. His hair slicked back, eyes focused, and a bead of water on his full bottom lip.

"Then don't go." His voice was low, and full sleep. But there was more than that. A vulnerability, an emotion I didn't understand from Jake.

I shook my head and looked into his eyes. I knew he was only half serious, but the intensity of his stare made my stomach flip. "I have to."

Something inside me unsettled. A tug deep down that warned me there was something wrong. I wanted him to tell me he'd miss me. That he loved me.

But he didn't say anything. His thumb ran over my lips, wetting them with warm water, then he bent down and kissed me...

I shook my head and pulled myself from my thoughts.

9:09

Where was Rick? I grabbed my phone and pulled up the itinerary he'd sent the day before. There it was, printed in all caps.

DEPARTURE: 9 AM SHARP

His SUV was still parked in the driveway, so I knew he was home. Maybe he was waiting inside?

*Shit!*

I tossed the phone, got out of the car, and raced up the walkway. By the time I made it up the flight of steps, I was out of breath and panicked. The oversized red door stared at me, and I took a calming breath before knocking.

He couldn't possibly be angry with me. He'd told me to wait outside—right?

An eternity seemed to pass with no answer. I knocked again, a little more forcefully this time, but nothing. Overgrown ivy covered the stone walls, and I began patting it down searching for a doorbell.

Just when I was about to give up and get my phone from the car, I found a button hidden in the leaves and pressed it.

Not even a minute later, Rick's groggy voice played through an intercom. "Yeah?"

I cringed. "Rick, it's Katie."

243

"What time is it?" he demanded.

"Nine fifteen."

"Shit."

A loud crash followed, then the intercom went dead. A minute later he yanked the door open wearing a pair of black boxers and nothing else and tossed me his keys. "I need you to load the truck." Then he turned and dashed back up the staircase.

The living room was full of his gear, and I tentatively got to work packing the equipment in the back of his SUV. What the hell? It wasn't in his character to be late, but then again, what did I know? This was only my second time working with him. Maybe it happened a lot.

I'd just gotten my bags from the back of my car when he appeared at the top of the stairs. "You drive," he ordered, then tipped a silver mug to his lips. "I'm still drunk."

It was an hour later when I realized I'd left my phone in my car. I patted down my pockets to be sure but came up empty and let out a sigh. The universe was trying to tell me something, I was sure of it.

"What's wrong?" Rick asked from beside me.

Surprised by his perception I forced my shoulders to relax and glanced over at him. "Nothing, why?"

"You're frowning."

"I just realized I left my phone in my car." I smiled for added reassurance, but his brows furrowed as he considered me.

I turned back to the road, my eyes locked on the license plate in front of me. "I'll be fine, I don't need it."

"You can use mine," he said after a pause, but when I looked at him again, his attention was once again focused on his laptop.

The wedding was over five hours away, on a private estate in Carmel. I knew it would be extravagant, but my jaw still dropped when I turned in to the long stone driveway. The estate was nestled on the edge of a cliff where manicured lawns and forty-year-old willows graced the front entrance. Beyond that, nothing but ocean.

Rick directed me to park around the back where a white fence contained a green pasture and two beautiful chestnut horses. I unbuckled my seatbelt and stepped out of the car as fast as I could. Foam-capped waves crashed into the mountainside, and the sun painted diamond-shaped facets in the water. Out in the distance, through a tuft of trees, a train of rocks was covered in a sheet of green—almost like tiny islands that tapered off into the sea.

"We'll be shooting out there tomorrow," Rick said, following my line of vision.

I turned to him and smiled. "It's the most beautiful thing I've ever seen."

He nodded, then seemed to assess me. I wasn't sure what he was looking at, but I got the feeling I pleased him in some way.

"Come on," he said, gesturing with his chin back to the truck. "We have work to do."

Moments later, weighed down with heavy gear, we were led through the back entrance to our rooms, and the wedding coordinator gave us a map of the property before she excused herself to let us get settled.

My room was large and very beautiful. A king-sized sleigh bed sat between two sizable windows that overlooked the ocean. Crown molding encased the ceiling, and large canvases broke up the pristine white walls with gentle shades of blues and greens. I placed my suitcase on the pale blue comforter and began unpacking.

This place was an oasis overlooking the sea. Somewhere you'd bring a loved one and never leave your room. A place I'd like to bring Jake...

"They're connected." Rick's voice shot through the silence and I jumped. When I turned, there he was, leaning against my bathroom door. Correction—our bathroom door.

His black shirt was unbuttoned at his throat, his hair tousled, as he pushed himself from the doorway and walked toward me. Something about the way he looked at me made me nervous. His eyes never wavered, his jaw tight and confident. I backed up a step and ran into the edge of the bed.

He stopped, turned his gaze to the window, then smirked. Trapped in silence, not knowing what to say, I shifted my eyes to the dark wood flooring.

"I'm not a predator, Katie." His tone was deep and even.

"I—I didn't..."

He shoved his hand in his pocket and pulled out his cell. "Be ready in ten minutes." He tossed the phone on the bed and turned back to the bathroom from where he'd come.

*Shit!*

After berating myself for my suspicious behavior, I called Jake to tell him about leaving my cell behind. His phone rolled to voicemail and I left a message. That same uneasy feeling grew inside, and I threw myself back to lie on the bed. I was losing my mind.

There was a quick tap on the door, and I joined Rick outside. We walked down the long prestigious hall, then stopped at the top of the stairs. The room before us was where all the magic would happen. The bride and groom would be announced from where we stood. Below, they would share their first dance in a room enveloped by windows. Wood beams curved around the concave ceilings and looked like the underside of a ship, and the view from the edge of the cliff took my breath away.

Rick nodded to me, as if acknowledging my awe of the scene before us, and for the first time, he looked at me like I was a peer. Like another artist appreciating the beauty we were presented with.

Regardless, he was nothing short of curt, barking orders and expecting me to be two places at once. But the apprehension I'd felt earlier began to fade. Even though he was demanding, he was completely professional. And by the time the rehearsal dinner was over, I felt guilty about my behavior back in my room.

"Good job today, Ms. McGregor," Rick said, passing me in the hallway.

"Rick, wait."

He paused, adjusted the heavy bag slung over his shoulder, and turned around. I pulled the phone I'd forgotten to give him earlier out of my pocket, and walked toward him. "Thank you."

His eyes locked with mine and his brows lifted in surprise. He took the phone from my outstretched hand then continued down the hall. "Katie," he said in a gruff voice before entering his room.

"Yes?"

"Be ready by five tomorrow. We have a sunrise shoot in the morning."

---

The day of the wedding, we rushed from one event to the next. Only stopping to change our clothes, eat, or rehydrate. Rick watched me like a hawk when we were together, but over half of the day I was on my own—and that was when I was able to relax. There were even a couple hours in the early morning when I got to walk the grounds and focus on photographing the landscape. Something I would have done without being paid.

Every couple hours we met in Rick's room and backed up our files on his hard drive. Just the thought of losing a single image from this high-profile wedding made me want to vomit. His room was much like mine, but there was a small table with two chairs set up on the far wall that held his laptop.

"I want you to take the groom's party this time," Rick said, before we parted.

"Okay," I replied, unable to hide my confusion. That was not on the plan he'd sent me earlier.

"See you at the ceremony."

The groom's party was secluded in the pool house out by the stables. Beer flowed on tap and shots were passed like water. I somehow corralled the rowdy bunch and took the obligatory photos without much trouble. The groom reminded me of Jake. Tall, dark wavy hair, built... Though he didn't have the dimpled chin or sideways smile that drove me crazy. There were five other men standing up with him, one of whom had a three-year-old boy with dark curls, big blue eyes, and carried a little bear in a tuxedo that matched his own.

"He's a ring-bear, just like me," the little boy named Peter told me in a tiny voice.

"Oh yeah?" I said, dropping to my haunches and smiling. "Can I see?"

He eyed me sideways, seeming to assess if I was a trustworthy person or not, then passed me the precious bear. "He's *berry* shy."

I smiled and took the stuffed toy from his chubby fingers. "What's his name?"

He scrunched his little face like he'd just tasted something sour. "Ring-Bear. I already toad you dat."

"Oh, yes, silly me." I bit my lip to keep from laughing. "Well, he's a very handsome bear. And so are you, I might add."

His chubby hand flew to his mouth to suppress a giggle. "I not a *real* ring-bear. I just pretending."

I threw my head back and laughed, and he joined me with more tiny giggles. "Can I take a picture of you, Peter?"

He nodded, took the bear from my hands, and smiled so big his eyes remained only as tiny slits.

The next hour was spent taking candid shots of the groom and his men. Peter stayed glued to my side the whole time. It felt natural and comfortable having a little shadow, and I couldn't help the longing that settled deep inside me to one day have a little boy of my own. A boy with chubby cheeks, dark curls, and big blue eyes. Just like Peter... Only with a dimple in his chin that matched his daddy's.

My heart squeezed. I needed to talk to Jake. To stop pretending like the future didn't exist. No matter how much I wanted to ride the waves and see where this thing took us, I was falling deeper and deeper in love with him, and pretty soon, I wouldn't be able to swim my way out. I wanted to get married, have kids, grow old together. Not a big wedding like this. This was beautiful and breathtaking, and something you'd see featured in a magazine, but it wasn't me... and it wasn't Jake... But what *was* Jake? What did *he* want?

My thoughts were consumed with him for the rest of the evening. Every tender moment I caught between the bride and groom, every laugh, and every kiss. Tiny feet that tapped on the dance floor, and Peter's chubby hands wrapped around his daddy's neck when he fell asleep.

It was just after midnight when I made my way to Rick's room, and my feet dragged with exhaustion. His door was left ajar and creaked open when I knocked. He stood in the center of the room, his shirt untucked and open at his chest, his feet bare, and a glass of dark alcohol in his hand. He was on the phone and waved for me to come in.

His computer was there on the table, so I dropped to the nearby chair to retrieve my memory cards.

Still on the phone, Rick poured a glass of whiskey and set it in front of me on the table. The invitation to have a drink with my boss made me nervous, but I took a tentative sip and got to work with the backup. In a few minutes the job was done, and I picked up my bag intending to slip out without notice.

"Are you in a rush, Ms. McGregor?"

I whipped around to face him, his phone now discarded on the nearby bed. "I didn't want to interrupt you," I said softly.

He picked up my abandoned drink from the table and walked over to me. "It's been a long day. Have a drink with me."

It wasn't a question, and something heavy dropped to the pit of my stomach. I took the glass from his outstretched hand, and he turned away to refill his own.

"Have a seat, Katie."

My heart hammered in my chest, and I eyed the empty bed as I made my way back to the chair.

He sat opposite me, his long legs splayed as he leaned forward and took another sip of his drink.

"I have a proposition for you."

All the twinges and unsettled feelings came crashing to my chest. This was it. The reason for all my apprehension. I had to fight the urge to run from the room, and my hands shook as I picked up my drink.

"You're warm, inviting, and people like you…"

I pressed the glass to my lips and pretended to take a sip. Time stood still, and long moments passed before Rick spoke again.

"I want you to come to work for me out of the field."

All the blood drained from my face and I blinked. "What?"

"I need someone like you. Someone with your artistic eye to fill my shoes when I can't be there. Other obligations are pulling me away more than I'd like, and I need someone I trust not to fuck it up. I'm impressed with your work, Katie. I've been looking for someone like you for a long time."

I couldn't speak. I was completely taken aback by his offer.

"I'll need you at my beck and call. Clients don't like to wait, and I need to know you'll drop everything when I need you."

He pushed back from his chair and stood. "You don't have to answer tonight. But you'll be compensated well for your time." He eyed me over. "You don't look well, Ms. McGregor. Go get some rest, and I'll see you tomorrow at breakfast."

I floated back to my room in a daze, then tossed and turned all night with excited energy. For the hundredth time that weekend, I missed Jake. I was anxious to get home and tell him all about my job offer. To ask him his thoughts so he could help me decide what to do. Being at the beck and call of Rick Henderson was intimidating, but on the other hand, how could I pass up an opportunity like this?

When the alarm went off the next morning, my body ached from little sleep. Rick's knock came way too soon, and I grabbed my bag to meet him in the hall. He narrowed his eyes as he examined my appearance. Basically confirming the fact I looked like shit, but I didn't care. In a few hours my job would be over, and I couldn't wait to go home to Jake.

"Plans have changed, Ms. McGregor," Rick said, as we made our way down the long hall to the dining room.

Why did this not surprise me? Nothing had gone as planned all weekend. I nodded and adjusted my bag to take some of the pressure off my aching shoulders.

"I need you to drive the Escalade back to Los Angeles. Something came up, and I'm leaving for Italy after I wrap things up here."

"Okay," I replied, trying to keep up with his hurried strides.

"You can leave after you have breakfast."

He barked the order like always, but I couldn't stop myself from getting confirmation. "You don't need me to help cover brunch?"

"Like I said, you can leave after you eat. I'll handle it from here." He paused before entering the dining room. "And Katie, make sure to drink some coffee. You look like shit."

The drive home was pretty uneventful, and I made it back to Rick's house by late afternoon. I thought about calling Jake when I found my phone in the front seat of my car, but it was dead.

*Of course.*

When I entered the living room twenty minutes later, the house was quiet, but I heard the shower running in the distance and smiled. I dropped my bag by the front door, toed off my shoes, and began unbuttoning my blouse, intending to join him.

When I walked into Jake's room, I first noticed the bra on the floor, then the trail of abandoned clothing, which led to the bed. There, lying in the middle of crumpled sheets, was Grace. And she was completely nude.

# CHAPTER TWENTY-SEVEN

I couldn't speak, could barely breathe. It was as if every system inside me had shut down in that single moment. Grace noticed me right away, but said nothing. She didn't even try to cover herself, or hide any part of her perfect body.

She smirked, looked me up and down, then glanced to the bathroom door where the shower still ran.

*He was still hers.*

As much as I wanted to believe he wanted me, that we could build a life together, I wasn't enough. *I was never enough.* Bile rose to the back of my throat and my hand flew to my mouth. I couldn't be here when he got out.

On legs that threatened to buckle beneath me, I stumbled to the front door. I needed to get away, get as far as I could and not look back. My shoes and bag were at the front door and I grabbed them, not even stopping to button my shirt as I made my way to the car.

I don't know how far I drove before I pulled to the side of the road and threw open the door. My whole body heaved out of control. Every last drop of my dignity expelled to the blackened asphalt below. With shaking hands, I wiped my mouth and sat back against the upholstered seat. I stared straight ahead and began to slowly button my blouse. Not because I cared if people saw me—because it was the normal thing to do. Because I was grasping for anything that would ground me to earth, so I wouldn't feel the only solid thing in my life running through my fingers like water.

An elderly couple walked by, watching me with a disapproving glare, but said nothing. Everything I knew as truth crumbled around me, and my body began to shake. I wanted to scream and throw things, but I was paralyzed by the pain.

Why would he *do* this to me? Lead me on like this and let me think we had a chance? Had this been going on the whole time? Had he even broken up with Grace?

God, I was so naive! My fists slammed into the steering wheel over and over, and I screamed at the top of my lungs. My voice was shredding, but I was desperate to feel anything to mask the searing pain that coursed through my heart. Was anything we shared even real? Were his late nights at work a lie?

I gripped my swollen hands to my chest as tears began to fall. I'd thought I'd reached rock bottom after Kevin, yet the way I felt now was incomparable. If I let myself experience the depth of my hurt, I would explode from the amount of pain that would erupt out of me.

Eventually the sun began to set, and I knew Jake would be expecting me. But how could I go back and stand under the roof of lies? Listen to excuses from the only person I thought I could trust? I looked to my phone in the center console, sure there would be messages, but grateful for its lack of charge so I didn't have to see them.

With bruised hands I gripped the steering wheel, eyes straight ahead—almost unseeing—and put the car in drive. I didn't know where I was going, only that I had to move. I drove in aimless circles until my car was on empty, and all the people on the road disappeared.

When I finally stopped, I looked up at Em's apartment building. I wasn't sure what brought me there. Maybe because she knew the heartache of infidelity? Or maybe because I had nowhere else to go and was afraid to be alone.

It was just past eleven when I found the front gate open and let myself inside. With my camera bag slung across my body, I climbed the rickety stairs to the second floor. All her lights were on, and my head fell to rest on the closed door. I was ashamed. The girl that men fucked but didn't want to create a life with. What would Em say? What would I tell her? How could I bear to relive the memory and give her an explanation? I took a calming breath and knocked.

Only a second passed before the door flung open, and she threw her arms around me. "Oh thank God!" She pulled me into the apartment and looked me over. "Where have you been? Are you okay? Are you hurt?"

She sat me on her bright blue couch, and I began to tremble. I was lost, a shell of the person I'd been only hours ago, and I didn't know what to say. I just shook my head and averted my eyes from her worried face.

"I'm calling Jake, he's been out looking for you. Did something happen at the wedding?"

I stood up and frantically shook my head. I couldn't see him. Not now. Not tonight when I was broken and weak. "Please don't call him. Please don't." My voice was hoarse, and it hurt when I spoke.

She put down the phone, her brows knit with confusion, and took my shaking hands in hers. "What happened, Katie?" Her voice was only a whisper, laced with fear and concern.

"I can't talk to him now. He can't see me like this. Please."

She pulled me against her chest and gripped my trembling body. I couldn't hold back the tears any longer. The dam of my sorrows opened up and poured onto her willing shoulders. Tears that came from the deepest part of me. Tears of heartbreak, the loss of my best friend, and the dream of a future I'd started to believe in.

I wasn't sure how long she held me, but eventually the tears ran dry, and I wiped my swollen eyes. Em didn't ask any more questions, and I was grateful for that. But I got the feeling she was afraid that if she did, I would snap. She pulled a pair of boxers and an oversized shirt out of her drawer and set me up in the bathroom with a fresh towel.

"Why don't you go take a shower? You'll feel better."

I nodded, and she closed the door behind me. With hands splayed on either side of the vanity, I looked at the reflection of a woman I didn't recognize. One with swollen, lifeless eyes. Eyes that had seen too much, experienced too many heartaches, and had finally given up.

The shower was quick and to the point. One I took to appease Em and offer her some kind of reassurance. I combed out my hair, got dressed, then opened the door just as Em entered the bedroom.

She closed the living room door behind her and approached me like I was a frightened animal she didn't want to scare off. "I called Jake." Her voice was soothing, but I couldn't help the sense of betrayal that flooded my insides. I didn't blame her. She was his friend first. But it was an aching reminder that I had no one to call my own. No one who was there for *me* above anyone else.

I turned around and squeezed my eyes shut to keep the tears at bay. "Why?"

"Katie, he was out of his mind looking for you. I couldn't—"

The bedroom door flew open, and I turned around to see Jake. He looked panicked and wild as he raked his hand through his hair. He rushed toward me, eyes searching mine, and pulled me into his arms. "Are you okay?" His voice was shredded and scared, and I fought back the tears that threatened anew.

I pushed out of his embrace, and my throat thickened with unbearable hurt. I wanted to tell him to leave, to never speak to me again, but I couldn't. If I spoke, I wouldn't be able to hide my pain, and I didn't want to give him that. He owned my heart, but this pain was mine.

He backed up a step, obviously thrown by my reaction. The blue depths of his eyes showed his anguish as he searched my face. *Damn him! I won't feel bad about this!*

Disgust bubbled inside me, and I pushed past him, the whole room spinning as I stumbled to the bathroom and fell to my knees by the toilet. My body heaved uncontrollably as I gripped my concave stomach that had nothing left to give.

"Shit, Katie." I heard Jake's distressed voice from behind me, then his hands were in my hair, holding it secure.

"What the fuck happened to her?" he shouted to Em, but she said nothing. She didn't know. Only I held this secret.

He stroked my hair, my face, my back. "It's okay, baby, it's okay."

My heart squeezed. How could he be so caring one minute and in bed with another woman the next?

I tore away and sat on the cool tile. Unable to meet his eyes, I rested my elbows on my knees and gripped my skull. "What are you doing here?"

"What happened? Did Rick hurt you? Did someone hurt you?" He crouched beside me.

"Rick didn't do anything to me." I looked up to his tortured face.

"What happened?" His voice was soft, ragged, and filled with a pain that stabbed me in the heart. He reached out to caress the side of my cheek, and I backed away from his touch.

"I don't want you here, Jake." My voice cracked with emotion, and my lips began to quiver. Using the wall behind me, I pushed myself to stand and he followed.

His eyes were pleading for answers, but how could he not

know? How could he be so confused when the only person in the world who could affect me like this was him?

"I saw her in your bed." My voice was cold, unfeeling, in total control—empty. "I came home early, and Grace was naked in your bed."

His hands raked through his hair and he stared at me. A host of emotions transformed his features. Shock, regret, relief, fear.

"When I got out of the shower she was there. I threw her out—"

I snapped. "I don't want your lies!"

He rushed toward me and gripped my face. "I threw her out, Katie. Nothing happened."

He looked so honest. His eyes boring into mine as he moved even closer. "I would never do that to you." His voice was only a whisper, and I took a ragged breath.

A part of me began to waver. I wanted to believe him, to believe he wouldn't do that to me. I wanted him to pull me into his arms and squeeze me so tight all my broken pieces squished back together. But I'd been here before. I'd been the fool. The trusting one. The girl who was blind to the lies and so naive that everyone around her laughed like an inside joke.

"Katie, look at me." His eyes were red rimmed and reflected my own pain. "Nothing happened."

I closed my eyes tight, my nails cutting into my palms at my sides. "I want you to leave," I whispered.

Moments passed as we stood there. Frozen together, but the bond between us ripping apart.

Eventually he let go and backed away. His jaw was tight, like he was using every drop of control not to touch me.

Em stood back in the doorway and slowly approached him from behind. She reached up and put one hand on his shoulder. "I think you should go."

His hand wiped over his face, and his eyes met mine one last time. He looked angry, hurt, confused—then he turned around and walked out of the room.

I heard Em trying to comfort him. "She's been through a lot... give her time... She'll feel better in the morning... I'll call you tomorrow."

And then the apartment door slammed, and he was gone.

# CHAPTER TWENTY-EIGHT

I blinked into the center of the room. My body stiff and still as I lay on the edge of the king-sized mattress. Last night Em had insisted her bed was large enough for the both of us, and I was too broken to argue about such a trivial thing as where I slept. Now in the light of morning, Jake's pleading eyes burned through my memory. His gruff voice played over and over in a continuous loop. *"Nothing happened."*

I wanted to so desperately to believe him, but I couldn't let myself be a fool again. Grace had been naked in his bed. The image would be imprinted in my memory for eternity. Not just a photograph like it had been with Kevin, but a living, breathing woman. How could I deny what I saw? I squeezed my forehead and sat up on the side of the bed. Every muscle was sore. Not from overuse, but from an exhaustive inability to relax. My throat was raw and hoarse, eyes swollen, and head pounding. But none of those hurts compared to the empty hole in my chest where a crushing ache now lived.

Not wanting to intrude on Em any further, I dressed in the clothes I'd worn the day before and walked into the living room to find my bag. My life was in shambles, and I needed to decide on a plan. *Charge phone, call Rick, find a place to live.*

Em sat in her tiny kitchen tapping away at her laptop, one foot curled under her bottom. When she noticed me, she jumped out of her chair and stood. "You're up." She tore her earbuds from her ears and placed them on the table. "I was trying not to wake you."

"You didn't." I tried to force a smile but couldn't quite manage one. I wasn't sure if I'd ever truly smile again. I pulled my phone from my bag and looked around the room. "Do you happen to have a charger?"

"Sure." She took the phone from my hands and plugged it into the charger on the kitchen counter. "Are you hungry? I have some orange juice and bagels. *Or...*" She pulled a box out of the cupboard and shook it at me. "Lucky Charms. My guilty pleasure."

I shook my head and let out a breathy laugh. "I'm okay. Still not feeling well." It hadn't been my intention, but as I watched her, I realized I'd stuck her in the middle of all this mess. Jake was one of her best friends, and now I was staying in her house. What kind of damage would that do to their relationship?

"I just need to make a few phone calls, then I can get out of your way."

"You're welcome to stay." Her words came out a bit too eager. She walked toward me, examined my red knuckles, then looked into my eyes. "You can stay here as long as you need."

My eyes brimmed with tears, but nothing fell. Not because I didn't want to cry, because there was nothing I wanted more. I wanted to crawl up in a tiny ball and cry so hard it would drown out the conflict going on inside me. I didn't want to trust anyone, not even Em. But I couldn't bear the thought of being alone. It had only been a few weeks since we'd met, but in that moment she was the closest person in the world to me, and I was grateful for her invitation.

"Okay," I said, swallowing the hard ache that balled in the back of my throat.

She opened a cupboard and pulled out a mug. "Coffee?"

I nodded, and she poured me a cup before we both sat at her tiny table.

"I can get you some fresh clothes."

I shook my head, suddenly feeling homeless, needy, and misplaced. "I'll be okay."

She raised her brows, and I looked down at my wrinkled blouse and black slacks.

I gripped my forehead and let out a small laugh. "Okay, but only for today."

She didn't say anything else, and I took that moment to calm myself before speaking again. "I need to go to the house to get my laptop. I'll get some clothes while I'm there." Jake would be at work until evening, and even though it now felt wrong entering without being invited, I couldn't deal with seeing him again so soon.

She nodded, but her eyes were sad. "I think he was telling the truth, Katie. I've known Grace longer than you and—"

"I know what I saw!" My voice was harsher than I intended; I glanced down to the table and squeezed my eyes shut. "Sorry. I just don't want to talk about it. I know he's your friend, but I know what I saw, and I can't let that happen to me again..."

She grabbed my hand across the table and squeezed. "You're right, I'm sorry, I just hate seeing my friends hurt."

I nodded, grabbed my coffee, and took a sip. My chest ached with a tension that wouldn't go away, and I searched my mind for a way to change the subject. "Rick offered me a new position." I looked up to assess her reaction, but her face showed nothing.

"I'm going to take it. It's not exactly what I wanted to do, but I really need a steady income now...." My voice trailed off, and I began to trace the grain pattern of the wood table with my finger.

"What will you be doing?" she asked.

"I don't know. Some kind of freelance work I think. I'll find out more when I talk to him."

My phone blared to life with new alerts, and my eyes flew to the kitchen counter. The device meant to connect me to the world now loomed like a snake ready to strike. I took another sip of coffee then walked to the counter and swiped through the messages from last night.

JAKE: I'm ordering dinner. Do you want pizza, or Chinese?

JAKE: Missing you like crazy. Come home ASAP

JAKE: Where are you???

JAKE: I'm getting worried. Call me.

There were three voicemail messages, but I scrolled past them to another text that came in an hour ago.

Jake: We need to talk.

My eyes shut. *We need to talk.* Those four little words I'd said to him only days ago. The same words that sent a feeling of dread down my spine every time I heard them.

Em cleared her throat behind me. "Everything okay?"

I opened up my voicemail and stared at the screen. "Yeah, fine." But inside I was fighting a battle between heart and mind. Part of me wanted to lock myself in the bathroom and listen to the messages over and over, analyzing and obsessing over every word. The other side knew I wasn't strong enough, that if I heard his voice now, I wouldn't be able to walk away. Focused on the task at hand, I deleted each voicemail, my heart breaking a little more with each one.

An hour later, I sat in my car outside Jake's house, my heart pounding in my chest. I'd driven by three times before I built up the nerve to stop. His truck wasn't there, so I knew he wasn't home, but a sense of dread consumed me.

I somehow managed to pry myself out of the car and slid the keys in the front pocket of the borrowed shorts. I'd lived there for almost a month, but now it felt like trespassing.

*In and out, Katie. Just get what you need, and be on your way.*

My hands shook as I punched in the code to the front door. The shutters were closed and beams of light shined through the wooden slats. A pizza box sat on the coffee table with a half-empty bottle of whiskey next to it. Something I'd never seen Jake drink before. His tortured eyes flashed through my memory, but I pushed myself forward, my chest aching with each breath. I didn't have time to think about that now. I had the rest of my life to torture myself with that moment, but I was here for a reason, and I needed to focus.

The door to my room was open, and I quickly got the suitcase out of my closet. The whole house smelled of him, smothering me with the male, earthy scent that would haunt me forever. I tossed the case to the bed, unzipped the zipper, then froze. There on the nightstand was an empty glass. One that hadn't been there before I left. I picked it up and held it to my nose. The scent of whiskey still lingered on the rim.

A photograph sat beside it, worn and tattered. I held it between my fingers and sank to the mattress. It was taken three years ago when Jake and I went to Disneyland together. Dave was supposed to have gone but backed out at the last minute because of the stomach flu. We'd just gotten off Splash Mountain and were both soaked to the bone.

I remembered it like it was yesterday. Jake had stopped an elderly couple to take our picture, then pulled me into his chest. I smiled at the camera, my hair and clothes plastered to my body and face—my heart beating a mile a minute. But Jake, he looked right at me. His smile wide and happy. His expression one of adoration and love. The old woman commented on what a cute couple we were, but I quickly denied it and pulled away...

The front door opened and I instantly stood. My breath caught in my throat, and I threw the photo to the nightstand, glancing around the room for a place to hide as boots hammered on the wood floor, moving closer, then stopped. I knew he was behind me, but I couldn't bear to face him. Not like this, caught with my tail between my legs, sneaking into his house like a coward.

He cleared his throat, letting me know I couldn't just stand there like a little girl playing hide-and-seek anymore. Ready or not, I had to face him.

I pulled in a breath and turned. His sandy blond hair was wild and unkept. His normally smooth face, now camouflaged by a thick beard. And angry, feral eyes skimmed over me. I gasped.

"Just give me the photos, Katie." Kevin's voice was low, calm, and chilled me to the bone.

My mind flashed to the conversation I'd had with Shelly, and all the blood drained out of me in an instant. "I—I don't have them."

"Stupid bitch!" He stepped into the room and closed the door behind him. "Where the fuck are they?"

"Kevin, I—"

His hand slammed across my face, and I stumbled back to the bed. I wanted to cry, to scream for help, but fear kept me silent.

His ungroomed face was wild and terrifying. "You know exactly what photos. The photos that cost me my career. The photos that ruined my life."

My cheek throbbed, but I ignored it, pulled myself from the bed, and backed toward the window. "I had nothing to do with that." My eyes darted around the room, looking for a way out, or something to protect myself with.

"Bullshit!" He walked toward me, each furtive step like a cat stalking its prey. Then his lips curled in a smile. "No one's here to see, no door to hide behind this time."

I took in a sharp breath. *It was him.* That night on the other side of the door. Not a stranger, but the man I'd lived with for two and a half years.

His teeth flashed with a smile. "You've become a lot feistier than I remembered. I wasn't expecting you to fight back."

He stopped two feet away and yanked the top drawer out of

my dresser. Bras and panties littered the ground when he threw it against the wall. "Where are they, Katie? In here?" He pulled another drawer. "Or in your little boyfriend's room?"

I'd never seen him like this. Crazy and feral, a desperation in his eyes that sent a stampede of alarm coursing through my body. "I threw them away. I left everything in San Diego. It wasn't me, Kevin, I wouldn't do that to you." My voice was calm, but inside I was frantic.

"Liar!" He came toward me, backed me into a wall, and stopped only inches away. "Don't fucking lie to me!"

My hands flew to my face to protect against further blows, but his gloved hand blocked me and gripped my throat. "I'm going to take your life, the way you took mine."

The front door slammed open and Kevin turned at the sound. I lunged toward the bedroom door, screaming for help, but my head yanked backward, and Kevin's fist was in my hair. "Stupid slut!"

The bedroom door flew open and crashed against the opposite wall. Jake stood in the doorway, his imposing form heaving. In a second, his eyes flashed from me to Kevin. His jaw pulsed, and he charged toward us.

Kevin hurled me with both hands, and my head crashed into the dresser. The room began to echo, my vision blurred, and right before the world went black, I saw Jake push Kevin against the wall.

# CHAPTER TWENTY-NINE

The first thing I remembered were the voices. Muffled voices like I was listening from the underside of a pool. I tried to concentrate, to focus on each syllable, but they were slurred and chaotic, and before long I was too exhausted to care. Then a low male voice boomed in the background—a familiar voice—and my body stiffened. My eyes fluttered open and darted around the room. *My room.* But something was different. Something wasn't right.

An overwhelming sense of confusion settled in my chest. What was going on? Why was I on the floor? Who were all these people? And then Jake's voice broke through the chaos, and I looked into his blue eyes. He squeezed my hand, his lips moved, but I was still under water. I couldn't understand.

A man appeared above me and wore a navy blue shirt that I recognized as a paramedic. He shined a bright light in my eyes and the water cleared. "Ma'am, can you hear me? Can you tell me your name? Ma'am, I need you to tell me your name."

His big brown eyes were covered by black-rimmed glasses, and I blinked up at him. "Katie. My name is Katie."

Jake let out a relieved breath, and some of the tension eased from my body. The medic continued to ask more questions, easy ones, like counting backward from ten to one, but weakness crept up my spine like a splintering pipe.

"Katie, I need you to keep your eyes open for me, can you do that?" Jake hovered above me, his voice gruff and strained. I smiled up at his handsome face and nodded.

The medic lifted my head, and cold, hard plastic wrapped around my neck. My eyes locked with Jake's and I began to panic. *What's going on? What happened?*

He squeezed my hand and told me to relax, that everything would be fine.

I was moved to a gurney, and the medic wheeled me out of the house and through the front gate. Red and blue lights flashed all around and emergency vehicles lined the street. Thrown over the back of one of the cars was a man, hands cuffed behind his back, head down and legs braced apart against the curb. He turned to me, his face beaten and bruised, a large gash under his left eye, nose swollen and bloody... *Kevin.*

I looked up to the sky and the clouds above began to spin. My heart slammed in my chest as the memory of what led to this point played in my head like a movie. Kevin's wild eyes, his hands around my throat, the fear that pulsed through me, and the inability to set myself free. What if Jake hadn't arrived when he did? What if he hadn't come at all? I squeezed my eyes shut, hoping that when I opened them again the last two days would just be some horrible nightmare. That I'd wake up in the hotel room in Carmel. That the attack, Grace, all the heartache could be washed down my throat with a cup of coffee.

A commotion of voices reverberated against the pavement and I opened my eyes. People I'd never seen before crowded the sidewalk. Watching, staring, like what I'd just been through was some sort of sick form of entertainment. We stopped at the back of the ambulance, doors open, and two medics made adjustments to the gurney.

"Sir!" a police officer called from behind us, and everyone turned. "I'm sorry, sir, but I'm going to have to get your statement before I can let you leave."

He was talking to Jake, whose eyes immediately shot to me. "I'll give my statement at the hospital." His tone was curt, dismissive, but the officer braced his legs apart and spoke again.

"I'm sorry, sir. I can't let you do that."

"She'll be alone, damnit!" Jake's lips pressed in a hard line, and his hand raked through his tousled hair.

With a feather-light touch he stroked my bruised cheek. "I'll be right behind you. I'll call Em. You're going to be fine." He kissed my head. "I'll be right behind you."

My throat tightened and I nodded. The threat was over, so why was I so scared? For the first time I noticed Jake's bloody knuckles, and a suffocating pressure began to choke me. I grabbed the steel rail at my sides, and the paramedic pushed me inside the ambulance. But my eyes never left Jake's, and inch by inch he disappeared behind the metal doors.

The same man with the glasses sat beside me and placed an oxygen mask over my face. His voice was soothing and deep in radical contrast to the sirens, which blared overhead. He kept me talking, asking me trivial questions, and I got lost in the hypnotic sounds of the road, his voice, and the turmoil rolling around inside me.

"I think I'm okay," I said, wanting nothing more than for the driver to pull over and drop me off on the side of the road. I didn't care that I had no car. I'd walk, take a cab, hitchhike, but I wanted away from this mess.

"It's just a precaution, ma'am. You hit your head pretty hard."

But I didn't hit my head. Not in the conventional way. I was thrown into a dresser... Something I could've never imagined happening twenty-four hours ago, but was my reality today.

Minutes later, the doors were yanked open, and the medics pulled me from the ambulance. I was wheeled down a long, narrow hall cluttered with medical equipment to a room divided by curtains. A team of people in pale blue scrubs waited for us. One of whom appeared kind and motherly. She squeezed my hand. "I'm Dr. Lear, and this will be your nurse, Mary." She nodded in the direction of a woman to my left who was wrapping a blood pressure cuff around my arm.

The smell of antiseptic and medicine overwhelmed me, and my heart raced. I hadn't been to a hospital since Dave's accident and all those familiar feelings came rushing back. Panic, fear, the loss of control, and the finality of never seeing my brother again. It was a place that represented death, and here I was, facing it alone.

Dr. Lear continued to catalogue my injuries, speaking medical jargon I didn't understand. She shined a light in my eyes and asked if I was in any pain, but all I could think about was the fact that the man I'd spent two and a half years with had just attacked me. Had hit me, had his hands around my throat. How could I have been so wrong about someone for so long? How could I have been so clueless?

The hour that followed came in a blur. I changed into a hospital gown, my wounds cleaned and wrapped, while an officer I hadn't seen before waited outside for me to give a statement. His questions were clear and direct. He wanted to know if I was in a relationship with Kevin, if he'd shown this type of behavior in the past, and if I was somehow involved in the loss of his career.

I told him everything. About the note in my in-box, hiring the private investigator, and how I threw all the photos away before I moved. Then I told him about Shelly, about Mr. Olson's wife, and gave him her number at the office should he have any further questions. When the officer asked if I'd like to press charges, I nodded, grasping at the only thread that held my sanity together. That Kevin would be in jail.

A short time later, Mary wheeled me down the hall for a CT scan. She helped me onto the cold table, adjusted a pillow behind my head, then pressed a button on the machine, and I slowly slid inside. The scene with Kevin played in my mind again and again, with only one thought: how could I have been so wrong about a person.

It seemed like an eternity, but in reality it was only about thirty minutes before Mary wheeled me back to my room. Em sat chewing her nails in the corner and rushed to my side when we entered.

"Katie, oh my God!" Her panicked voice rang through the room, stirring the emotions I was trying so hard to keep tucked away. "Are you okay?"

I nodded, but at the same time my throat constricted with unshed tears. I wasn't okay. I was scared, confused, thankful for my life, yet completely lost in the pieces that were left scattered on the floor.

Her face contorted with emotion and she dropped her bag to the ground. "I was in spin class when Jake called. I came as soon as I got the message."

I nodded, and Mary helped me from the wheelchair to the bed.

"Have you heard from him?" I didn't say Jake's name. I couldn't.

She shook her head with immediate understanding. "I think they took him to the station. He's probably going crazy."

"Did you tell him I went to the house?"

She looked to the floor, then let out a breath. "He called to check on you. I couldn't lie to him."

"It's okay..." How could I possibly be upset with Em? Had she not told him, who knows what would have happened?

The nurse patted my shoulder, showed me where the call button was, then closed the door behind her as she walked out to the hall.

The room was thick with tension and unasked questions. Em sat on the side of the mattress and squeezed my hand. "What happened?"

"I pick the wrong people." I laughed a little and began picking at an imaginary something on my gown. But I knew—there was nothing funny about what happened with Kevin.

A twang of longing gnarled in my belly, and I shook my head. I wasn't sure if it was from being in the hospital, or because I knew how protective they were of me, but I wanted my dad and brother so desperately.

It was still light outside, and I looked to the window trying to swallow back tears. "When I was a little girl, my dad and Dave used to talk about all the hoops they'd make boys jump through before they could date me." I met Em's eyes and a sad smile tugged at the corner of my mouth. "It always started with the boy coming to the front door to ask their permission. I always rolled my eyes and said the only one who needed to give permission was *me*, but deep down I loved that they were so protective."

Em pulled her leg up into her lap and smiled.

"Next would come the weapon cleaning on the coffee table, a lecture about how to treat a woman, and how they were always watching." I laughed under my breath.

"The final step would be the DNA swab and his fingerprints. Of course, I was mortified and embarrassed, certain that no boy would ever go through such trials for *me*, but my daddy always said that if the boy was worth it, *he'd walk through hell just to hold my hand.*"

I wiped at tears with my thumb. But there were never any boys who came to the door while my daddy was alive, and I didn't put men through trials. I gave myself over, trusted, and loved without question—look what it got me.

I cleared my throat and sat up a little—Em said nothing. Not that I expected her to. She was probably so confused—just as I was. Someday I'd tell her more about what happened with Kevin, but right now I didn't have the strength. I wanted to forget—for her to take me back to her apartment so I could sleep for a thousand years.

There was a commotion down the hall, and Jake appeared at the door. His jaw was tense, his hands bandaged with white gauze and tape, and he hurried to my side. Em stood and offered him her spot, and he said beside me not saying a word.

He just leaned over and pressed his lips to my forehead, my nose, my lips. A part of me knew I should push him away, but I was selfish and weak, and in that moment, I needed him. I needed the friend he'd always been to me. The friend I hoped not to lose forever.

When Dr. Lear came in later that afternoon we all sat up in attention. "Ms. McGregor, your scans have come back clear, and you've given me no reasons for concern.

"Given you have someone to watch over you," she looked from Em to Jake, "you'll be free to leave within a half hour."

She continued to go over protocol of what to look for throughout the night. Vomiting, loss of vision, any erratic or uncharacteristic behaviors. Jake took all the literature and thanked her for taking good care of me, but my heart began to race. I couldn't go home with him. Go home and pretend like everything I saw hadn't happened.

Mary came in with the discharge papers, and I fumbled over each signature. I couldn't concentrate. I needed to spit it out, but the words were locked away at the back of my throat.

"Do you want to change?" Jake asked, and my heart sank to the pit of my stomach.

"I'm not going home with you." The words came in a breath of a whisper, but Jake's expression hardened.

"What?"

I looked him in the eyes and spoke again. "I'm not going home with you." My chest was heavy and my ears began to ring, but I stood up and began collecting my things from the table.

"Is this still about Grace?"

There was a shuffle in the corner, and Em dropped to pick up her bag. "I'll give you guys some privacy." Then she turned and left the room, closing the door behind her.

He walked closer. "Do you still not believe me?" His voice was low and gruff.

I shook my head. What had changed? Just because my life had suddenly become ten times shittier didn't mean Grace hadn't been naked in his bed. "I don't know." My eyes shifted to my hands. "I don't know anything anymore."

He closed the gap between us and gripped me around my waist. The pain that flashed in his eyes was almost my undoing. *I wouldn't feel bad about this!* He'd saved my life, but how could I trust anyone ever again?

"I'm broken, Jake. Scared to death to trust my own judgment anymore. I can't do this."

His face paled like I'd struck him. "You've known me for twenty damn years. Do you really believe I'd do that to you?"

My lips began to quiver, but I forced myself to speak. "You saved my life back there—but honestly, I don't know what to believe anymore."

He sucked in a breath, but before he could speak I pushed him away. "I can't do this."

He swallowed. "Do what?" He searched my face.

"This. *Us.*" I couldn't quite meet his eyes.

He grabbed me again, forcing me to look up. "I was in the shower," he began. "She used the code to get in the house. She was crazy, pissed, I don't know, but you came home at the worst possible moment." He let out a breath. "I know it looked bad, but I promise...nothing happened."

My brows furrowed, and I jerked away from him.

"You've been through a lot. Let's not talk about this here. Let's go get something to eat. Get some rest."

"No, Jake. I don't need food. I don't need rest." My heart squeezed tighter. "I need you to leave me alone."

Just then a nurse poked her head in, undoubtedly from our raised voices, but I nodded that everything was okay, and she closed the door again.

He stood motionless, as if waiting for me to wake him from a nightmare. But we weren't waking up. This wasn't a dream.

"Shit." He gripped the back of his neck, and turned away. "Maybe you're right, Katie. Maybe all this was just one big mistake." He let out a hollow laugh, and even though this was exactly what I was asking for, I couldn't stop the stabbing pain that twisted inside my heart. He was right. It was all a big mistake, but hearing those words left me unbalanced, and I gripped the side of the bed for support.

He turned to face me again. The pain in his eyes seared through me. "People need me at work, every fucking thing is falling apart, and no matter how hard I try, you don't want to believe me."

He said it as a statement, but his ocean-blue eyes asked a million questions. None of which I was willing to answer.

"When you're ready to talk you know where to find me." He pulled his keys from his pocket, yanked open the door, then stopped. I wanted to run to him, to tell him I was wrong, that I believed him, that I knew he was telling the truth. But I couldn't.

I gripped my gown with both hands, walked into the bathroom and closed the door. Because if I stayed, if he turned around, I wouldn't have been strong enough not to throw myself in his arms.

# CHAPTER THIRTY

Ten days. It had been ten days of living without Jake. Ten days of sorrow, heartache, and a hurt so deep that tears wouldn't even surface. But ten days felt like an eternity without him. An eternity because even though we'd lived apart for three years, I always knew he was there for me. But now, sitting on the couch in Em's dark living room, the bright display of my phone the only light in the room, I couldn't even bear to look at his texts. Bear the thought of listening to his messages, and even the sight of his name on the screen made me nauseated.

I didn't hate him. The complete opposite. I loved him so much I felt crippled by it. So much that in the wee hours of the night, I began to doubt everything I saw, regret everything I said.

He'd left me alone for five days, and that was when he began calling. In my heart, I knew he deserved to be heard, but I wasn't strong enough yet. I'd been through too much in the past few weeks, and I didn't know my mind anymore. Let alone trust my judgment enough to know if he was telling the truth.

Exasperated, I gripped the bridge of my nose, and read Rick's email for the tenth time.

*Ms. McGregor,*

*You're either in, or you're out.*

*I need you to do a shoot for me tomorrow evening. I'll give you until midnight.*

*Rick*

Simple and direct. Either I went to work, or he'd find someone else. I had twenty minutes left to decide.

*Fuck.* The tune of *Jeopardy!* played in my head. I wasn't ready, but what could I do? My excuse about the bruises didn't hold water any longer, and deep down I knew I had to move on. Em had been nothing but gracious, but I couldn't live with her forever. I had to face my life and pick up the pieces that were left for me.

Keys jingling in the lock pulled my attention, and Em's hour-glass silhouette appeared in the doorway.

"You're still up," she stated, then closed the door behind her.

"Yeah."

She flicked on the kitchen light, gestured to the phone in my hand, and asked the question she'd asked at least a dozen times since I'd moved in. "Did you talk to him?"

My shoulders slumped. I didn't have to say anything—my silence was answer enough.

She nodded, kicked off her heels, and pulled a pint of Häagen-Dazs Dulce De Leche out of the freezer.

"How was your date?" I asked, needing to change the subject. She cared about me, she cared about Jake. I understood that. But I wasn't ready.

She shrugged, took two spoons out of the drawer, and joined me on the couch. "You can't avoid him forever." Her voice soft and pleading. "If you only knew how much he was hurting—"

"Him?" I cut her off, my chest so tight that I could barely speak. "Do you think this has been easy for *me?*" I was dying inside. Could she not see that?

I stood up and began pacing the floor. Trying to get a grip on my emotions before I said something stupid. "Do you think I like *this?*" I waved my hand over my body, still in the boxers and T-shirt I'd worn to bed the night before, the hair I hadn't washed in three days. "But I need to move on, Em. It's better this way. It's better it ends now than in ten years when I wouldn't be able to survive."

"Oh, because you're surviving so well right now?" She didn't yell, but her voice was firmer than I'd ever heard before.

I stopped and covered my quivering lips with my fingers. I wanted her to see my pain only a minute ago, but now I felt vulnerable—weak.

"Katie, he loves you..."

I closed my eyes, trying to shut her out. To go to the blank place in my head that kept me from feeling the magnitude of my hurt. But she wouldn't stop.

"Do you know how we met?"

I didn't answer, but she continued anyway. "We were both shit-faced in a bar, and he kept talking about this girl. A girl who was beautiful, and smart, and the only person in the world who knew the real him. The girl he was too stupid to hold on to.

"I was suspicious when he told me about his friend *Katie* who was moving in with him, but when I saw the way he looked at you when he thought no one was watching...I knew. He'd been talking about *you.* He loves you."

I wiped at tears with the back of my hand. "He was mourning the loss of his best friend."

"Yeah, *you.*"

I shook my head.

"You know the code to his house?" She continued. *"Five four eight, five two eight?* That's you, Katie. *Kit Kat.*"

I turned to face her. Tears clouded my vision, and she pulled me into her arms. "Just talk to him."

But I couldn't. I wasn't ready. I needed my heart to heal. I needed to get over him first... "I can't."

She didn't push me any further. I think she sensed I'd had enough. But as I sat on the couch after she went to bed, I realized she was right. I wasn't surviving. I was wallowing in hurt, self-pity, and it was time for me to get over it.

I picked up my phone from the coffee table and punched in my reply to Rick.


*We need to talk. Meet me tomorrow, 10 a.m. Starbucks on Melrose and Fairfax.*
  *Katie*


Part of me feared I was making a big mistake, but the other part was proud. I was taking a stand for myself, and I wouldn't back down.

I forced myself to take a shower, dressed in fresh pajamas and climbed in beside the already-sleeping Em. My hand found the sea glass under my pillow, and my stomach twisted in knots about my future. Consumed with all the things Em had told me about Jake I began to think—had it really been me he'd told her about all those years ago? I rolled over on my side, grabbed my phone from the nightstand, and punched out the code Jake had given me the first day I'd come home. Five four eight, five two eight.
  *Kit Kat.*

---

Parked in front of Starbucks the next day, I glanced to my makeup-clad face in the rearview mirror, then covered the remaining bruises with a pair of sunglasses. Rick's curt reply had been waiting for me when I woke up that morning.

*O.K.*

That was it. No signature. No nothing, and my stomach had been in knots ever since. I fished some change from my bag, climbed out of my car, and fed coins in the meter. My eyes locking on Rick right way. He was leaning back in a chair the way he'd been the first time we met. He looked exactly the same: designer jeans, white linen shirt, his legs stretched out in front of him. But this time *I* was different. This time I wouldn't be intimidated. I might not have control over whom I fell in love with, but I was in total control over my career.

"Rick," I said in greeting as I approached the table.

"Ms. McGregor." He sat up. "Can I get you something to drink?"

He started to stand, but I shook him off and sat in the chair across from him. I wasn't here for coffee. I would say my piece, and if he didn't like it, I didn't need a reason to have to stick around.

He eyed me over, and I touched the rim of my glasses, hoping their camouflage was large enough to cover the still-yellowed bruise.

"I've come to negotiate." I cleared my throat and sucked in a breath before I spoke again. "I'll take the job, but I won't be your beck and call girl." My tone was firm, final, confident; I was proud of myself.

He sat back in his chair, his dark brow cocked, but he actually grinned a little. Not in facetious way—he looked happy. "Go on."

"I'll require twenty-four hours notice, and there *will* be times I say no. I have my own clients, and they come first."

He pressed his fingers to his lips, considering me. "And if I don't agree?"

I sat a little straighter. "Then you'll have to find someone else."

He grinned—wide and casual. "You surprise me, Ms. McGregor. All the time, you surprise me."

Relief flooded me, and my shoulders relaxed a little. He

surprised me, too. I wasn't sure what I'd been expecting, but this wasn't it.

He sat forward again. "What makes you think I'll agree to this?"

"Because I'm good. You said so yourself." I hoped it was true. I needed the money, but I wouldn't put my own clients second.

He chuckled. "So I did." He took a sip from his paper cup. "I'm usually more guarded than that." The right corner of his mouth lifted. "Fine. I'll give you twenty-four hours." He braced his elbows, then sat forward. "Now, tell me what happened to your face."

I shouldn't have been surprised. He was a photographer; his job required him to notice details—but there was genuine concern in his eyes I didn't know what to do with. It was in that moment, staring into the questioning eyes of my boss, that I realized I'd misjudged Rick Henderson. Yes, he was odd, gruff, but I sensed he really cared about my well being.

I didn't know why, maybe because I needed someone to talk to, or maybe because in that moment I saw him as a friend, but I opened up to him. I told him about all that transpired after I left him at the wedding. About finding Grace, Kevin's attack, all my uncertainty about Jake, my future—and he listened. *Only* listened. He didn't offer advice, didn't tell me what to do or whome to call. And it was exactly what I needed.

# CHAPTER THRITY-ONE

A week later, I placed my mug in the center console and checked the address Rick sent me again. This was only the second job he'd given me after our conversation at Starbucks, and I was still nervous as hell. I would've been nervous under any circumstance, but the field before me looked like the kind you'd see on CNN in a missing-persons report. A deep-set panic churned in my belly, but I pushed my fears aside. My job description could easily be "Single girl for hire, ready to meet you in any abandoned or secluded location of choice. Will bring incredibly overpriced equipment for your disposal." I needed to get over my fears.

I threw the car in park and pulled the visor down to check my reflection. There was a hint of a yellow bruise on my left cheek, but with the disguise of makeup, you could barely see it. My hair was brushed and pulled back into a high ponytail, and I was dressed in my normal photography garb. Black slacks, black top, and comfortable shoes. Nothing fancy, but it was a vast improvement from the state I was in only days ago.

As much as I wanted to hide away, I couldn't run scared anymore. Kevin was behind bars and the likelihood of a psychopath booking a photographer just so he could kill her in broad daylight was slim to none. Regardless, I made a mental note to sign up for a self-defense class before I climbed out of the car.

A couple parked cars sat beside mine, but I was twenty minutes early and didn't see any sign of the client anywhere. The field was overgrown and golden from the summer sun, and a bank of trees swayed off in the distance.

Something fragrant and earthy hit my nose, and I let my thoughts linger on in the cool breeze. The sun was low in the sky, and its amber light was cast over everything it touched. Just then, off in the distance, a flash of color caught my eye high above the tree line. *Red.* I squinted, and stepped to the side to get a better look. Maybe it wasn't the field I was here for after all.

*Damn.* I fired off a text to Rick asking for more details, but nervous flutters began to beat away in my abdomen, and I knew I needed to investigate.

The crisp weeds crackled under my feet as I moved across the field. Spurs from foxtails clung to my wool slacks, and I became nervous about holes and snakes I was sure lingered under the brush.

When I looked up again, there behind the tall trees were a whole rainbow of colors. A patchwork illuminated by the setting sun. The hot air balloon was secured to a large wicker basket with its door swung wide open and tethers anchoring it to the ground.

My phone buzzed in my pocket, and I pulled it out to see a text from Rick.

RICK: He had my number from when you borrowed my phone in Carmel. Sorry, but you both seemed so miserable.

Alarm squeezed my chest, and I turned around to the empty field behind me. There in the distance, coming from the opposite side of the parking lot was Jake. He was dressed in jeans and a white button-up shirt. His hair freshly cut, face clean-shaven, and more beautiful than I'd ever seen him.

At first I was confused. *What was he doing here?* But then I realized what was going on. There *was* no client. He'd planned the whole thing.

Without acknowledging his presence, I began tromping through the field, no longer caring about holes or snakes, but only the need for the shelter of my car. My hands shook with panic—I couldn't face him like this. Caught off guard without time to prepare. I wasn't ready.

"Katie, wait!" Jake shouted as he made his way toward me.

"I don't know what you're trying to do, but it's not funny!" All my energy was focused on keeping the tears from my vulnerable eyes and placing one foot in front of the other.

But he was faster than me, and before I knew what was happening, he threw me over his shoulder like a sack of feed.

"What are you doing?" I screamed. But he didn't answer as he turned around with determined strides and headed back to the balloon.

"Up!" he bellowed as he stepped into the basket.

The little man I hadn't noticed before released the tethers, and when the balloon lifted from the ground, Jake returned me to my feet.

I backed away until my legs hit the edge of the basket. My heart was slamming in my chest, my breath heavy, and hands fisted at my sides. "What the hell are you doing?" I screamed.

"Trying to get you to listen to me!"

"So you kidnapped me in a hot air balloon?"

He actually grinned, then folded his arms across his chest and rested against the basket opposite me.

He looked smug and satisfied with himself, and my eyes narrowed. I didn't see the humor in the situation. I looked over at the man controlling the balloon, and he smiled too.

"Do you think this is funny?" I demanded. Balloon guy quickly sobered and turned around. Offering us the limited privacy of his back.

I turned to Jake and stared at him. Trapped by the open sky—

overwhelmed by anger and hurt—but I couldn't think of a word to say.

He ran his hand through his hair, eyes searching mine. "I've been trying to talk to you for two weeks, but all you did was ignore me. You left me no choice." His voice was low and calm.

"There's nothing to talk about."

"I think there is." He began to move toward me, but I stiffened, and he stayed put.

"Please just listen to me. If you still feel the same way when I'm done, you can walk away and I'll leave you alone."

My throat tightened and I nodded.

He relaxed against the basket, but said nothing. We stood in silence as the balloon climbed higher and higher. The sun moving lower as it began to set into the hillside.

"I've run this over in my mind a thousand times, but now that I have you here I don't know where to begin." His lips lifted in a sideways smile, but his eyes were sad and distant. "Why are you running from me?"

I looked to my hands, not sure how to answer. Not sure I understood my own motivation anymore.

"Is it because of Grace?"

Just the sound of her name turned my stomach, but I knew that wasn't the reason. With each passing day my subconscious told me he was telling the truth. This was Jake. The man who'd never lied to me about anything in the twenty years I'd known him. Not even when he was a child...

"Shit, Katie, I'd do just about anything to prove to you that nothing happened, but I can't. All I can do is promise on every fiber of who I am that I would never do that to you. I'd never hurt you like that..."

"It's not that." I turned out toward the sky, and took a deep breath. "This thing between us will never work." My throat was tight and voice so weak it was barely audible.

"Why?"

I took a deep breath, my heart aching. "Because I want a family."

Three long seconds passed before he answered, "So?"

"So?" I turned around again. "You don't want that! You've never wanted that."

He shook his head. "I was a kid, I didn't know what I wanted." His eyes locked on mine. "But I do now, and I want *you*. I want everything with you."

I swallowed the ball of tears that clogged my throat, and my mind raced for an excuse—any excuse to push him away and protect what was left of my heart. "We've known each other too long, Jake. There's too much history between us."

He stepped closer. "Isn't that a good thing?"

"No. Maybe. I don't know!" I gave him my back again and sucked in much-needed air.

I felt him move behind me, so close his breath was in my hair, his deep voice demanding a better answer. "Why, Katie?"

I broke. "Because something is bound to happen—because I can't risk losing you." I choked on the words. All the emotions I'd been holding on to came pouring out of me. My insecurities, all my fears of being left behind by every single person I cared about. "It's too much of a risk. I can't lose another man I love." I gripped the side of the basket, needing its support so I didn't fall to the floor in a puddle of sorrow.

His smooth jaw grazed my cheek, and he let out a breath. His hands came up on either side of the basket, caging me in. "Is that what you're afraid of?"

My chest ached at the understanding in his voice, but I couldn't speak.

"You love me, Katie, and I love you so much I can't see straight." His words wrapped tight around my heart. I'd never heard him say them before. To anyone.

He gripped my shoulders and turned me around. "I can't let you run away from me again." His eyes met mine. "After Dave died, I thought I needed to take care of you. I thought that if I let myself fall for you, I was somehow betraying him."

I looked down, but he caught my chin and lifted until our eyes met again. "I was wrong." His voice lowered to a whisper. "I was *so* wrong.

"I want to be with you, Katie. I want to protect you and be everything you've always believed I am. I want to build a life with you. I want to have a dozen kids who look exactly like you. Ones that throw tantrums, wear their heart on their sleeve, and whose noses scrunch when they laugh. I want that so much. I love you."

I gripped his shirt and smothered a sob in the crook of his neck. "I'm afraid."

He pulled back and cupped my face in his hands. "Why?" he whispered.

Tears streamed down my face, but I couldn't hide anymore. "Because I don't have anyone left. You're it, Jake."

A storm of blue emotion stared back at me. "I know I'm not the easiest man to live with. I'm stubborn as hell, and I can take an eternity to see what's standing right in front of me. But I promise you... No one will ever love you as much as I do."

His lips grazed mine, his warm breath giving me life. "Do you trust me, Katie?"

I closed my eyes, my throat so tight I could barely breath. What was I supposed to say? I wanted to trust him. I wanted to give him everything—just didn't know if I could.

He trailed a hand down my cheek, my neck, my shoulder, until he took my hand and held it over my heart. "Trust me with this. Trust me because you know me better than anyone. Trust me when I tell you there's nothing more I've wanted in my whole life than spending the rest of it with you. I love you, Katie."

I crushed my body to his, gripping fists of his shirt to pull myself closer. "I love you, Jake. I love you so much."

He buried his face in my hair, and his voice came low and rugged. "I thought I lost you."

My hands laced around his neck and I whispered, "You could never lose me. I've been yours since I was fourteen."

He took my face in both hands and kissed me. A kiss that poured emotion. A kiss that healed hurts and left no doubt in my mind that he loved me.

"I'm so sorry. I should've trusted you, but I was so scared." I gripped him to me, not sure I'd ever be able to let him go again.

"Just talk to me. We can get through anything, Katie. Don't you know that?"

I leaned back and looked into the eyes of the man who'd already seen me through life, death, good times, and bad. And for the first time realizing that I meant as much to him as he did to me.

"I do." I tucked my head into the crook of his neck. Tears of relief, love, and devotion rolled down my cheeks as I pressed my body against his, savoring each breath, each heartbeat, the warmth of his skin.

The little man in the corner began to hum a low tune, a love song, and my shoulders began to shake between tears.

Jake pulled away and looked at me. "Are you laughing?" He smiled and brushed my cheek with his thumb.

"It's just—this!" I waved my hand in the air, encompassing all there was. The open sky, the balloon, the little man who still stood in the corner, humming.

He smiled, showing his adorable dimple and white teeth. "Now you can cross it off your list."

I shook my head and wiped at my face. "When did you plan this?"

"Remember that phone call I told you to trust me about?"

In the bar. How could I forget? "You're crazy." I smiled.

"That's not my fault, you make me crazy."

I hit him on the shoulder.

He laughed, pulled me closer, and pinned my hands to my

sides. "I'd live in an asylum the rest of my life as long as I got to take you with me."

Tears blurred my vision as I looked up at him. "I love you too, Jake."

"I'd walk through hell just to hold your hand."

And that's when I knew. Sometimes life didn't send you a road map. Sometimes pieces to a puzzle went missing, and you had to patch it together with scraps of paper and tape. And sometimes... Sometimes you have to jump, and trust that someone will be there to catch you.

That day, with the open sky as my canvas, miles up in the air with the man I'd loved my whole life, I jumped.

And he caught me.

THE END.

# ACKNOWLEDGMENTS

I am very grateful to a multitude of friends and family whom without, this book would've never come into being.

To my husband— I would be lost without you. Thank you for always picking up the slack when I need you. Thank you for always encouraging me, especially in the moments when I felt like giving up.

To my three children— You make my life better just because you're a part of it. Don't ever forget how much I love you, don't ever stop being you, and never give up on your dreams!

Mom— Thank you for instilling in me that nothing is beyond my reach. That there's nothing that isn't possible if I want it badly enough.

Dad— You were the first example of what a man should be, and I miss you every day.

My big brother— You will always be the *other* man in my life. Thanks for being the best brother a girl could ever wish for.

My little sister— The one who introduced me to the world or romance novels, who still calls me with the gross details in life, and will always be one of my best friends.

My brother-in-law— I will never be able to express how much your support and encouragement means to me. Thank you!

My soul sister, Kate — The one I didn't find until I was twenty-six. I know we'll be friends until we're little old ladies. Without you, I wouldn't have done half the crazy things in my life; including (but not limited to) writing this book.

All my SG friends— You ladies have been with me through so much! Thank you for your constant support through love, loss, life, and publishing my first book! You all mean more to me than you'll eve know. Thank you for everything.

Marianne— Because your shoulder is the most comfortable one to cry on, and I'm *so* glad I met you!

Anna—I can always count on you for your honesty. Thank you for holding my hand through this whole process.

Kelly— What can I say… I *fucking* love you, my sweet, supportive friend. ;)

Jeff — Thanks for being my comic relief and partner in crime.

Mika — You're the person I count on you to push me out of my comfort zone. Thank you for always encouraging me.

Ann — Thanks for your constant support and always being there to lend the perfect word.

Kishan — Thanks for always sharing your wealth of Knowledge and constant support. You're such a wonderful friend.

C.C.— Thank you for always being there to answer my endless questions!

To all my Beta readers: Tabetha, Kristen, Nancy, Polly, Kate, Nancy, Nesreen, Kelly, Marianne, Emma, Carmen, Heather, Dawn, Jamie, Lisa, Nikki, Ryann, Kathryn, Brandy, Stevie, Megan, THANK YOU! With all my heart!

I really hope I haven't forgotten anyone, but if I did, I blame it on lack of sleep, and too much coffee!

# ABOUT THE AUTHOR

Taylor is a contemporary romance author who loves writing stories about real people. Ones with hopes, dreams, fears, insecurities, and flaws. She loves to read as much as she loves to write, and is trilled to share her writing with you.

When Taylor isn't writing, she can often be found with her nose in a book, her face behind a camera, or spending time with her husband and three young children.

Taylor would love to hear from you.

**Website:** TaylorSullivanAuthor.com

**Email:** Taylorsullivan.author@gmail.com

**Facebook:** https://www.facebook.com/TaylorSullivanAuthor

**Twitter:** https://twitter.com/@AuthorTSullivan

ALSO BY TAYLOR SULLIVAN

Waiting for Tuesday

ALSO BY TAYLOR SULLIVAN

The Boy I Hate

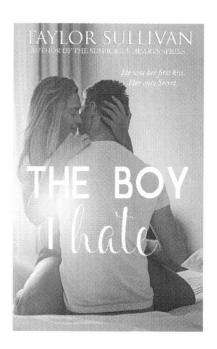

Made in the USA
Columbia, SC
05 June 2019